TANDEM

Keep the Home Guard Turning

Far from the paternal eye of the War Office,
the inhabitants of Great Todday and Little
Todday, as yet unaware of the possibilities of
whisky-filled wrecks off their coasts, have
weighty matters to consider in the fateful summer
of 1940.

Hitler is on the rampage. Undoubtedly his first
objective will be the Hebrides, and just as
certainly the men of the two Toddays will stick
at nothing, face any hardship and difficulty –
provided it does not interfere too seriously with
their daily lives – to defend their beloved islands
from the invader.

Anyone who has read *Whisky Galore* will know
how the men of the two Toddays, ably seconded
by their wives and daughters, can rise to the
occasion, and in KEEP THE HOME GUARD
TURNING they show the spirit that made even
Little Todday great. ROCKETS GALORE and THE
RIVAL MONSTER, two more of Compton
Mackenzie's famous Island comedies, will be
published in Tandem editions during 1972.

Map of the Islands

Keep the
Home Guard Turning

Compton Mackenzie

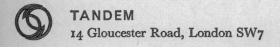

TANDEM
14 Gloucester Road, London SW7

Originally published in Great Britain by
Chatto & Windus, 1943
Six impressions

First published by Universal-Tandem
Publishing Co. Ltd, 1972

© Compton Mackenzie 1943

Made and printed in Great Britain by
C. Nicholls & Company Ltd

CONTENTS

My dear Colonel,

The process of keeping the Home Guard turning has had the effect of making this dedication retrospective because the Battalion as you commanded it no longer exists. It might imperil the whole future strategy of the war if I were to reveal what has taken its place, and so I shall say no more than a word of gratitude to you for your unfailing appreciation of Home Guard problems in the Islands, so many of which have been solved by laughter.

I fear you will not recognize in these pages anybody who served under you, and I may add that I have seldom gone to so much trouble in a book to avoid living models for what really are imaginary portraits.

Slàinte mhath!

Yours ever,

Compton Mackenzie

Isle of Barra, Outer Hebrides
July 14, 1943

Chapter 1

THE TWO TODDAYS

EVERY lover of the Outer and Inner Hebrides has his or her favourite island, and no reflection is cast upon the judgment of the devotees of Lewis, Harris, the two Uists, Benbecula, Barra, Rum, Eigg, Muck, Canna, Skye, and a hundred smaller islands when it is boldly claimed that the two Toddays, though they may be exceeded by many others in size and population are excelled by none in beauty and romantic interest.

The testimony of Hector Hamish Mackay who is the author of nine books about the Hebrides cannot be disregarded. This is what he writes in *Faerie Lands Forlorn* :

"And so after sailing for the whole of a fine summer's day along the magical coasts of Tìr nan Òg the gallant *Osprey* reached Snorvig, the picturesque little port of Great Todday (Todaidh Mór) where we dropped anchor and soon afterwards went ashore to enjoy the hospitality of the Snorvig Hotel and the tales of 'mine host', Roderick MacRurie, the 'uncrowned king' of the island. After a lordly spread, of which a magnificent lobster was the *pièce de résistance*, we sat outside on a terrace of shingle to pore spellbound over a scene of natural beauty which is nowhere surpassed in all the wondrous West.

"Down below we could hear the voices of children playing about among the various merchandise lying all over the quay and pier until Iain Dubh, the piermaster, should find time to put it away in the store—sweet Gaelic voices that seemed to reach us like the 'horns of elfland faintly blowing'.

"Mr MacRurie, with a grave shake of his impressive head, assured us that the Snorvig children were getting out of hand. Only last week two of them had ridden into the sea a motor-bicycle just arrived from the mainland for the schoolmaster at Bobanish on the other side of the island.

"Soon, however, all discussion of modern youth was hushed by the splendour of the sunset beyond Little Todday (Todaidh Beag) which was turning the mighty Atlantic to a sheet of molten gold. Kiltod, the diminutive port of Little Todday, lies opposite Snorvig from which it is separated by a strait of water two miles wide. Little Todday is not so very much inferior in superficial area to·its sister island and probably earned its qualifying adjective by the comparative lowness and flatness of the vivid green machair land framed by long white sandy beaches, which. contrasts with the more rugged aspect of Great Todday. Here the soil is peaty and the shores are rockbound, while three of its hills, of which Ben Sticla (1400 ft.) is the most conspicuous, rise above a thousand feet. The contrast in appearance between the two islands is so remarkable that we are not surprised to learn the inhabitants of both have preserved for hundreds of years an equally remarkable independence of one another, and differ considerably not merely in character but even in religion, Great Todday being Protestant and Little Todday Catholic.

"Both of the islands were formerly under the protection of St Tod who is said to have sailed there from Donegal on a log, his monkish habit providing the sail, his arm uplifted in benediction the mast. He built a church at Kiltod the foundations of which beside a holy well are still discernible close to the port. My grief! Nowadays even on Little Todday the old tales of the saint are passing from the memory, and the store of legend has been sadly depleted.

"In our time the two islands display no more than a friendly rivalry, but in the old period of clan feuds the MacRuries of Great Todday were always raiding the cattle of their neighbours, and the Macroons of Little Todday were not less adept at making inroads upon the MacRurie sheep. Authorities disagree about the comparative antiquity of the two clans. The Macroons claim to be descended from a seal-woman who loved an exiled son of Clan Donald and bore him seven sons every one of whom brought himself back a mortal bride from the mainland. The MacRuries on the other hand claim to be descended from an exiled Maclean called Ruairidh Ruadh, reputed to have stood seven feet six inches without his brogues. This Ruairidh Ruadh was a noted pirate who stole at least one wife from almost every island in the west. The fact that there is no legend of his having stolen a Macroon wife is held by those who support the claim of the MacRuries to greater antiquity to prove that the Macroons had not yet appeared upon the scene.

"We shall not venture an opinion on this vexed question. The air is too soft and balmy upon this June evening for genealogical controversy. Let us lean back in our deckchairs and watch the great sun go dipping down into the sea behind Little Todday. Is that St Brendan's floating isle we see upon the western horizon? Forsooth, on such a night it were easy to conjure up that elusive morsel of geography. And now behind us the full moon clears the craggy summit of Ben Sticla and swims south past Ben Pucka to shed a honey-coloured radiance over the calm water of the Coolish, as the strait between the two Toddays is called. Why, oh, why, the lover of Eden's language asks, must the fair Gaelic word Caolas be debased by map-makers to Coolish, so much more suggestive of municipal baths than of these 'perilous seas'? Alas, such sacrilege is all too sadly prevalent throughout Scotland. We turn our gaze once more to rest spellbound upon the beauty of earth and sea and sky and to let our imagination carry us back out of the materialistic present into the haunted past.

"We see again Ruairidh Ruadh's dark galley creep out from Snorvig and sweep with measured strokes northward up the Coolish on rapine bent. We see again the seal-beaked galley of the Macroons off Tràigh nam Marbh—the Strand of the Dead—and we hear the voices of the rowers lamenting their own dead Chief as they bear his body to the burial-place of the Macroons on the little neighbouring isle of Poppay. Alas, for these degenerate days, although Poppay is still a breeding ground for the grey Atlantic seals, the Macroons no longer use it as a burial-ground.

"But hark! What is that melodious moaning we hear in the west? It is the singing of the seals on Poppay and Pillay, the twin small isles that guard the extremities of Little Todday, their fantastic shapes standing out dark against the bloodstained western sky. Would that the present scribe possessed the musical genius of Mrs Kennedy Fraser that he might set down in due notation that melodious moaning!

"And now in the entrance of the hotel we notice our host beckoning to us. With one last lingering look at the un-earthly beauty of this Hebridean twilight we turn to answer the summons. In our host's snuggery the glasses reflect with opalescent gleams the flicker of a welcome fire of peats, and as we raise the *uisge beatha* to our lips with a devout '*slàinte mhath, slàinte mhòr*', we feel that we are indeed privileged visitors to Tìr nan Òg, and rejoicing in our own renewed youth we give thanks to the beneficent fortune which has brought us once more to the two lovely Toddays, there to dream away a few enchanted days on the edge of the world."

It was in that room of Roderick MacRurie thus commemorated in Mr Hector Hamish Mackay's poetic prose, a commemoration of which Roderick himself was justifiably proud, that on a morning in June 1940 the owner of the Snorvig Hotel was reading one of the Glasgow papers, the whole of his huge frame expressive of the profoundest alarm and despondency.

"*A dhuine dhuine*," he muttered, "these Chermans are worse than the Polshevicks."

Roderick rose from his chair and dragged his great bulk gloomily to the window. His dark eyes under black tufted eyebrows gazed sombrely across the Coolish to Little Todday. He was wondering whether in view of what Winston Churchill had said over the wireless it would not be as well to close down the hotel and remove himself and his family to Glasgow. Glasgow was seeming less vulnerable than Great Todday on this June morning. There was a sound of footsteps on the shingle of the terrace, and a moment later a thin man with a sharp slightly upturned nose, dressed in voluminous cigar-brown plus-fours of Harris tweed, came into the hotel.

Roderick hurried to meet him:

"Ah, I'm glad to see you, Mr Waggett," he exclaimed. "Terrible news. What do you think about it all? Will these Chermans get a hold of Glaschu, do you think?"

"I've come to discuss the business of raising Local Defence Volunteers," the newcomer announced, the serenity of an impregnable self-esteem communicating itself even to the perturbed owner of the Snorvig hotel.

"Will you take a dram, Mr Waggett? Come in, please. Do you think we will be invaded?" Roderick asked woefully as he ushered the guest into his own parlour.

When Paul Waggett at the age of forty-five sold out from his partnership in a firm of London chartered accountants and retired to Great Todday some five years before the outbreak of the Second World War, his associates in business wondered what the idea was. The idea was perfectly simple. The idea was to enjoy the romantic sensation of being a landed proprietor at a cost within his means. For years the arithmetical wastes of chartered accountancy had been brightened for Paul Waggett by day-dreams of his own little shoot and his own little fishing. He had joined syndicates to shoot partridges in Hampshire or pheasants in Hertfordshire and with the increasing profits of the business even grouse in Perthshire, but the magic of individual possession had been lacking. As the member of a syndicate of hard-headed London business men he could not issue an invitation to a fellow clubman to come down next week to his own little place. "I think I can promise you some good sport at my little place in Hertfordshire. We have a lot of birds this year," or "Why don't you take a run down to my little place in Oxfordshire next week? The mayfly will be up, and I can promise you some very decent sport."

Then one year Paul Waggett had joined a syndicate to rent some sea-trout fishing in the Hebrides, and on his way back south he had heard that the Department of Agriculture which had taken over the two Toddays wanted to sell the tumbledown house of the last of the MacRurie chieftains with a lease of the shooting and fishing of the two islands. A few grouse, a few salmon and sea-trout, brown trout galore, snipe and plover and woodcock in abundance, plenty of geese on Little Todday, everything in fact that a sportsman could want except stags.

When the Department of Agriculture had first taken over the Toddays as the fag-end of a great estate which had been broken up, the optimistic bureaucrats in Edinburgh had supposed they would be able to sell Snorvig House for almost as much as they had paid for the whole of the two islands. Ten years had gone by, and Snorvig House had stood empty. Tenants had been found to lease the sporting rights from time to time, but nobody would look at Snorvig House at £9000. The Department of Agriculture, threatened with a question in Parliament from the Labour Member for Wester Inverness, a lively young sprout from the laurels of Eccleston Square, suddenly brought down the price of Snorvig House from £9000 to £1000 with a long lease of the shooting and fishing at £40 a year. This was Paul Waggett's opportunity. He broke his journey at Edinburgh, and when he reached the London offices of Messrs Blundell, Blundell, Pickthorn, Blundell, and Waggett, he offered the senior partner his share in the business.

"You're going to live in the Hebrides, Paul?" the senior partner had wheezed in amazement. "You'll be blown away, won't you?"

"Wonderful shooting, wonderful fishing," Paul Waggett had

murmured. "Of course to all intents and purposes I shall be laird of the two islands. It'll cost me a bit to put the house in order, but I think I have a bargain."

That evening Paul Waggett had broken the news to his wife. His light-grey eyes, which usually brightened only under the influence of greed or cocksure knowledge, had shone like those of an eager child at the start of the summer holidays catching his first glimpse of the sea from the train.

"Is it a very long way from London, Paul?" fluffy-headed little Mrs Waggett had asked tremulously.

"Almost as far as it's possible to be without going abroad," her husband had replied complacently, his sharp nose tilting upward in admiration of his own cleverness. "The twins will love it, Dolly. I'll turn them into real sportswomen. And I shall get an Irish setter. Or a couple," he added dreamily.

Dolly Waggett did not belie her name, for at the age of forty her face suggested like those of so many once pretty English blondines the face of a china doll which has survived six or seven years of hard nursery life. This face now confronted Paul with the same expression of faintly timorous and utterly vacant perplexity as that with which it used often to confront one of his leads at bridge.

That had been five years ago on this June morning of 1940. The twins—Elsie and Muriel—had joined the W.A.A.F. at the outbreak of war, and if their father was to be believed, they were already the two most vital plumes in the wings of the Royal Air Force. Their mother was looking a little more chipped by nursery life and what roses were left of her girlhood's complexion had been turned into pot-pourri by five stormy Hebridean winters. One of the Irish setters had been shot for sheep-running, and the other had grown into what looked more like an auburn-haired St Bernard than an Irish setter. While Paddy's master was discussing the military future of the two Toddays this morning the thud of his benevolent tail could be heard thumping the floor of the passage outside Roderick's own small sitting-room.

"No thanks, Roderick, I never touch a dram before dinner," said Paul Waggett, in a tone of reproachful condescension. "You know that."

The landlord's Hebridean courtesy did not allow him to drink alone; with a resigned sigh, he pushed the dimpled bottle of Haig's Gold Cap beyond the temptation of an absent-minded hand.

"You know, of course, that I was right through the last war?" Paul Waggett went on.

Roderick knew it all too well. He was a good hand at a tall story himself, but since Paul Waggett had come to live on Great Todday he had had to succumb so often to Waggett's florid recklessness of invention that he had ceased to compete nowadays except in Gaelic.

"I believe you were, Mr Waggett. That's a beautiful piece of tweed. Where are you after getting that?"

Paul Waggett looked down complacently at the cigar-brown billows of his plus-fours.

"You're like my tailor in London, Roderick," he smiled. "He said he would pay thirty shillings a yard any time for such tweed. Any time," he echoed in that voice of childlike wonderment he kept for his own astuteness. "But of course I had to tell him that it was a special weave which only I could obtain."

"Man, man, thirty shillings a yard!" Roderick gasped. "What's his name? And where does he have his shop?"

Within a few seconds in fancy Roderick had driven to the other end of the island, called upon the Widow Maclean at Bobanish, beaten her down for a length of crotal-dyed tweed from three shillings to half a crown a yard because their grandmothers had been second cousins, sent the length to London carriage forward, and made a profit of £10 : 12s. on the transaction less the cost of the petrol to Bobanish.

"I'm afraid that's a secret too, Roderick. But he's one of the best tailors in London."

"Ay, he would be," the landlord agreed with a devout sigh. "Oh, well, if he's wanting any more tweed, Mr Waggett, I wouldn't say but I might not be able to find him a darling of a length."

"Look here, we mustn't start yarning," said Waggett austerely. "I've come to tell you that Colonel Lindsay-Wolseley of Tummie has written to ask me if I will raise a company of Local Defence Volunteers from the Toddays. He's raising a battalion at Fort Augustus, and he is responsible for these islands."

"Och, I know the Colonel well," Roderick exclaimed. "We're in the Council together. And does the Colonel think the Chermans are coming to the Toddays?"

"I suppose like all of us in these days he's prepared for any-thing. However, the first thing to be done is to call a meeting in the hall and I'll explain the position. Macrae the constable has the enrolment forms. I don't quite know what the police have to do with it. I should have thought it was a purely military matter. But apparently the police have to satisfy themselves that all recruits have a clean sheet."

"Ah well, you see, the Colonel is Convener of the Police Committee. He wouldn't be pleased to do anything against the police. Have you spoken to Mr Morrison for the hall?"

"Not yet. I'll go along to the Manse presently, and I'll send word over to Father Macalister at Kiltod so that the men from Little Todday can come across."

Roderick shook his head.

"You'll have to hold a meeting over there, Mr Waggett. The Little Todday men would sooner see the Chermans land on us than have it said they took second place to keep them out. Och, I know them. Hitlers every one of them over there."

"Surely at a time like this we should all pull together."

"Och, we'll all pull together right enough," Roderick declared. "But we'll each keep to our own side of the rope."

A moment later the tail of Paddy beat a tattoo to welcome his master, and then he rose and followed the new military commander of the Toddays up the winding road behind the hill to the Manse.

Chapter 2

TO ARMS, GREAT TODDAY!

THE Snorvig hall was crowded two evenings later, and it was as well that Paul Waggett had taken Roderick's advice and summoned another meeting at Kiltod on the following evening, for there would have been no room for the representatives of Little Todday.

The platform was packed with local notabilities, so closely packed indeed that in a burst of patriotic applause John Beaton, the schoolmaster of Bobanish, very nearly sent Mr

Andrew Thomson the bank agent and his chair plunging over the edge into the venerable audience. The adjective is not used lightly. So many of the younger men of the island were already on the seven seas in the mercantile marine that this gathering of those still at home suggested to a superficial glance an average age of seventy. Partly this was due to the fact that the two front rows were filled by a drift of snowy beards. A closer examination revealed that the majority of the audience were between fifty-five and sixty and that the back of the hall was occupied by youths and small boys eligible as yet for nothing except mischief.

Much of the interest had been roused less by the gravity of the military situation than by three or four posters which Paul Waggett who, as he modestly put it, 'dabbled a bit in paint', had sent round to various townships of the island:

TO ARMS!
MEN OF TODDAY, SHOW HITLER
WHERE HE GETS OFF!

And underneath this stirring invitation was a picture in extremely vivid colours of a kilted warrior plunging a bayonet into what was intended to represent a German soldier, though perhaps on account of the speed with which the artist had worked the figure resembled rather a deep-sea diver in the uniform of a postman. The appearance of this picture on the doors of the schools in Bobanish, Watasett, and Garryboo caused a rumour to spread that Mr Waggett was exhibiting a picture 'fillum' of the war, and the lorries that served these outlying populations were crowded to capacity in consequence.

"Oughtn't friend Waggett to have invited us to show Hitler one place where he didn't get off?" Dr Maclaren, the jovial, hard-drinking, and thoroughly competent medical man who served both the Toddays, suggested to Mr Thomson the bank agent.

"Imphm," the latter replied, with the passionate eloquence of Midlothian.

The chair that evening was taken by the Minister, the Reverend Angus Morrison, a native of Harris, whose countenance still kept the slightly puzzled expression it had taken on when he first saw himself in a mirror wearing a clerical collar. He was a kindly, rather solemn young man in his mid thirties, whose profoundest conviction for the first two or three years after his call to the ministry had been that the Lewis ministers were prospering in the sight of Almighty God just a little more than he, setting aside any prejudice he might retain against them as a Harris man, felt that they quite deserved to prosper. However, down here out of hearing of the sough of the Lewis aspirates except at Presbytery meetings he had been able to forget that Lewis prepotency due to a combination of brains, drive, and sublime self-confidence. Moreover, as a minister half in communion with Rome, as he would say with a grave jocularity, he felt he was in his own humble way a cosmopolitan compared with his reverend brethren in the north of the Long Island. Mr Morrison was not an eloquent divine ; he was a good simple soul who with the help of a somewhat nervously ladylike young wife from Glasgow did his best to justify his parents' investment, and he was very well liked by his parishioners, whose respect he had won and kept— neither a particularly easy achievement on Great Todday.

"*Ach, duine beag bochd!* Poor wee man, he tries so hard!" the Todday womenfolk would declare, and it was with genuinely respectful and affectionate applause that his small figure was greeted that June evening when he rose from the chair and stepped forward, rubbing his hands nervously, to give the Church's blessing on the martial occasion.

"At an hour of national peril like this, my friends, it behoves every Minister of the Gospel to demonstrate that he is indeed a Minister of the Church Militant, and I have pleasure in calling upon our friend Mr Waggett to address us on what Todaidh Mór can do to help in the great emergency with which the Lord has seen fit to test us."

With these few words in hesitant English which followed a much longer exhortation in Gaelic Mr Morrison sat down, and Paul Waggett, who had put on a dinner-jacket for this solemn occasion, stood up.

"Mr Chairman, gentlemen, my Todday friends, you all know that a good soldier never wastes words, and I shall not waste any time this evening on words. You know the situation. At any moment the Germans may land at Snorvig. . . ."

Here the proposed commander of Snorvig's defences was interrupted by a gasp from old Bean Eachainn Uilleim who had bumped into Snorvig on the lorry from Garryboo to see the 'fillum' and could not be persuaded that it was an entirely male gathering.

"Och, the Lord be good to us and don't let the Chermans come till I'm back home in my little house," she wailed in Gaelic.

"*Ist thu*," the shocked stern voices of several bearded ancients exclaimed.

"Keep your tongue quiet, woman," admonished old Simon MacRurie, who owned the largest general store in Snorvig. "It's not you that will be keeping the Chermans away from us."

"I'm afraid I must repeat my warning," the speaker went on when Bean Eachainn Uilleim had been hushed. "I should not be doing what I conceive to be my duty to my country if I pandered to any spirit of false confidence."

This last sentence ploughed furrows of perplexity on the brows of his audience, and the speaker felt he would be wiser to avoid abstract eloquence and stick to simple facts.

"However, as I said just now, a good soldier never wastes words. What I am asking for to-night are Local Defence Volunteers, men who will defend Todaidh Mór against the Huns as their forefathers used to defend the island against the Macroons of Todaidh Beag."

Loud applause greeted this piece of local chauvinism, and Waggett made a mental note to use the same phrase the other way round when he addressed the recruiting meeting at Little Todday the following evening.

"A battalion of Local Defence Volunteers is being raised at Fort Augustus by Colonel Lindsay-Wolseley of Tummie and it will be attached to the Duke of Clarence's Own Clanranald Highlanders. MacDonald of Ben Nevis, Cameron of Kilwhillie, Sir Hubert Bottley of Cloy, and some of the other Wester Inverness lairds are forming companies and platoons. It has been suggested that I should raise a company from the two Toddays. Constable Macrae is standing by with the enrolment forms, and I hope the response will be a good one. I am accepting recruits up to the age of seventy-five—I'm sorry, I should have said sixty-five. Now, before you sign on perhaps some of you may like to ask a few questions. I shall be very happy to answer them to the best of my ability."

Few silences are so profound as those which greet an invitation to a Hebridean audience to ask questions, except of course

. a Conservative candidate's invitation: that wins an immediate acceptance from hecklers. When Paul Waggett resumed his seat and smiled with encouraging condescension his audience sat still and mute as waxworks, every member of it determined as a schoolboy not to give his classmates a chance to deride him.

At last John Beaton, the schoolmaster of Bobanish, who had already drawn attention to himself by nearly knocking the bank agent off the platform, rose to his feet and broke the spell. He was a burly Skyeman in his mid forties with sandy hair and a high complexion, a good Gaelic scholar, a disciplinarian and something of a bard, who was married to a Todday woman reputed to be the most competent housewife in the island.

"Will Mr Waggett tell us what arms we will be given?" he asked.

"Ah, of course, that's a question I've been asking myself," Waggett replied. "And I have to admit frankly I do not know yet. Assuming, however, that we are able to muster at least a hundred men between the two islands, I shall ask for a hundred rifles and bayonets, half a dozen machine-guns, a couple of anti-aircraft guns, and perhaps a fairly heavy gun to deal with any U-boat that tries to be—er—funny in the Coolish. I might obtain half a dozen mortars as well and some Tommy-guns."

There was a murmur of approval round the hall.

"Perhaps I should add that of course owing to heavy demands elsewhere we are not likely to get any arms at present," Waggett went on. "But I'm authorized to appeal to all owners of shotguns, miniature rifles, pistols, and revolvers to hand them over to Constable Macrae at the Police Station as soon as possible."

A certain amount of dubious coughing from the audience greeted this announcement. Since Mr Waggett had become the owner of Snorvig House and the tenant of the sporting rights there had been one or two arguments about shotguns owned by some of his neighbours, and this surrender of them to the police was sounding more like a convenience for Mr Waggett than a duty to the country.

"Of course, any such weapons handed over will be returned to their owners as soon as the situation grows easier," Paul

Waggett went on. Nevertheless in spite of that assurance the coughing continued, and the audience was evidently unconvinced. The Minister thought it wise to intervene.

"I would remind Mr Waggett that there are two field-guns on either side of the War Memorial. Might they not be usefully employed against the enemy in view of the fact that the Ministry of Waste couldn't see their way to removing them in the salvage drive?"

The mention of salvage brought the headmaster of Snorvig school to his feet. Alec Mackinnon like his opposite number at Bobanish was a Skyeman, but there the resemblance stopped, for Mackinnon was as tall as a bean-pole, as thin as a lath, and as dark as a Spaniard. He responded with passionate enthusiasm to every announcement on the wireless that seemed capable of helping the war and was conversely as passionately indignant when such responses were not appreciated by those who had been entrusted with its conduct.

When the Minister of Waste broadcasting to the nation after the nine o'clock news had urged the vital importance of collecting scrap, Alec Mackinnon had flung himself into the campaign with the ardour of a fanatic. The housewives of Snorvig dared not leave so much as a kitchen knife in sight of Mackinnon's schoolchildren lest it should be carried off to be flung on the dump of scrap that was rising a little higher and spreading a little wider every day upon the quay and the pier. In vain did the skipper of the *Island Queen*, the mailboat that called three times a week, curse the obstruction. In vain did Iain Dubh the piermaster curse the obstructors. In vain did Mrs Simon Macrurie, when she tore her best Glasgow frock on the rusty ribs of a bedstead contributed by the children of the Watasett school, appeal to her husband's cousin Roderick, the County Councillor of Great Todday, to have the dump flung into the harbour. Alec Mackinnon called for more scrap and still more scrap. He had been in communication with the Ministry of Waste which had been in communication with the Ministry of Supply which had been in communication with the Ministry of War Transport which had referred the whole question of the salvage dump on Great Todday Island, Orkney, Inverness-shire, back to the Ministry of Waste. And the dump grew larger. Mackinnon waited for the magic letter of congratulation from the Ministry of

Waste conveying its appreciation of the work done by Great Todday in the national drive for salvage and announcing that a boat was ready to take it away.

But no boat came.

Alec Mackinnon went on board the *Island Queen* one day and harangued her skipper, Donald MacKechnie.

"There comes a moment, Captain MacKechnie, when matters of national importance must override personal convenience. The nation requires scrap. It is your duty to load the Todday salvage dump on the *Island Queen* and unload it at Glasgow."

The voice of Captain MacKechnie was high-pitched at any time. When he grew angry the pitch of his voice sharpened. At Alec Mackinnon's demand it trembled upon the air like the rarefied squeak of an infuriated bat.

"Tam you and your plutty tump," he piped. "Do you think my ship is a plutty tustcart?"

"I will complain to the Ministry of Waste about your obstructiveness," the headmaster threatened.

"*A mhic an diabhoil*, do you think the moon rises in that old woman's pottom of yours that *you* are telling *me* what *I* must be doing?"

So the headmaster wrote one more desperate letter to the Ministry of Waste, and received this reply:

Ref: 496421/M.W./Z27/1642.
Dept.: A (sec. 14)

Ministry of Waste
Bellevue Hotel
Morecambe
Cumberland

Great Todday Salvage Dump

Dear Sir,

I am instructed by the Minister to acknowledge with thanks the receipt of your letter of the 9th inst. and to say that while he much appreciates the work you have done in connection with the National Salvage Drive he regrets that owing to the need to conserve shipping space he is unable to avail himself of the scrap collected on Great Todday Island, Orkney, Inverness-shire.

He desires me to express his thanks to the Great Todday District Council for their public-spirited offer of the two field-guns presented by the War Office to the local War Memorial after the Great War for Civilization 1914–1918, but regrets that under the circumstances adverted to above he is unable to accept the aforesaid two field-guns.

In reply to your query as to what should be done with the scrap

*already collected I am empowered by the Minister to suggest either that
the aforesaid scrap should be replaced or failing the feasibility of such a
measure that the aforesaid scrap should be dumped into the sea after
consultation with the Naval authorities and subject to their approval
as to the most suitable portion of the sea for the absorption of such
material.*

Yours faithfully

A. *Mackinnon, Esq.,*   [an illegible signature]
Schoolhouse,
Snorvig,
Great Todday Island,
Orkney,
Inverness-shire,
  Scotland, N.B.

That was the letter which led Alec Mackinnon to strap any
of his pupils nowadays who showed the slightest hesitation
about the position of Orkney on the map, and caused the word
'salvage' to loosen his tongue more potently than half a bottle
or whisky.

"What I want to ask Mr Waggett is whether he can give us
any guarantee that when we have raised a company of Local
Defence Volunteers on this island we will not be invited by the
War Office to massacre the lot."

From the back of the hall a bunch of Snorvig schoolchildren
cheered shrilly.

"Silence, boys," their headmaster commanded.

"I consider such a question extremely unpatriotic," Paul
Waggett declared. "And I cannot believe it reflects the
spirit in which Todday men wish to confront the threat of
invasion."

"I'm not concerned with your opinion of me, Mr Waggett.
You asked for questions. I've given you one to answer," said
Mackinnon hotly.

The Minister rose to bring the soothing influence of the
Chair into play.

"I'm sure the last thing—the very last thing—our friend
Mr Mackinnon would wish was to ask an unpatriotic question.
I know we are all united in our resolve to resist invasion and
protect our homes. I'm sure you'll withdraw your remark,
Mr Waggett."

But Mr Waggett's nose was tilted a little higher as if it were

seeking to escape a more than usually bad smell, and the headmaster of Snorvig school sat fuming.

Dr Maclaren, as so often on such occasions, came to the
rescue.

"What I want to know is what the police have to do with
a military affair like this? Why must the police approve all
recruits?"

Waggett's nose came down.

"I am in complete agreement with Dr Maclaren. Why
indeed? However, that's the rule, and at a time like this the
more rules we keep the better we are serving our country.
And now with our chairman's permission I should like to call
upon Mr Roderick MacRurie to address the meeting."

Loud applause saluted the great form of the hotel-keeper
when he rose in response to this suggestion, for in spite of his
ruthless business methods, his tall tales, his ferocious whisky,
and it was believed his enormous wealth, Great Todday was
proud of Roderick MacRurie. So long as he represented the
island upon the County Council Great Todday knew that it
would benefit, in a minor degree to Ruairidh Mór himself it
is true, but still that it *would* benefit from the road or jetty
or new school or water-tank or additional bursary that its
representative extracted from the ratepayers of Inverness-
shire. Hector Hamish Mackay did not exaggerate when he
called him the uncrowned king of the island. The people of
Great Todday felt that Ruairidh Mór came as near to the
giant pirate they acknowledged as their original patriarch as
any Great Todday man had come since the immense form of
the redoubtable Ruairidh Ruadh himself vanished from the
eyes of men.

Roderick MacRurie like the Minister before him opened
with a long speech in Gaelic, no word of which, to judge from
the delighted and almost continuous laughter of his listeners,
was suggesting the imminence of the danger which earlier
speakers had hoped to impress upon them. Paul Waggett,
whose ability to follow Gaelic after five years with the sporting
rights of the two Toddays hardly extended beyond recognizing
the conjunction 'and' every time he heard 'agus', was inclined
at first to resent so much merriment. Then he consoled himself with the thought that Roderick who two days before had
been contemplating flight to Glasgow with his family was now

so much reassured by his own assumption of the military command that he could afford to laugh at Hitler. Nevertheless, he decided to lean across and ask the Minister what *was* making everybody laugh so heartily, himself included.

"I hope Roderick isn't making light of the invasion threat?" he whispered.

"No, no," the Minister whispered back. "He's just now telling them the story of how the *Island Queen* was chased all down the Minch by a German submarine in the last war. Roderick himself was on board at the time, and he's telling how he shot the periscope clean off with his own guns. He's encouraging them to hand over their shot-guns now. It's very very funny if you could be following it in the Gaelic."

"I'm sure it is," Waggett agreed. "Of course, I only get bits of it here and there."

There was a particularly loud laugh at this moment, and the Minister explained Roderick had just observed that nobody had to take out a gun licence to shoot Germans.

"But it sounds better in Gaelic," he chuckled.

At last the speaker turned to English.

"For the benefit of those poor souls who through no fault of their own cannot speak the tongue spoken by Attam and Eve in the Garden of Eden I will now say a few words in English. We are proud to find that our friend Mr Waggett is taking the grand responsibility to put the two Toddays in a suitable condition to beat off the enemy from our shores. We are. crateful to him for the splendid manner in which he has answered the call of duty. We do not know if the Chermans will come to Snorvig, but if they do come, for once in a way we will not show them the hospitality we like to show our visitors. They will receive another kind of a Highland welcome altogether. It'll be warrum enough, oh yess, by Chinko, it'll be so warrum that they'll be glad to chump pack into the sea to make themselfs cool."

If any had been inclined to hold back before Roderick MacRurie spoke, his enthusiasm banished all doubts. Fifty-nine Local Defence Volunteers had filled in enrolment forms when their commander went back to Snorvig House that night.

"Did you have a successful meeting, dear?" asked his wife, looking up with a sweet cracked smile from her task of knitting comforters for the armed forces of the Empire. She was waiting for her husband in the brightly-papered 'lounge' to which the Waggetts had transformed the musty old drawing-room of Snorvig House that used to look like an empty tank in an abandoned aquarium.

"Fifty-nine recruits. I've made John Beaton my section leader at Bobanish. He's a very sound fellow, I think. Mackinnon didn't enrol."

"Didn't he? That's very slack, isn't it?"

"He says he has too much to do already. Busybody of course. As a matter of fact I'd sooner not have him. But I'm afraid it's personal. I had to put him in his place for making an unpatriotic remark."

"Oh, Paul dear, how frightful! He's surely not a fifth columnist?"

"I wouldn't go as far as to accuse him of that, Dolly, but he seems to think that every announcement over the wireless is made to him personally, and I suppose he resents Lindsay-Wolseley writing to me about the L.D.V.s."

"He listens a lot to Lord Haw-Haw, you know."

"I'm afraid they all do, Dolly. I suggested to Mr Morrison that he should say something about it in Church, but apparently he listens to Haw-Haw himself. Most extraordinary. I cannot understand what pleasure people get from it except of course people like me who listen intelligently in order to find out what really is happening in Europe."

Mrs Waggett smiled affectionately and proudly at her husband.

"But you're able to judge for yourself, Paul. We haven't all got your knowledge of politics."

"Oh, I don't claim to be an expert," said Paul modestly. "I read the *Daily Express* very carefully and I listen to Haw-Haw with an open mind. And of course I was right through the last war. I always said the French would let us down. Sometimes one wishes one wasn't always right."

"But they're fighting very well, aren't they?" Mrs Waggett almost pleaded with that fact-facing husband of hers. He smiled compassionately.

"I don't want to depress you, old lady, but in my opinion the French are finished."

"Oh, well, you're always right, Paul," she sighed. "By the

way, what part is Dr Maclaren playing in your L.D.V.s?"

"Says he hasn't the time to be of any real use, which of course
is ridiculous. Quite ridiculous. Doctors never believe that
anybody except themselves ever do any work. The trouble
is that very few people have yet grasped how serious the situation really is. However, I suppose we shall muddle through
as we always have in the past. Well, I'm feeling rather tired
and I have the Little Todday meeting to-morrow. What
about Bedfordshire for the two of us? I wonder if we shall
get letters from the chicks to-morrow?"

"Oh, that reminds me, Paul, Mrs Neil MacRurie came in
with a dozen eggs. What a nice woman, she is. She wouldn't
hear of my paying for them . . . let me see, what did something remind me of? Oh yes, her eldest girl Morag has joined
the Waafs, and what do you think has made the most impression on her so far?"

"The balloons, I suppose."

"No, the only thing that seems to have excited her at all
was a free issue of brassières. You would think a girl going
down to England for the first time from an island like Todday
would have had something more exciting to write home about
than brassières."

Paul smiled charitably.

"Little things please little minds," he said. "How many
eggs have you collected now, old lady?"

"I have over thirty dozen in waterglass already."

"Bravo, I'll see if I can collect some at Kiltod when I go
over to-morrow."

Chapter 3

TO ARMS, LITTLE TODDAY!

WITHOUT venturing to compete with the descriptive pen
of Hector Hamish Mackay some attention really must
be paid by the present chronicler to the beauty of Little
Todday on that golden June evening when Paul Waggett set
out to inspire the inhabitants with ardour to defend their
island against the invader. It was that sweet season when

the young grass·had won back from the salty blasts of·winter its vivid green and was spread with a bright veil of buttercups and daisies right across the surface of the island that undulated in knolls as gently as the lazy summer ocean from which it nowhere raised itself higher than a hundred feet. Apart from a small cluster of houses round the diminutive haven of Kiltod beyond which stood the towerless church of Our Lady, Star of the Sea, and St Tod, there was nothing like a village in the twenty square miles of machair. Isolated houses, all at different angles, were dotted everywhere, each one with its patchwork croft, and everywhere all at different angles the cattle and ponies of Little Todday were tranquilly grazing. There was one metalled road, which had been exacted from the County Council less because the inhabitants really wanted it than because, in view of what was being spent on the roads of Great Todday, Joseph Macroon, their councillor, was determined not to let Roderick MacRurie have things all his own way in Inverness. From this one road tracks far better suited to the local traffic of ponies than the metalled road wandered off in every direction. Joseph Macroon, who was·the postmaster and leading merchant of the island, in the exultation of securing this road for the electors had tried the experiment of running a lorry; but as the noisy second-hand machine could traverse the island only from Kiltod to Tràigh Swish, the long white sandy beach that gleamed almost the length of the western boundary four miles away, the alarm and despondency it caused to the cattle and ponies was considered a waste of enterprise. The lorry was sold to Simon MacRurie, the leading merchant of Snorvig, at a small profit, and Little Todday was disembarrassed of the monster, which went to swell the volume·of mechanical transport on Great Todday, round which half a dozen lorries rumbled and rattled all day long under the impression that their activity was helping Great Todday out of the past into the present.

"They're so snop over there."

This was the verdict of the people of Little Todday upon the people of Great Todday, and they would throw a defiantly scornful glance at their neighbour across the Coolish as if the very hills of Todaidh Mór—Ben Sticla, Ben Pucka, and Ben Bustival—were daring to look down upon the daedal carpet of Todaidh Beag with a sneer of superiority.

On this June evening Paul Waggett had not exposed the
'snoppery' of Snorvig to further criticism by donning a dinner-
jacket to address the meeting at Kiltod. He was wearing
instead a tweed suit the predominant light blue of which was
framed in dark-blue lattices, a pattern which gave his plus-
fours the appearance of a crinoline hoop.

"Camouflaged as a lobster-pot," Alec Mackinnon had
observed sarcastically when he saw the owner of Snorvig
House step aboard Joseph Macroon's motor-boat, which had
come over to fetch him.

Half-way across the Coolish the engine of the *Morning Star*
stopped, and the crew consisting of Kenny Macroon, Joseph's
youngest son aged fourteen, and Michael Gillies, his handyman, a tall melancholy piper who was still lamenting the dis-
appearance of the lorry, hastily twisted knobs, loosened screws,
swung the handle of the starter, blew down pipes, and did
all the things that are done when a marine motor ceases to
chug. The water of the Coolish gurgled mockingly against
the sides of the *Morning Star* as the boat drifted idly along with
the tide.

"Is it a choke?" Waggett asked.

"I don't know what it is, Mr Waggett," said Michael Gillies
gloomily. "I don't know at all."

"It's himself," declared Kenny, whose habit it was to blame
his father for everything. · "It's a new engine she's wanting."

"Ay, a new engine would be good, right enough," Michael
admitted.

"Well, what are we going to do?" Waggett asked a little
impatiently. Five years of life in Tìr nan Òg had not yet
taught him that one does not waste emotion on the caprice
of motor-boats.

"Maybe we will have to row," Kenny suggested.

"That's just what we will have to do, Kenny boy," the other
member of the crew agreed.

"Where are the oars?" asked Kenny.

"Are they not in the boat?" Michael exclaimed. "They
must have been left on the pier."

"That's where they will be right enough," said Kenny.

"Well, what are we going to do? I really don't want to be
late for the meeting," Waggett pressed.

"Och, we won't be late. The new time is on now. What

time is the meeting?" Michael asked.

"The meeting is at eight o'clock sharp," Waggett snapped irritably.

"By the new time?" Michael pressed.

"By summer time, of course."

"But there's no new time on Todaidh Beag," Michael explained. "And with the long way it is to Kiltod it'll be ten o'clock by the new time before they will all be at the hall. We haven't any lorries on Todaidh Beag. It's a different kind of a place to Todaidh Mór."

"Well, whether the meeting begins at eight or at ten," Waggett protested, "we won't reach Kiltod by sitting here and drifting with the tide. The engine won't start up of its own accord."

The crew looked at one another.

"What Mr Waggett's after saying is right enough, Kenny," Michael admitted. "We'd better have another look at the engine."

There was a fresh bout of blowing and twisting and unscrewing and screwing up and tapping and swinging of the handle; but the engine remained silent.

Suddenly Kenny had an idea.

"Did you fill up before we came along?" he asked Michael.

"I thought there was plenty petrol in the tank," Michael replied. "Your father said there was plenty petrol."

"Ah, there you are, it *was* himself," Kenny said severely. He examined the tank. "Not a drop. That's why she's after stopping."

"Och, yess, right enough, Kenny boy. That's just what it is. No petrol. Look at that now, and us blowing the heart out of ourselfs because we were thinking the feed-pipe was choked."

"What are we going to do then?" the indignant passenger demanded.

"Maybe we'll see another boat and get a tow," Michael speculated hopefully, and lighting a cigarette he settled down comfortably in the bows to wait for assistance. Kenny made himself equally comfortable amidships, and Waggett who had the tiller tried to keep his temper while the *Morning Star* drifted with the gentle tide. Gradually the sun's gold deepened. The craggy steeps of Great Todday were aglow. The grey

houses above the harbour of Snorvig stood out sharply from
the bulk of Ben Sticla instead of looking as they often did in
misty weather like a heap of boulders which had rolled to the
foot of the mountain behind them. The scattered houses of
Little Todday grew tralucent-seeming against the fast westering sun.

"Nine o'clock," Waggett exclaimed at last in exasperation.
"Are we going to spend the night out here?"

It was at this moment that Father James Macalister closed
his breviary with a sigh of relief, raised his portly shape from
the deep armchair in which he had disposed of vespers and
compline, put on his hat and started to stroll down from the
Chapel House to the pier.

Groups of Little Todday men were creeping at a snail's pace
across the daisy-powdered buttercup-gilded green toward the
hall at the west end of which some early arrivals were leaning
against the warm corrugated iron and puffing tobacco-smoke
into the sun's eye.

"Good evening, Joseph," Father Macalister said to his most
substantial parishioner who was standing outside his shop,
looking across the Coolish through a decrepit spy-glass.

"Good evening, Father James, good evening indeed," the
postmaster responded. He was a small sharp-featured man
with a trim grey moustache, quick in his movements, who
always wore a knitted red cap such as trolls wear in illustrated
fairy tales.

"What are you looking at, Joseph?"

"I'm looking to see where he is."

"Where who is?"

"Mr Waggett."

"Where would he be?"

"That's what I'm after asking myself."

The postmaster lifted the decrepit spy-glass to his eye again,
and when it had stopped rattling he gazed at the Coolish.

"*A Dhia, Dhia!*" he exclaimed.

"What's the matter now?"

"They must have broken down. I can see them a mile away
to the south."

"You'd better send and give them a tow in," the parish
priest advised.

A quarter of an hour later a crew was mustered for the

rescue of the *Morning Star*. By half-past ten the meeting began. Even so at least three of the proposed defenders of Little Todday managed to miss the first five minutes.

There was not quite the same atmosphere of expectation as there had been at Snorvig the previous night. Waggett had not had time to send round stirring posters, and Father Macalister in his opening remarks, to judge by the laughter of his audience, hardly seemed to take the situation as seriously as the local commander would have liked. Waggett wondered what on earth he could be saying. That was the worst of Roman Catholics: they were always inclined to take their own political line. At last the Gaelic flow dried up and the burly priest turned to the visitor.

"You must pardon me, Colonel, if I now proceed to massacre your mother tongue by my very peculiar English."

Waggett smiled as amiably as he could. He thought it was rather bad taste of the priest to call him 'Colonel'. But it was no use getting angry with him. He had a very elementary notion of humour.

"I have been telling them, Colonel, that I expect every man in Todaidh Beag who can stand upon his feet to do his duty. Perhaps you will now explain to them what that duty is."

Paul Waggett rose from his chair and stepped to the front of the platform.

"Father Macalister, gentlemen, my friends of Little Todday . . ."

"*Glè mhath!* Very good," ejaculated the Chairman.

"You all know that a good soldier never wastes words, and I shall not waste any time this evening on words."

"Beautiful," the Chairman interposed enthusiastically.

"I must apologize for being late, but . . ."

"Don't apologize at all," said the Chairman. "We cannot be late on Todaidh Beag. Thank God, it's a lovely and beautiful impossibility!"

"But unfortunately the good ship *Morning Star* broke down."

"She would," cried the Chairman with an exuberant guffaw, slapping his thighs.

"The *Morning Star* has carried you many a time, Father," Joseph Macroon put in.

"Under protest, Joseph. Always under protest."

"Well, I'm afraid I must get back to what I was saying," Waggett cut in, to stop this cross-talk. "As I was coming over the Coolish . . ."

"As you *weren't* coming over," the Chairman corrected with a sonorous gravity.

"Father James will have his little joke."

"His pound of flesh," the Chairman chuckled to himself.

". . . I was thinking how very vulnerable Little Todday is to any attempt at an enemy landing. Very vulnerable indeed. Still, that is all the more reason why the men of Little Todday should take on the responsibility of defending it. I have come here to-night to ask for Local Defence Volunteers who will defend Todaidh Beag against the Huns as their forefathers used to defend it against the MacRuries of Todaidh Mór."

"Good shooting!" the Chairman ejaculated. The audience clapped vigorously, and Paul Waggett feeling that at last he had brought home to his listeners the seriousness of the situation tried to explain how Little Todday would be expected to confront it. He was so far successful that thirty-eight recruits had been enrolled when at half-past eleven the meeting broke up and the members of the audience scattering seemed to float away into the twilight like moths.

"You'll come round to the Chapel House before you go back, Mr Waggett," Father Macalister suggested. "And you'll come too, Joseph," he added on a note of authority.

"It's rather late," Waggett demurred.

"Not at all. Not at all. You'll require just a sensation before you entrust your *corpus vile* to the *Morning Star* again."

So Paul Waggett yielded, and presently in the priest's cosy sitting-room he was fortifying himself with a sensation under the benignly pastoral glance of His Holiness Pope Pius XII whose portrait hung over the mantelpiece.

"I suppose the Italian declaration of war upset you rather, Father?"

"Ah well, I never thought they would come in against us. Never. I was a student in Rome, you know."

"Well, of course, I'm not quite as familiar with Italy as you are, Father. I was never actually there myself. But I'm bound to say I've never believed there was the slightest chance of their keeping out. I've said so from the start. It's really rather extraordinary, but I've been absolutely right about everything from the day the war started."

"Have you indeed, Mr Waggett?" the priest exclaimed, his face so credulously solemn that Joseph Macroon, who knew that expression, nearly forgot himself by winking broadly. "And now you really think the enemy will try to capture Todaidh Beag?"

"I don't go as far as that. I only say we must be ready for anything."

"Yes, yes, the way we all got our gas-masks," the post-master agreed. "Ach, what a nuisance those gas-masks were. It's to be hoped these L.D.V.s won't be such a nuisance as them. There won't be a lot of shooting, will there? A bullet would travel a long way on Todaidh Beag. There's nothing to stop one between Kiltod and Tràigh Swish."

"Except one of your stirks, Joseph," the priest put in.

"Ay, that was the very thing that was in my mind."

"You needn't worry about that, Joseph," the Commanding Officer assured him. "The men will all be trained. I intend to make a great feature of our musketry. Oh, and that's something I wanted to consult you about. Who do you think I ought to approach as local commander here?"

"Duncan Macroon," said Father Macalister without a moment's hesitation.

"Duncan Bàn!" the postmaster exclaimed in horror. "Duncan Bàn loose on Todaidh Beag with a gun? *A bhobh bhobh*, we'll all be dead before the Germans arrive."

"He's your man, Mr Waggett," the priest insisted. "No doubt about it at all. He's the very man you want."

"But he wasn't at the meeting to-night," Waggett objected.

"Ah, well, poor Duncan wasn't quite himself this evening," said the priest with a profoundly tolerant sigh.

"Too much himself," Joseph observed severely.

"But that's a fault with all of us, Joseph. We're all too much ourselves," the priest pointed out. "No, no, Mr Waggett, don't you be prejudiced against poor Duncan just because once in a while he takes a hefty one. I know he's the man you're looking for. Who is to be your second-in-command on that up-to-date island opposite?"

"John Beaton."

"Ah, well, he and Duncan will get on gloriously together.

Duncan was going to be a schoolmaster himself till his grand-mother died and he got the two crofts. He was at the university for two years. He's the very man for you. You leave him to me. I'll put him in touch with the whole situation, and you'll find him a real Napoleon."

Waggett was not sure that he wanted a real Napoleon as his second-in-command on Little Todday, but he thought it unwise to oppose Father Macalister, who if Roderick MacRurie was the uncrowned king of Todaidh Mór was certainly the unmitred bishop of Todaidh Beag.

"Well, Father Macalister, you know best, of course, and if you feel Duncan Macroon is the right man to command what I suppose will be the Little Todday platoon, I shall accept your opinion."

Joseph Macroon burst into some extremely emphatic Gaelic, which to judge by the tone of his voice and the number of 'aguses' suggested to Paul Waggett that he was putting forward a catalogue of objections to Duncan Bàn.

"No, no, Joseph," the priest insisted. "Duncan is the only man for the job. A pity he wasn't quite himself this evening, poor fellow. But he'll come over and see you, Mr Waggett, and you'll have a good man and a good shot."

"I know he's a good shot," Waggett agreed. "And so do my geese."

"Ah, well, you'll have to excuse that, Mr Waggett. You'll always find it very difficult to persuade us on Todaidh Beag that the wild geese belong to anybody except the man who shoots them. But don't forget that the man who can shoot geese can shoot Germans. And now what about another little snifter?"

"No, thank you, Father Macalister. I really must be getting along."

" Just the smallest sensation," the priest insisted, lifting the bottle of Haig's Gold Cap. "A *deoch an doruis*."

But his guest thrust forward a firm hand to shield his glass from excess of hospitality, and soon afterwards he was walking down to the pier with Joseph Macroon, the figure of his reverend and burly host framed in the lamplight of the open door to speed him on his way.

"Aren't you the Chief Warden here, Joseph?"

"Yes, yes, I'm the Chief Warden right enough," the postmaster replied, obviously quite unaware of any implied criticism in the question.

"Don't you think Father Macalister should be warned about his door. And his windows?" Paul Waggett added. "There is a black-out, you know."

"Ah, yes, the black-out," the Chief Warden agreed. "I've had a lot of trouble with that black-out."

"We're much stricter on Great Todday."

"I believe you will be."

"Especially in Snorvig."

"I'm sure of that."

"And everything will have to be tightened up now. After all, it's no use having rules and regulations if people don't pay the slightest attention to them."

"No use at all."

"The last thing I want to do is to interfere, but when the L.D.V.s get really going and we take over the defence of the two islands we cannot have one system for Great Todday and another for Little Todday. Let me put it another way. We *must* all pull together."

"When do you think this war will be over, Mr Waggett?"

"In my opinion it hasn't begun yet."

"Not begun yet!" Joseph Macroon gasped. "*A Dhia, Dhia,* what are you telling me?"

"So you see the importance of a really effective black-out," Waggett went on, coldly oblivious of the postmaster's despair. "I don't say an effective black-out will win the war, but I do say that it may shorten it by several years. And I think it's up to Little Todday to put its back into the black-out."

"You'd better have a word with Father James yourself," Joseph suggested. "He'll say a word about it from the altar if you tackle him. The people think I'm making money over the black-out just because I stopped Kate Anne and Peggy reading in their beds and the price of paraffin has gone up."

"Well, I shall give you all the support in my power, Joseph."

At this moment they came round the corner into the light streaming from the windows of the post-office.

"That isn't a very good example for the Chief Warden to set, is it?" Waggett asked reproachfully.

"But it's so dark down by the quay," the postmaster objected. "In winter-time anybody might step over the edge for the want of a little light. I wouldn't like a poor soul to be drowned just for the sake of the black-out."

Paul Waggett sighed deeply. As he said to his wife when he reached home about half-past one o'clock after an uneventful crossing of the Coolish in the *Morning Star*:

"It's very difficult to make the people of Little Todday understand there is a war on."

"Were they sticky about coming forward to enrol?"

"No, I got more than I expected. Thirty-eight in fact. Some of them are a bit old, but I didn't like to refuse any volunteers. No, it's their attitude towards rules like the black-out. However, I shall tighten things up presently."

"I'm sure you will, dear. And how was Father Macalister?"

"He was very helpful. Very helpful indeed. I had a dram with him after the meeting. We didn't start till half-past ten."

"I wondered why you were so late."

"The usual lack of staff work. There was no petrol in Joseph Macroon's boat and we stopped half-way across. Finally they had to send a boat to tow us in."

"How tiresome for you. So I don't expect you had time to get any eggs?"

"I'm afraid I didn't. But I found four saucepans in Macroon's shop and I bought them all in case there's a shortage of saucepans. I bought twelve boxes of matches too. There's bound to be a shortage of matches. We ought to build up a reserve. Don't bother about the eggs. I'll have to go over again in a day or two to give instructions to my second-in-command."

"Who's he going to be?"

"Duncan Macroon—Duncan Bàn."

"Wasn't he the crofter you had trouble with about shooting your geese?"

"Yes, we did have a little spot of bother, but Father Macalister was anxious for some reason or other that I should make him my second-in-command, and I thought it would be politic to agree."

"But isn't Duncan Macroon a very heavy drinker?"

"He has bouts of it. But perhaps if he's given a responsible job we may keep him off it."

Mrs Waggett looked dubious.

"Well, you know best, dear."

If Mrs Waggett could have seen Duncan Bàn at this moment,

sitting with a bottle of whisky on Tràigh Swish and declaiming Gaelic poetry to the flowing tide, she might have wondered whether in this case Paul did know best.

Chapter 4

THE L.D.V.s

EVEN as upon a chill and dark-browed winter's day snow-flakes begin to fall sparsely at first but presently swirl ever faster and thicker until they obliterate the familiar landscape, so now against Snorvig House the blizzard of paper swept more furiously every time the mailboat called at the island.

"I must say I hadn't realized when I took on this job that it was going to mean quite so much correspondence," Paul Waggett admitted to his wife.

"Couldn't I help, dear?"

"I'm afraid not, old lady. A good deal of it consists of secret orders," he replied, with a smile half appreciative of her wifely dutifulness, half censorious of her feminine presumption. "I think I'll take the old bus over to Bobanish and see if John Beaton can give me a hand. I may get some eggs from Mrs Beaton."

Differently though it might be spelt, the name sounded upon Mrs Waggett's ears like a tucket blown upon the horn of plenty.

"Yes, that would be splendid. Mrs Beaton's such a good henwife."

Mrs Waggett was proud of this Scotticism she had just acquired and her blue eyes sparkled with the faint roguishness of her flapperhood in anticipation of a verbal pat on the back.

But the commander was too deeply absorbed by military problems to notice her new word.

"I only hope we shall get some weapons soon," he said.

So far the total equipment of the island defences, apart from the local shot-guns amounting to eight in all, a pistol without any ammunition, and two assegais contributed by Captain Alan MacPhee, a retired mariner of eighty-seven, consisted of six waterproof capes, six pairs of anklets, four battle-blouses which would have been a tight fit for a boy of fourteen, and six gummed labels inscribed in red with the letters L.D.V. One of these last was stuck on the window of Waggett's veteran 16 h.p. Austin.

Bobanish lay on the east side of the island protected from the savage west by Ben Sticla, from the furious south-west by Ben Pucka, and from the ferocious north-west by Ben Bustival. The east wind assailed it across the Minch without mercy. To reach Bobanish from Snorvig one could either start by driving north with a view of the Coolish and Little Todday on the left or by driving south with a view of the Coolish and Little Todday on the right. By taking the northerly route one drove through Garryboo, the only fairly level stretch of country on that side of the island, and then came round to the east side past the sharp aquiline headland facing due north called Sròn Ruairidh from its resemblance to the nose of the redoubtable Ruairidh Ruadh. By taking the southerly route one drove through the township of Watasett, the houses of which were clustered along either side of a winding inlet once the harbourage of a dozen fishing-boats, but now that the boats had vanished before the destructive activities of trawlers, empty and suggesting to the passer-by the question why people should have chosen so bleak a site for their habitation. Bobanish itself was situated at the head of another inlet, and though here too fishing-boats were no longer in evidence, the land round if not so level as at Garryboo was cultivable.

The school was old and inconvenient, but at least it was wind- and water-tight. The schoolhouse itself was a low gabled residence with a sizable garden to which two fuchsias, a veronica, a stunted contorted laburnum, and a musk-rose over the porch gave a semblance of luxuriant vegetation, so stark was the landscape in which it was set.

"Mr Beaton is not out of school yet," his wife told the visitor who had chosen to approach Bobanish from the south and return to Snorvig by way of Sròn Ruairidh.

"He won't be long?"

"Not more than a few minutes. It's nearly four o'clock. Will I go and fetch him?"

"Please don't bother, Mrs Beaton. I'll wait."

"You'll take a cup of tea, Mr Waggett?"

"Thank you, I should like a cup of tea very much."

Mrs Beaton, a dainty little woman with quick bright eyes like a bird's, bustled off to her kitchen which was famous all over the island for its polished brass and neatly arranged crockery.

Waggett waited for his second-in-command in the sitting-room, the window of which was gay with sharp-scented pelargoniums. He sat in a comfortable saddle-backed armchair long ago broken in to the human seat by John Beaton's father, gazing at a Great Northern Diver in a glass case, and wondering if John Beaton had shot it himself, and if he had whether it was before the Department had let the sporting rights of the two islands to the owner of Snorvig House. The cuckoo's door in the loudly-ticking clock hanging on the wall beside the fireplace flew open and the wooden bird mocked him four times. Outside there was a shrill sound of children's voices. A minute or two later the headmaster of Bobanish school came in and gripped his visitor's hand in a cordial welcome.

"I was going to ring you up, Mr Waggett, to ask if any rifles had come for us yet. We'll be in better fettle altogether with rifles."

"No rifles yet. It's disappointing, isn't it? But I've had a lot of instructions and enquiries," Waggett added.

"Ah, I expect you will have."

"And I was wondering if you'd care to act as my adjutant and deal with any queries that have to be answered. I don't want all my time to be taken up with paper work."

"I'll be glad to do anything I can to help, Mr Waggett."

"What I thought was that I would read through all this correspondence which is arriving faster and faster by every post and send it along to you. They seem very anxious in Fort Augustus about road blocks."

"Road blocks?" the schoolmaster repeated in perplexity.

"Against enemy tanks," his commanding officer explained as nonchalantly as if enemy tanks were a feature of the sporting amenities of Todday. "I thought we'd have one block where the road narrows between Sròn Ruairidh and that boggy stretch below Ben Bustival, and another where the road turns off to Watasett."

"What kind of blocks were you thinking of, Mr Waggett?"

"I haven't worked out the details yet. But roughly I should say tree-trunks to work from cement blocks built out just the

width of a lorry allowing an inch on either side.   And barbed
wire of course."

"I think we will find cement and tree-trunks a bit of a
problem to manage out here," the schoolmaster said, shaking his
head.   "And where do you expect these tanks to come from,
Mr Waggett?   I don't see how the Germans can land tanks
on Great Todday very easily."

"Didn't you read the accounts of the campaign in Norway?"
the Commanding Officer asked compassionately.

"I believe I did, and pretty thoroughly.   I'm afraid it's
the old story.   Muddle through."

"Don't you remember that light tanks were dropped by
parachute?"

"Yes, but what would be the Germans' idea in dropping
light tanks on Great Todday?   Or Little Todday either for
that matter.   I don't see what they'd do with them, Mr
Waggett, when they had dropped them."

"Well, whatever they try to do with them it will be our
business to stop them doing it.   That's why I shall construct
two blocks.   If we had only one block the tanks might go
back right round the island and attack us from the other
side."

"I don't at all want to put up my opinion against yours,
Mr Waggett," said the burly sandy-haired headmaster of
Bobanish, assuming, though he was unaware of it, the expression he assumed when he was wrestling with the obtuseness
of a pupil at the bottom of the class.   "Still, I cannot for the
life of me see why the Germans should use tanks against either
of the Toddays.   Parachutists, yes, or a landing from a submarine, yes.   Mind you, I don't think it's probable, but I
know we must prepare ourselves as much against possibility
as probability.   But tanks . . ."

John Beaton shook his head.

"You don't read the *Daily Express*, do you?" his Commanding
Officer asked.

"No, we take in the *Glasgow Herald*."

It was Paul Waggett's turn to shake his head.

"I don't want the L.D.V.s under my command to be caught
napping.   And though you may not think there is any likeli-
hood of enemy tanks appearing on Todday, Mr Beaton, when
you've read through all those communications I've had from

headquarters at Fort Augustus you'll see that road blocks against tanks are considered of primary importance."

"Road blocks won't be much use without rifles, will they?"

"But we shall get our rifles in due course. I've asked for 150 so that we have some in hand for new recruits. But the most important business at the moment is all this correspondence."

Paul Waggett produced a quantity of pieces of paper of every size from folio to duodecimo out of the ample pockets inside his shooting-jacket and offered them to his second-in-command.

"You'd better start a file. Some want answering, some are really unanswerable, and some don't require an answer," he said.

"I understood there was a paper shortage," the schoolmaster commented grimly.

"So did I. Mrs Waggett wrote the other day to Glasgow for sixty rolls of toilet paper—I feel sure the war will last for a very long time as you know—and the stores where we deal could only send her ten rolls."

At this moment Mrs Beaton came in with tea, and the subject of paper was dropped.

"You still have plenty of jam," Waggett observed a little enviously. "That's going to be scarce. And in my opinion tea will be rationed soon. Mrs Waggett and I have started to build up a reserve. If you're wise you'll do the same."

"Oh, dear me," Mrs Beaton exclaimed, "if they ration tea we'll begin to realize that there really is a war going on. We don't feel it here, do we, Mr Waggett? Except for the young men away at sea."

"We're going to try and bring the war to the Toddays, aren't we, Mr Beaton?" Waggett announced, with the benevolent smile of a Santa Claus. "You won't know the islands when you see us all in uniform."

"In uniform?" the schoolmaster's wife exclaimed. "Goodness, you'll want to be careful, John. The children will laugh plenty if they see you in uniform."

And in anticipation of the pupils' delight trim and plump little Mrs Beaton began to laugh merrily herself.

John Beaton squared his broad shoulders.

"Well, we will have to see the effect when our uniforms arrive," he said. "Nothing yet, Mr Waggett?"

"Only a few anklets, and some battle-blouses which won't fit anybody. But, as you'll see, they're sending us fifty L.D.V. armlets which the women folk must stitch on. By the way, Mr Beaton, what do you think of Father Macalister's idea that Duncan Macroon should command the Little Todday platoon?"

"Duncan Bàn!" exclaimed the schoolmaster. "Oh, he's a grand bard, right enough, but . . ." he paused, unwilling, good man, to criticize another favourite of the Muses.

"Well, as long as you don't let Duncan loose with a gun on Todaidh Mór, Mr Waggett, it'll be Father Macalister's responsibility," observed Mrs Beaton.

"Father Macalister's funeral in fact," said the Commanding Officer, his nose tilting up to allow full play to a complacent smile at his own wit. "Duncan is coming over to see me this evening. I hardly liked to go against Father Macalister. I think we must give him a trial."

"Yes, yes, yes, every man has a right to a trial," John Beaton agreed emphatically.

"Are your fowls laying well, Mrs Beaton?" Paul Waggett enquired tenderly.

"We've nothing to complain of. No, indeed. We've been very lucky. I must send some eggs to Mrs Waggett. Would it be troubling you to take them with you in the car, Mr Waggett?"

"Not at all. It's very kind of you, Mrs Beaton. But you're sure you can spare them?"

Mrs Beaton made a quick gesture to dispose of so ridiculous a question, and when Paul Waggett drove off northward with two dozen eggs for which Mrs Beaton had indignantly refused to accept payment, he was so much exhilarated by his successful visit to Bobanish that he approached the corner where the road narrowed between Sròn Ruairidh and the bog below Ben Bustival at such a pace as nearly brought him into headlong collision with Dr Maclaren's Morris Minor coming from Garryboo.

The two cars pulled up with a grinding of brakes.

"Hi!" shouted the Doctor, leaning out of the window. "What does L.D.V. stand for? Licenced to Drive with Velocity? My god, Mr Waggett, did you think I was a German tank?"

"Curious you should say that, Doctor, because this *is* just where I'm planning a tank-trap. John Beaton and I have been discussing it this afternoon."

"Get away, you're joking!"

"I'm not joking at all. I don't joke about matters of life and death," said Waggett stiffly.

The Doctor got out of his car and came along to find out if he had heard aright.

"You're not seriously telling me you expect German tanks on Todday?" he asked, his jovial florid face puckered in a grin.

"I don't expect them, but that's all the more reason why I should prepare for them. The fundamental principle of all military operations is to expect the unexpected. In the last war I remember when the Germans attacked us at Haut Camembert I said to the Brigadier, 'In my opinion, sir, the enemy will make their main thrust against us,' and he said, 'Well, Waggett, you're usually right, I'll get in touch with D.H.Q.' And at that very moment the Brigade-Major—a fellow called Bickerstaffe—came in to say that the Commanding Officer of the 10th Herefords had just telephoned. . . ."

"Here, but wait a minute, Mr Waggett," the Doctor interrupted. "What bearing has the last war on the question of German tanks on Todday?"

"The point is that the attack was expected at Petits Fours and that it came at Haut Camembert."

The Doctor shook his curly head.

"Well, as long as you didn't start monkeying with the surface of the road I suppose you and John Beaton can dream of German tanks without worrying the rest of us. I'm surprised at John, though. I thought he had more sense."

"Are you suggesting that I am deficient in sense?" Waggett asked, his leathery countenance taking on the deeper tan of indignation.

"It might be more than a suggestion," said the other, with a chuckle.

"Look here, we may as well get things clear at the start, Doctor. I have been asked to make myself responsible for the defence of the two Toddays against invasion. I can't admit your right to criticize any measure of security I feel the situation requires. If I decide that for the defence of Great Todday it is necessary to construct tank-traps and road blocks, I shall do my duty regardless of what anybody says. Anybody," he repeated in a tone of dreamy obstructiveness.

"And supposing the Germans land to-morrow morning?" the Doctor asked. "Do you think that with Captain Mac-Phee's assegais and a few anklets you'll be able to repel them?"

"This isn't the moment for defeatist talk. That's the kind of talk which has led to the present crisis. And now if you'll back your car a bit I shall be able to get past, Doctor. I want to be home as soon as I can, and I expect you have patients to see."

The Doctor returned to his Morris Minor and backed to a part of the road wide enough to allow the Austin to pass. The two drivers went their separate ways each convinced the other was the stupidest man he had ever known.

Mrs Waggett was admirably sympathetic when her husband reached home and told her about Dr MacLaren's utter lack of imagination.

"But you must make allowances, dear," she told him. "You must remember he has not had your experience. His whole life has been spent in the islands except for a few years at Glasgow University. And you must also remember that he *is* very fond of . . ." she coughed.

"He was quite sober this afternoon. Well, if he thinks he is going to be the Great Todday Quisling he'll find it won't be too pleasant for him. No sign of Duncan Macroon yet? It'll soon be time for the six o'clock news."

Mrs Waggett went over to the window and looked out across the daisied lawn for the expected visitor making his way up from the pier, but there was no sign of him. She could see Mr Morrison pacing up and down in front of the Manse in earnest colloquy with Simon MacRurie, his leading elder. She could see Mrs Morrison wheeling the Morrison baby in his perambulator along the drive. She could see the large shape of Roderick MacRurie on the shingled terrace of the hotel gazing through his binoculars at Kiltod. She could see Alec Mackinnon hurrying along the little main street of Snorvig. She could see Iain Dubh the piermaster chasing a party of boys away from the diverse collection of merchandise waiting for a lorry to collect it. She could see a great blue and white sky and the green carpet of Little Todday and the pale Atlantic immense and tranquil beyond.

But there was no sign of Duncan Macroon when her husband

switched on the wireless for a fussy female voice to pant through a catalogue of players in some Children's Hour racket of tushery and finish only just in time not to leave one of them out before the six squeaks played their overture to the sombre tale of French catastrophe, to which her husband sat listening with the gratified expression of a major prophet who had not been let down by Jehovah.

Toward the end of the disastrous news there was a tap on the door. Mrs Waggett jumped up quickly and went across the room on tiptoe to open it and admit a man with tumbled fair hair, a glowing countenance, and eyes as blue as the wing of a kingfisher.

"Here we are then," exclaimed Duncan Bàn. Both Paul and his wife put their fingers to their lips and pointed to the wireless cabinet. Mrs Waggett still on tiptoe led the new arrival to a chair.

"Wonderful reception," Paul Waggett murmured, and at once put his finger to his lips again to prevent the visitor's loud and enthusiastic agreement.

"We'd better wait and hear the announcements," Waggett said when the tale of catastrophe was finished.

It was well he did so, for he had the gratification of hearing that the line of the protected area which guarded north-west Scotland and most of the islands had now been extended to include a little more of the mainland and all the rest of the islands.

"That means a permit will be required in future to visit Great and Little Todday," said Waggett with relish. "Well, it was high time. I could never understand why they weren't included last March."

"Then Gladys will require a permit when she comes to stay with us next month," Mrs Waggett exclaimed in dismay.

"She should apply to the Permit Office as soon as she can," a severe brother-in-law declared. "She'd better say she's staying with the local commander of the L.D.V.s. That will help."

"Do you think the Germans will apply to the Permit Office before they come to Todaidh Beag, Mr Waggett?" Duncan asked in a voice of grave innocence.

"I'm afraid not, Duncan."

"Then what's the use of having permits?" the other pressed.

"To prevent important information leaking out and to keep a check on the activities of fifth columnists. I'm very pleased indeed about it. Very pleased. As I said, I can't think why it wasn't done earlier."

Had he but known, the reason was a simple one. When the magic line was drawn round No. 12 Protected Area the authorities had not noticed that small square in the bottom left-hand corner of the map in which the two Toddays were framed because their position made it impossible to fit them into their proper place on the map of north-west Scotland. They had been discovered at last by an earnest young subaltern who had just been timeously evacuated from a hushy job in Paris to an even hushier job in London. Not Captain Cook himself ever felt a keener thrill of gratification than that young subaltern of Intelligence who put the two Toddays on the map.

"But what important information could anybody find on Todaidh Beag?" Duncan pressed.

The man who was to be his commanding officer smiled indulgently.

"If you do your job as well as I count on your doing it, Duncan, I hope there will be plenty of important information to be gleaned from Little Todday presently."

"Is it true then what Father James is after telling me?"

"That I want you to command the Little Todday platoon? Yes, perfectly true."

"But it's all just a piece of nonsense, isn't it? What could we do if the Germans did come?"

"Fight it out to the last round and the last man," said Waggett in the tone of Leonidas giving his final instructions to the immortal Three Hundred.

"Is it really true then we will be having rifles?"

"Of course."

"Och, that's a different matter altogether. I wasn't believing it. I'll make a fine song about it when we get these rifles. *A Dhia*, I might have a chance to take a pot shot at Joseph Macroon."

"It's a pity you weren't at the meeting in the Kiltod hall."

"Yes, yes, it was a pity, right enough, but I had a date with a fairy-woman that night. A good kind crayture. She's been washing my clothes for me all winter."

Mrs Waggett's china face was hair-cracked with bewilderment, for Duncan did not sound as if he had been tippling.

"I don't understand. Do you really mean that a fairy has been washing your clothes all this winter?" she asked.

"Sure," Duncan replied earnestly. "But she's away now. She just faded clean away like a dream of the morning. You'll remember, Mr Waggett, that it was a fine clear warm evening when you came to Kiltod. Well, she'd finished my washing for me and she was sitting the way she would always be sitting in the chair in the corner, and 'Duncan Bàn,' she said to me—only she said it in Gaelic, you'll understand, 'O Duncan Bàn,' she said to me, 'you'll never see me again, and who's going to wash your clothes next winter,' she said, 'I'm sure I don't know.' And when I was going to speak back the kind crayture was gone. Well, I thought, I may as well walk along to the hall and hear what Mr Waggett has to say about these L.D.V.s. And I started off, but instead of finding myself in the hall I found myself next morning on Tràigh Swish with a beautiful song in my head about that fairy-woman. Isn't that strange now?"

"Very strange indeed," Waggett agreed drily. "But I hope you'll concentrate now on the defence of Little Todday. Father Macalister said you were the best man to command the platoon, and it'll require a great deal of concentration."

"Well, here I am, Mr Waggett, and I'm sure you never saw a more concentrated man in your life. Ach, I'm just a cup of mental Bovril, I'm so concentrated."

"Have you filled up your enrolment form? I'll sign it if you have."

Duncan Bàn slapped his thigh.

"Ah, dash it, I left it behind when I came over. Ah, well, I'll send it over with the post to-morrow. And what do you want me to be doing?"

"I'll let you have two pairs of anklets, which is all I can spare at the moment. And I want you to bring over all the shot-guns you can collect and hand them over at the police station."

"That'll be a trick of Macrae to screw gun licences out of us, I believe."

"Nothing of the kind," said Waggett a little irritably. "We must know what firearms are available on the two islands. As soon as the uniforms come you will have to muster your men

and get them fitted. Oh, you'll find there'll be plenty to do.
Plenty. I'll come across as soon as I can and discuss the plan
of defence for Little Todday. I think we may have to dig
trenches. There's so very little cover on the machair."

When Duncan Bàn had departed the Commanding Officer
turned to his wife.

"You don't think Father Macalister was trying to be funny
when he suggested I should put Duncan Macroon in command
of the Little Todday platoon?"

"It would be very bad taste, dear, to try and be funny at a
moment like this," said his wife severely.

"Very bad taste indeed, Dolly. But sometimes there's a
curious kind of flippancy about Father Macalister when one
would expect a man in his position to be serious. However,
we shall see. I think I'd better give Duncan a chance. Did
he seem quite sober to you this afternoon?"

"I did think for a moment he must be a little tipsy when he
was talking about that fairy, but I don't think he actually was."

"Bother!" Waggett snapped.

"What is it, dear?"

"I meant to ask him to collect some eggs for me on Little
Todday."

Chapter 5

EQUIPMENT

EVEN if it were possible to catalogue the variety of equipment
which throughout the first three months of its existence
arrived three times a week by the *Island Queen* for the Todday
Home Guard, it would obviously be undesirable to take the
slightest risk of providing the enemy with information he must
be thirsting to obtain. The contemporary chronicler of martial
events inevitably suffers from a self-imposed aphasia. Nevertheless, without too gross an indiscretion a few facts can now be
divulged.

As soon as L.D.V. armlets had been issued for fifty volunteers and their wives had patriotically sewn them on, the
initials were abolished in favour of the more inspiring designa-

tion Home Guard. Love's labour may have been lost, but the new name was received with general satisfaction. The Todday L.D.V.s became G Company of the 8th Inverness-shire Battalion of the Home Guard, sporting in their bonnets a square of Clanranald tartan and a tin Macdonald lion for badge, which proclaimed that they were related as soldiers, however distantly, to that famous regiment the Duke of Clarence's Own Clanranald Highlanders (the Inverness-shire Greens). What is more, Paul Waggett became Captain Paul Waggett, John Beaton became Lieutenant John Beaton, and Duncan Bàn became Lieutenant Duncan Macroon. Uniform was a problem at first because it was extremely difficult to equip a man with a perfect fit in every direction. A volunteer might appear with a blouse that impeded his breathing and with many-pocketed trousers into which he was liable to vanish like a potato into a sack, or he might appear with a blouse like a balloon and with trousers that made him look like a Kate Greenaway schoolboy. Bonnets seemed to have no happy mean between extinguishing the features beneath them or balancing on top of the head like a rook's nest in the wind. The greatcoats, too, alternated between the threatened annihilation of their wearers by smothering them with multeity or by strangling them with exiguity. Even those burly volunteers who did manage to acquire the component parts of a uniform all of which fitted them more or less were so much embarrassed by the mirth of the children when they donned them that for some time not a Home Guard would put his nose outside his own door when dressed for parade unless he was assured of the support of at least three other Home Guards in uniform to enable him to conquer his self-consciousness.

In fact it is doubtful whether the Home Guard of the two Toddays would have lasted a month even on paper if it had not been for the boots. It was the boots which saved the military situation. That issue of boots convinced the men of the two Toddays that there really might be something sweet and suitable in dying for one's country. The blouses, the bonnets, the trousers, and even the greatcoats had left them unconvinced; but the fame of those boots travelled round the two islands like the fiery cross in the fierce old days when MacRuries and Macroons gathered to knock one another about. Recruiting for the Home Guard went up with a rush after the first consignment of boots arrived; but Battalion Headquarters had laid down that the ceiling of G Company was not to exceed 120 because at that date there were not arms for more than a quarter of that number. Nobody has yet discovered why the word 'ceiling' was substituted for the word 'strength', and that scholarly little official pamphlet called *Military English* offers no explanation. Possibly it was an early attempt by the War Office to cooperate with the Air Ministry.

The unnecessary word gave keen pleasure to Captain Waggett, and he was never tired of talking about his ceiling. A strength of 120 sounded so feeble: a ceiling of 120 put him in tune with the infinite.

"Your ceiling on Little Todday will be fifty, Mr Macroon," he told his subaltern when the new word had been introduced to him in a communication from Captain George Grant, the adjutant at Fort Augustus.

"Fifty what?"

"Fifty non-commissioned officers and men."

"They'd make a very uncomfortable kind of a ceiling, Mr Waggett."

"One moment, Duncan. I'm speaking to you now as a friend, and so I call you Duncan. But didn't you notice that just now I called you 'Mr Macroon'?"

"I did indeed. I was wondering if you were turning me into an aristocrat of the democracy."

"No, no, no. The point is that I was speaking to you then as one of my subalterns. Lieutenants are addressed as 'Mr'."

"Ach, don't bother with 'Lieutenant' or 'Mr'. Just call me Duncan."

"Not when we're both in uniform. When we're in uniform I call you 'Mr Macroon', and you call me 'sir'. Similarly if you were to address one of your sergeants in uniform you call him 'sergeant' and he addresses you as 'sir'."

"*A Dhia na gràs*, there's not a man on Todaidh Beag would be calling me 'sir' if he didn't want to have his face pushed in. He'd get a smack on the jaw from me he'd never forget."

Captain Waggett sighed. It was hard work fighting the conviction of his Home Guards that they were not really soldiers at all, and his task was not made any easier by the fact that the War Office, the Admiralty, the Air Ministry, and the

Home Office seemed to share this conviction.

Still, once their boots arrived, the status of the Home Guard took a sharp upward curve in popular esteem. The wives of volunteers might consider it their right to wear the battle-blouses themselves when they went to milk the cows on a chilly evening. The children of volunteers might suppose that the battle-trousers were meant as a convenient protection against the rain on the way to and from school. The boots of the volunteers were sacred to the volunteers themselves, and they wore no other kind of footgear from the moment that it was issued to them. There were hitches of course in the issue, like the asperities in the path of true love, and when four pairs of left-footed boots arrived and started an impassioned correspondence in which Battalion Headquarters, the Territorial Association, the Army Clothing Department, North Highland Command, Scottish Command, the L.M.S., the MacPain Steamship Company, O.C. G Company, and every other Company Commander, all took a hand. In the end the missing right-footed boots were traced to C Company commanded by Major Donald MacDonald of Ben Nevis. After this Major (Acting Lieutenant) Norman MacIsaac, the senior subaltern of the Ben Nevis company, and Lieutenant John Beaton played a game of long-distance tennis with those boots across the Minch, trying to match the right-footed ones with their left-footed opposite numbers. In the end one right-footed boot was lost either by the L.M.S. or by MacPain's or possibly on Snorvig Pier, and under Captain Waggett's orders the odd left-footed boot was retained as a hostage by G Company.

Two personal letters from this vast correspondence are worth printing:

> *To Lt.-Colonel A. Lindsay-Wolseley, D.S.O.,*
> *H.Q. 8th Bn. Inv. H.G.,*
> *Fort Augustus*

Dear Lindsay-Wolseley,
> *Who is this fellow you have put in command of G Company? MacIsaac tells me he has had the impertinence to keep back a boot belonging to us. I don't feel inclined to put up with this sort of thing. Can you do anything about it?*
> *Yours sincerely,*
> *D. MacDonald of Ben Nevis*

To Major D. MacDonald of Ben Nevis,
Glenbogle Castle

Dear Ben Nevis,

I have spoken to George Grant who says he thinks it will save trouble if we try to get you another pair of boots. You must realize that communication with Todday is slow and difficult, and I do not think anything will be gained by prolonging this already lengthy correspondence. We are out to save paper, as I know you'll appreciate.

I have complete confidence in the fitness of Captain P. Waggett to command G Company.

Yours sincerely,
A. Lindsay-Wolseley

"In my opinion, MacIsaac," said the Chieftain of Ben Nevis, "Lindsay-Wolseley is turning into a nincompoop."

Major (Acting Lieutenant) Norman MacIsaac, who was the Chamberlain of Ben Nevis in private life and had served with distinction in the last war as a major in the 8th Service Battalion of the Clanranalds, tried to look as much like a lieutenant as his White Knight's face and moustache would let him.

"Colonel Lindsay-Wolseley is very much preoccupied with the invasion threat, Ben Nevis," he suggested.

"Well, I'm not going to have one of our boots calmly stolen by these island thieves. I suppose I must let the matter stand over for the time; but I don't intend to forget that boot, and you're not to forget it either, MacIsaac. Who is this fellow Waggett?"

"I believe he is an ex-chartered accountant who has settled on Great Todday."

The twenty-third MacDonald of Ben Nevis snorted majestically.

Far away across the Minch in Great Todday Captain Paul Waggett, happily unaware that he had offended the pride of Mac 'ic Eachainn, was debating how to send back six boxes of .304 ammunition which had been sent him for the sixty .302 rifles issued to G Company.

"It's a nuisance right enough, Mr Waggett," said Macrae, the genial constable responsible for the control of crime on the two Toddays, and still, much to the company commander's annoyance, intimately associated with the Home Guard, which at this date was regarded as an illegitimate child of the Police they were trying to foist on to the Military.

"It's more than a nuisance," Captain Waggett said angrily. "It's holding up the whole defence scheme for these islands. How do they suppose I'm going to beat off the enemy if the cartridges won't go into the rifles?"

"Ay, it would be a bit awkward right enough."

"It would be more than awkward. It might lead to the whole of Scotland being overrun. It's just the kind of thing that was happening in France."

"Ay, I believe it was."

"Can't you compel Captain MacKechnie to take back those boxes of ammunition, Constable?"

"I'm afraid I can't, Mr Waggett. He says he's not allowed to carry explosives by the Board of Trade regulations," Macrae explained.

"But they arrived here with the *Island Queen*," Waggett expostulated.

"Yes, yes, but Captain MacKechnie says he didn't know they wass explosives. He's not allowed to carry explosives with the mails on board."

"When is the *Kishmul* expected?" This was the cargo steamer that in pre-war days used to call at Snorvig every three weeks.

"Ach, I don't think she's expected at all, Mr Waggett."

"Then do you mean to say this .304 ammunition will have to remain here indefinitely? I can't get any .302 till this .304 goes back to ordnance. I had a telegram from Fort Augustus about it this morning."

The constable took off his diced cap, ruffled his curly hair in perplexity, smoothed it again, and replaced the cap.

"Would it be all the same if we sent back the .302 rifles and kept the .304 ammunition against an issue of .304 rifles?"

"No, it wouldn't be the same at all. I have five hundred rounds of .302 ammunition and I haven't any .304 rifles. You'd better come down with me to the boat and we'll try to make Captain MacKechnie see reason."

"But the man has the regulations to think of," Macrae objected.

"He should have thought of them when he brought the ammunition here."

"So he would have, Mr Waggett. So he would have, if he'd known they wass explosives."

"I don't intend to let the Germans capture Great Todday for the sake of a lot of obsolete regulations," the company commander avowed. "I'll go down to the ship at once."

"Captain MacKechnie will be up at the hotel just now," said Macrae.

And there they found him sitting in Roderick's own room.

"I'm very sorry, Mr Wackett. I'm very sorry inteet to causs you any inconvenience, but it's impossible for me to accept those poxes of ammunition."

Roderick said something to the captain in Gaelic.

"Shut my ice?" the latter piped indignantly. "How the deffil can I shut my ice to six poxes of ammunition?"

"But you did bring them here," Waggett argued.

"And amn't I after telling you a tussen times, Mr Wackett, that the ammunition wass put aboard when I titn't see what it wass. A rule iss a rule and a reckulation iss a reckulation, and you'd petter have a trink with me and say no more about it."

It was no use arguing with Captain MacKechnie. So the glasses were filled and under the influence of the kindly spirit peace reigned in the sitting-room of Roderick MacRurie.

In the end the two Toddays gained by Captain Mac-Kechnie's observation of the rules, because Captain Waggett received twenty .304 rifles to fit the immobilized ammunition on condition that he returned twenty .302 rifles to ordnance. In due course this was done, but by a happy mistake the twenty rifles like hikers in the days of peace travelled all round Scotland for two or three weeks and then returned to Snorvig.

So instead of sixty rifles for their ceiling of 120 G Company had eighty rifles, probably a higher proportion than any other Home Guard company in the country at that date.

But it must not be supposed that G Company was dependent upon rifles of one calibre or another to defend the two Toddays against the invader. They had six pikes also. The word suggests medieval pageantry. In point of fact these pikes were lengths of thin gas-piping to which bayonets had been soldered.

"They'll be more useful on Little Todday, I think, than on Great Todday," the company commander decided.

And in a way they were, because Joseph Macroon was able to use one of them to open an obstinate packing-case.

It was not only by supplying the Home Guards of the two

Toddays with lethal weapons that a grateful Administration showed its appreciation of what they were doing for the country in this hour of peril. With pikes and rifles and bayonets and Lewis guns and directions for the manufacture of a home-made grenade known as a Molotov cocktail in those unregenerate days when Lord Haw-Haw was still obsequiously stroking the Russian bear, Todday men would repel a direct assault upon their coasts; but they had to be protected against the enemy within as well as the enemy without. And this is where the strong arm and the fine intelligence of the Military Permit Office combined to protect the islands. It was realized at the War Office that for anybody to be able to travel from Obaig to Snorvig without restriction must gravely affect the security of the whole of Great Britain, and so anybody who was not in Great Todday or Little Todday on a specified night in June, whether a native, an immigrant or a mere inquiline, could never thereafter visit the islands without filling up a form, sending it in to the Military Permit Office, and, after a delay long enough for the sleuths of the Military Permit Office to ascertain all about him or her being granted a permit. Very often such a permit was refused, and if it was refused not even a Member of Parliament at question time could extract from the Secretary of War the reason for such a refusal. Stupid people who did not appreciate what a protection against Hitler the Military Permit Office was, used to grumble when the daughter of a Todday crofter could not come home for her holiday from domestic service in Glasgow because her holiday was over before the permit was accorded to her. Such people deserve to be Germanized and taught what life is like under a really competent bureaucracy.

It is a tribute to Captain Waggett's common-sense patriotism that when his sister-in-law Mrs Gorringe was refused a permit to pay her annual visit to Snorvig House, he accepted the decision of the Military Permit Office without question.

"But, Paul, dear," his wife protested, "I really cannot understand why poor Gladys has been refused."

"There must be some very good reason," he replied, his philosophy reinforced by remembrance of the way Gladys always went back to her home in Upper Norwood laden with local produce. Such acquisitive behaviour had annoyed him even in peace-time; in war-time it would be unbearable.

"But it seems such a reflection on *you*, dear. After all, if you are fit to be entrusted with the defence of Todday you are entitled to have your wife's sister to stay with you. And I know poor Gladys made a particular point of your being her brother-in-law. I think you ought to write a very strong letter to the Permit Office."

Captain Waggett shook his head.

"We must trust the people on the spot," he said. "They have their reasons. I may have some very disagreeable tasks to perform both here and on Little Todday before long, and I shouldn't like my reasons to be questioned. Gladys used to attend meetings of the British Union of Fascists. That may be the reason for refusing her a permit."

"But so did you, Paul, in the days before the war."

"Only out of curiosity."

"Poor Gladys only went out of curiosity."

"Don't worry, old lady. War's war, and we've all got to give up something. I'm not going to keep the Twelfth this year. Poor old Paddy," he added to his auburn-haired dog. "No grouse for you this year, old man."

The outsize setter flogged the floor with his plumose tail, and his master could not resist exclaiming as usual in astonishment at the way Paddy understood every word he said to him. "That dog's intelligence is uncanny," he declared.

"It's a pity he's not employed at the Military Permit Office," Mrs Waggett said tartly.

"You're letting the war get you down, Dolly. You mustn't do that. I'm sorry about Gladys, but don't forget the chicks will be getting their leave soon."

"Perhaps they won't get permits," Mrs Waggett observed.

"Oh yes, dear, they're members of His Majesty's Forces," their father reminded their mother proudly.

"Well, I still think it's ridiculous to refuse Gladys a permit." And Mrs Waggett might have thought it even more ridiculous if she had known that the reason for refusing her sister a permit for a fortnight's visit to Great Todday was the similarity between her married name 'Gorringe' and 'Goering'.

"I don't suppose there's anything in it," said the Major entrusted with the decision. "But I think it's wiser to refuse this woman."

"Quite, sir," the subaltern agreed reverently, and presently a strapping young orderly in the pink of condition for active service carried away a sheaf of rejected applications to the room where three equally strapping young women entered them up in a card-index, cross-referenced them, and finally filed them away in the limbo to which such rejected applications were consigned.

Some days after this Captain Waggett received an eighteen-inch envelope O.H.M.S. in which was enclosed another envelope O.H.M.S. of a quarter the size stamped SECRET in purple ink. Inside this on a quarto of battered tissue paper, which might have served as a splendid advertisement of the War Office's campaign to save paper if it too had not been stamped SECRET in red ink, was a description of the various identity cards the holders of which were entitled to travel without let or hindrance :

"Pink identity card with green stripes shows that the bearer is a Member of Parliament.

"Mauve identity card with a yellow half moon in lower left-hand corner shows that the bearer is authorized as an official of the Ministry of Waste to travel in prohibited areas."

And so on and on through a polychrome of identity cards with which Captain P. Waggett was instructed to familiarize his Home Guards so that if the bearer of one of them was challenged he could establish his right not to be shot, bayoneted, piked, or blown up with a Molotov cocktail by the defenders of the two Toddays.

Finally precautions were taken to ensure that one Home Guard should recognize another Home Guard. This was effected by stamping the national registration cards of Home Guards with 8th Inverness-shire Bn. H.G. in green within a green lozenge. Efforts were made by the authorities on the mainland to have photographs affixed, and it took a good deal of correspondence to persuade them that neither of the two Toddays supported a professional photographer. So, unwillingly, the authorities at last agreed to accept the stamp as a guarantee of the individual Home Guard's authenticity. At the same time, they never felt perfectly sure that the Todday Home Guard was not a collection of fifth columnists so long as there was nothing but the imprint of that green rubber-stamp to convince them, and finally Captain Waggett, whose eager imagination was already playing with the idea of being made an O.B.E. for his energy and devotion as a company commander, tried to import a photographer from Glasgow. When the latter applied for his permit and stated the object of his visit to Snorvig he was refused, and after being tailed round Glasgow for a few days by Security Intelligence sleuths he was arrested on suspicion of espionage. The name of this photographer was John Anderson, which explains the strong rumour that ran round Glasgow in the summer of 1940 that Sir John Anderson had taken advantage of his position as Minister of Home Security to do a Vichy with Hitler and had been lodged in the Tower where he was being watched day and night by a couple of Beefeaters.

Chapter 6

ACTION STATIONS

ONCE more in our island story it was about the lovely close of a warm summer day that somewhere in the south-west of England the wild alarum clashed from all the reeling spires. In Macaulay's fragment the news of the Armada reached no farther than the burghers of Carlisle. On that September day in 1940 the superiority of the telegraph to the beacon as a transmitter of news gave the signal on Todaidh Mór before the sun had dipped into the ocean beyond Todaidh Beag.

Captain Waggett had just risen from the dinner-table when the telephone rang and, lifting the receiver, he heard the gentle voice of Mrs Donald MacRurie, the wife of the postmaster:

"Hullo, is that 101 Snorvig?"

"Yes."

"Can I speak to Mr Waggett, please?"

"This is Mr Waggett speaking."

"Oh, I'm sorry, Mr Waggett. I didn't recognize your voice. We have a priority telegram here and we think it may be for you."

"Oh, yes?"

"It's addressed to Ochome Guard, Snorvig."

"To what?"

"Ochome Guard."

"Spell it, please."

"O-C-H-O-M-E-G . . ."

"Oh, O.C. Home Guard! Yes, yes, yes, that's me. O.C. of course is Officer Commanding."

"I'm sorry, Mr Waggett, that was the way we had it from Fort Augustus."

"Never mind, Mrs MacRurie. It is Mrs MacRurie, isn't it? What does it say?"

"Baboon."

"What?"

"Baboon."

"Will you spell that, please."

"B-A-B-O-O-N."

"Baboon?"

"Yes, just that. And the sender is Hog. H-O-G. We thought it was rather peculiar. Would you like us to get it repeated? There must be some mistake."

"Don't bother, Mrs MacRurie. Put me through, will you, to Mr Beaton at Bobanish?"

A few seconds later the emphatic voice of the second-in-command spoke.

"This is Bobanish 122. Who is speaking?"

"Captain Waggett."

"Oh, good evening, Captain. What a beautiful day we've had."

"Mr Beaton, will you look through the files and see if you can find those code-words they sent from Fort Augustus two or three weeks ago. I've just had a telegram with one word— Baboon."

"Baboon?"

"It *must* be a code-word, I think. It came from Fort Augustus."

"Oh, it must be," the schoolmaster agreed. "Who would be calling anybody a baboon in a telegram? If you'll hold on, Captain, I'll have a look at the files."

Presently John Beaton came back to the telephone.

"I can't find 'baboon,' Captain. Would it be a mistake for 'balloon'?"

"What does 'balloon' mean?"

"Action stations."

"Action stations?" the Commanding Officer gasped. "Good god, the invasion must have started! Call out all your section, Mr Beaton, and get them in position at once. If the landing forces are too strong to be resisted, fall back fighting a delaying action and take up a position on the easterly slope of Ben Sticla to harass the enemy. The men should take as much food as they can carry. And don't let them forget their respirators. I'll get round as soon as I can and visit all stations. Place a patrol on the road, stop every lorry and car, and put the magnetos out of action. I must warn the Garryboo and Watasett sections now. Good luck to you."

As her husband put down the receiver and stood there, tight-lipped, his eyebrows meeting in a determination to do or to die, she who had sometimes wished he would not talk quite so much about what he had done in France and Flanders realized that she was indeed the wife of a hero and yielded him all the admiration of her heart, which had not always supported the loyal wifely service of her lips.

"Paul, I think you're wonderful," she murmured.

He acknowledged the tribute with a smile half sweet, half steely-stern, and lifted the receiver again.

To George Campbell, the schoolmaster at Garryboo, and to Norman MacLeod, the schoolmaster at Watasett, he gave similar orders to those he had given to John Beaton. And then he was faced with the problem of passing the news to Little Todday where the telephone had not been installed.

While he was pondering this problem a ring came through from the post-office.

"Is that you, Mr Waggett?"

"Yes, what is it?"

"We have another telegram from Hog for O.C. Home Guard, Snorvig."

"What does it say?"

"You cannot count on any repeat any reinforcements stop establish contact with R.N. or R.A.F. immediately."

"Get me 18 Portrose, Mrs MacRurie. It's very urgent. And meanwhile put me through to Mr Thomson at the Bank."

A few seconds later the voice of the bank agent was asking who was speaking.

"Is that Sergeant Thomson?"

"Imphm!"

"This is Captain Waggett, Sergeant."

"Good evening, Mr Waggett."

"I've just had news from Fort Augustus that the invasion has started."

"Is that so, Mr Waggett?" came the voice of the bank agent without a trace even of surprise let alone of excitement.

"I want you to get all the Snorvig section to their action stations as soon as possible."

"I'll do that right away."

"And, Sergeant, will you get hold of Corporal Archie MacRurie . . ."

"Which of the two Corporal Archie MacRuries?"

"The Biffer."

"Imphm."

"And tell him to get across to Kiltod as soon as he can and inform Lieutenant Macroon that his men are to take up action stations at once. I will try to get across later myself. And, Sergeant!"

"Yes, Mr Waggett?"

"Please tell Corporal MacRurie he's not to waste half an hour talking about the invasion on the quay. He's to go at once. He'd better commandeer Iain Dubh's boat."

"Wouldn't it be easier if he went in his own boat?"

"Yes, perhaps it would. I'm trying to get in touch with the Rear-Admiral at Portrose."

At this point the wife of the postmaster broke in to say Mr Waggett's call to Portrose was through.

"Hullo, is that the Rear-Admiral's office?"

A bluebottle buzzed a faint reply.

"Can you hear me?"

The bluebottle buzzed again.

"This is Captain Waggett, Officer Commanding the Home Guard, Great and Little Todday."

The buzzing was more protracted but fainter than before.

"I want to know if in the event of the enemy landing on either of the Toddays I can have a destroyer?"

The defender of the Toddays fancied he heard a gnat ping for a moment at the other end of the telephone. Then silence followed, a silence from which no amount of 'Halloaing' could extort a response.

Waggett rang up the exchange again.

"Get me the R.A.F., Obaig, if you can. I don't know the number."

While he was waiting for the call to be put through, Captain Waggett went up to put on his uniform. When he was dressed he tested his respirator and at that moment he heard the telephone ring. Mrs Waggett had seen her husband in this respirator often enough, but always when she had been prepared for the transformation it would effect in the human countenance. Now when he burst into the 'lounge' like a deedy orang-outang she dropped the receiver with a scream of horror. From the muffled recesses of the respirator she was urged to pull herself together. And as Paul picked up the receiver and disembarrassed his face of the respirator he said reproachfully:

"I'm counting on you to set an example to the other women, Dolly."

"It was only a momentary jump you gave me," she pleaded.

He held up his hand for silence, and this time it was the slow voice of Donald MacRurie himself who had just come in from an evening's fishing.

"Haven't you got R.A.F. Obaig yet?" Waggett expostulated.

"I'm sorry, Mr Waggett, but they won't give me the number."

"Did you say it was a matter of urgent military importance?"

"No, I didn't say that, Mr Waggett," replied Donald, who was twenty years older than his wife and a brother of Simon the merchant, with an equal sense of his own importance.

"Well, the point is, Mr MacRurie, that the invasion has started and I've been ordered to get in touch with the R.A.F."

"Will I tell them that at the Obaig exchange?"

"You'd better."

There was a pause, and then the slow voice of the Snorvig postmaster came through again.

"They say they have orders not to give the number of the R.A.F."

"This is ridiculous. Suppose I get a message in a minute to say that enemy forces have landed at Garryboo? Ring up the police station at Obaig. . . . Hullo, is that Obaig police station?"

"Yes."

"This is Captain Waggett, Officer Commanding on the

islands of Todday. I want to be put through to the R.A.F.
I have important information about the enemy."

"I'll fetch Inspector Macfarlane. Will you please hold on."

Waggett put his hand over the mouthpiece and turned to
his wife.

"This is the kind of thing that led to Dunkirk," he said
bitterly. "Hullo? Oh yes, that's Inspector Macfarlane, is it?
Good evening, Inspector. I want to be put through to the
R.A.F. . . . What do you say? You can't give me the number?
But surely it's for the R.A.F. to judge that . . . yes, I know those
are the orders, but surely now that the invasion has started . . .
no, I don't say Germans are actually landing on Great Todday
at this moment . . . I'll accept the responsibility . . . it's not my
place to accept responsibility? . . . I say, what do you mean?
. . . hullo? . . . hullo? . . ."

Captain Waggett hung up the receiver.

"They've rung off," he told his wife indignantly. "What
they want in Obaig police station is a Hun bomb to make them
realize that there's a war on. I'm disgusted. Perfectly disgusted. Well, it's lucky for the islands that *I'm* not swathed
up in red tape like an Egyptian mummy. I'm off now, Dolly,
to inspect my dispositions."

"Oh, Paul, I hope nothing will happen to you."

He shrugged his shoulders.

"The fortune of war, old lady."

"But suppose the Germans land and you're at the other side
of the island?" she asked tremulously.

"Don't you remember the instructions over the wireless to
the civil population? You stay put. Everybody in Great
Todday except the Home Guard must stay put."

He patted her on the shoulder and in a moment was
gone.

On the way down to inspect the preparations made by the
Snorvig section to give the enemy a warm reception Captain
Waggett turned aside to offer a word of advice to the Minister.

"It's true then what they are telling me?" Mr Morrison exclaimed. "I thought it was just another Todday tale. Well,
well, this is indeed an historic occasion."

"I'm counting on you, Mr Morrison, to keep the women
quiet when the firing starts," said the commander. "You
know how excitable they are. Ah, good evening, Mrs Morri-

son," he added as the Minister's wife came into the room.
"You've heard the news?"

"It's terrible, is it not, Mr Waggett? And only last week
my mother was writing to beg me to bring Baby with me to
Glasgow."

"I think you're far safer here, Mrs Morrison," the Commander assured her. "I expect Glasgow will be bombed to
pieces."

"Is that so? What a pity I did not write and tell my mother
to come here. But it's so difficult with this permit business,
is it not? And how is Mrs Waggett? Is she feeling very
worried about the invasion? I'm sure she'll be anxious on
your account."

"Indeed yes, Mr Waggett," the Minister added. "And we
are all very grateful to you for the trouble you have taken with
the Home Guard. It gives us a real sense of security."

"We shall do our best," Captain Waggett modestly assured
him. "And if the firing does start I'm relying on you to keep
the civil population calm."

"Angus!" exclaimed Mrs Morrison. "Will there be firing?
What will I do with Baby if there's firing?"

"We will trust in God, Janet."

"Oh, I know we will, Angus. But I'd like awfully much to
find a nice quiet place for Baby," Mrs Morrison insisted.

"We'll talk that over when Mr Waggett has gone, Janet.
I'll just walk along with him to the gate."

"You mustn't let Mrs Morrison worry too much," said the
Commander when he bade the Minister farewell. "After all, the
Germans have not attacked us yet. And perhaps they won't."

There was a note of wistfulness in the Commander's voice
which touched the little Minister's kind heart.

"I believe you'll be disappointed, Mr Waggett, if they don't
attack us," he said.

"Oh, I won't go as far as to say that," the Commander
replied. "But of course one can't help being curious to know
if one's preliminary hard work will stand the test when the
time comes. I remember in the last war when we were in
billets at Foiegras after the German break-through in March
1918 I worked out a plan for our counter-offensive and it was
exactly the same as the plan that Foch worked out afterwards.
Most extraordinary. There was I a subaltern in the Stock

Exchange Rifles and there was he a Marshal of France and we both hit on exactly the same idea.   Ironical, isn't it?"

With what he fancied sounded like a light-hearted chuckle over the whimsicality of fortune Paul Waggett made his way down the road into Snorvig.   Here he found the Civil Defence organization mustered in full force and Alec Mackinnon issuing orders.

"May I ask what you think you're doing with that stirrup-pump, Mr Mackinnon?" the commander of the Home Guard enquired coldly.

"I'm giving instructions what to do in the event of a landing by the enemy, Mr Waggett," said the tall schoolmaster, who was dressed in blue denim overalls and wearing a steel helmet.

"Well, please call your men in until you get word from me that their services are required.   I wish all civilians to stay put while the emergency lasts."

"I don't accept your right to order about Civil Defence workers, Mr Waggett," the schoolmaster declared hotly.

Captain Waggett's nose tilted up like an anti-aircraft gun at Alec Mackinnon's steel helmet.

"Perhaps you'll accept being put under arrest for subversive conduct?" he asked.

"Who's going to put me under arrest?" the schoolmaster demanded.

"The senior military officer on the island, who happens to be myself."

"You'll put *me* under arrest?"

"Certainly, unless you obey my orders."

At this point MacRae the constable intervened.

"I'm sure Mr Mackinnon is only anxious to be helpful, Captain Waggett."

"If he wants to be helpful let him take that idiotic stirrup-pump away.   Nobody can work it, and if anybody could it wouldn't contribute anything to the repulse of the enemy, which is all we have to concentrate on for the present."

"And suppose an enemy plane starts dropping incendiaries?" the schoolmaster asked.

"I'm not expecting to be attacked from the air," said Captain Waggett coldly.

"I'm not compelled to accept your expectations as my authority, Mr Waggett.   However, as I don't want to be the cause of dissension when the enemy is at the gate, I'm prepared to withdraw the stirrup-pump and accept your orders."

"Ah well, I like the spirit of that, Mr Mackinnon," the constable declared enthusiastically. "Ah well, my goodness, that's a fine spirit right enough."

There was a murmur of '*seadh gu dearbh*' from the Civil Defence workers echoing in Gaelic that 'right enough' of the constable.

"I accept your· offer in the same spirit, Mr Mackinnon," the Home Guard Commander said, with majestic condescension. "And I appreciate very much your readiness to—er—co-operate. Ah, there you are, Sergeant."

This was addressed to the bank-agent.

"Good evening, Mr Waggett."

"Everybody at his post?"

"Imphm," Sergeant Thomson informed him with a nod.

"I must drive round the island now and see what's happening to the other sections. You will be in command here of course. Tell Donald MacRurie from me that nobody—I repeat nobody—is to use the 'phone except yourself while I am away."

"What if there's a call for the doctor?" Sergeant Thomson asked.

"You must decide whether it's urgent or not."

"That's putting rather a heavy responsibility on me," said the cautious Midlothian man.

"I've every confidence in you, Sergeant. Corporal MacRurie has gone over to warn them in Little Todday, I suppose?"

"The Biffer's gone over, yes."

"When he gets back tell him to stand by with his boat. If everything's all right here I'll go across myself later on. By the way, don't forget to immobilize all the lorries and cars in Snorvig."

Captain Waggett swung round and walked rapidly up the hill to Snorvig House.

"What a man!" Alec Mackinnon commented.

"Imphm," Andrew Thomson grunted, but whether he was assenting to the sarcasm of the schoolmaster or expressing a genuine admiration of his own was beyond the detection of the nicest ear for a subtle inflection.

Paul Waggett found his front door locked against him when he reached Snorvig House a few minutes later.

He drew his pistol from the holster and hammered upon it.

Presently the voice of Roderick MacRurie was heard asking who was there.

"Captain Waggett," the master of the house rapped out. The key turned in the lock.

"Chust as well to be prepared," said the big hotel-keeper, his tone touched with a slight sheepishness. "Mistress Waggett was feeling a wee bit nervous. Well, well, what terrible news to be sure! And when do you think the Chermans will be here? I was after coming round to ask your advice, Mr Waggett. The wife's in a fix what we ought to do."

"Stay put," said the commander of the Home Guard curtly. "There may be an attempt by the enemy to land to-night."

"*A Thighearna bheannaichte*, don't be saying such a thing. Will we all be murderred in our beds?"

"You've nothing to worry about at all, Roderick, nothing at all. If the Germans captured the island you might get taken as a hostage for the good behaviour of the civil population. That's the worst that could happen to you."

"*A Thighearna*, a hostitch? What kind of a hostitch would I make?"

"What is it, Paul? Have they been sighted?" Mrs Waggett came out of the 'lounge' to ask anxiously.

"No, of course not. Do you think I should be here if the enemy had been sighted?" her husband replied irritably. "I'm just off to drive round the island and see that everything's in order."

"Oh, well, well, it's a mercy you're here, Mr Waggett," said the big hotel-keeper. "Well, I was never the one to laugh at the Home Card. It's not a fun at all. I'm always telling to them 'Wait you till the Chermans come and then you'll see if the Home Card is a fun.' Ah, well, it's not for us to be questioning the ways of the Lord, but *och, a charaid*, it would take a wise man to puzzle out chust what His idea was when He created a trash like Hitler."

"I'm afraid I can't spend the evening discussing theology with you, Roderick," said the man of action. "Would you like to drive round the island with me?"

"Drive round the island with you?" Roderick exclaimed in consternation. "No, no, no, if the Chermans are coming I'll be more at home with them in my own house. Is it whisky they like best, or rum, or chin?"

"You're surely not thinking of offering them drinks?"

"No, no, but I was thinking that many a man's heart has been softened by a tram at the right moment."

And when Captain Waggett was speeding northward to Garryboo through the twilight this remark of Roderick's came back to him, and his nose tilted in disgust at the memory of it as the nose of General de Gaulle might tilt in disgust at the thought of Laval.

Chapter 7

THE VIGIL

THE section leader of Garryboo was George Campbell who was the headmaster of the school. He was a small shy man with a light tenor voice, whose father had been factor of the Toddays before the Department of Agriculture acquired the islands. Originally the Campbells had come from Mull and George Campbell's rendering of *An t'Eilean Muileach* was a feature of every *céilidh*, his light voice being swallowed up by the enthusiastic participation of his listeners who always made the song their own, not because they had any great admiration for the island of Mull but because it was such a catchy tune.

George Campbell was a bachelor living with a majestic old mother in the new school at Garryboo, which had looked such an improvement upon the obsolescent schools of Bobanish and Watasett for at least three months after it was erected, but which now six years later looked more like a cracked egg-shell than a new school, a monument while it should last to the dishonesty of a builder and the incompetence of county councils.

In the little sitting-room of the schoolhouse the flimsy shoddiness of which was made more pitiably obvious by the solid mahogany furniture of old Mrs Campbell, Captain Waggett was received by the old lady herself.

"You're not feeling nervous, Mrs Campbell?"

"Nervous," she exclaimed contemptuously, "what would I have to feel nervous about at my age?"

"I thought perhaps the prospect of the invasion . . ."

"You're surely not believing all that rubbish, Mr Waggett?" the old lady scoffed. "What would the Germans want to invade Todday for?"

"We have to be prepared, Mrs Campbell."

The old lady eyed him balefully.

"If people spent more of their time preparing to meet their Creator and less of their time behaving like a lot of silly children this would be a better island in the sight of the Lord. I'm surprised at Mr Morrison for encouraging such wicked nonsense."

"There *is* a war on, you know, Mrs Campbell."

"There's always a war on, Mr Waggett, a war with Sahtan, with Sahtan, Mr Waggett, and it's no use calling out the Home Guard against him. *He* invaded Great Todday years ago, and he's walking about the island at this very moment, laughing to himself because people who ought to know better are dressing themselves up to make clowns of themselves and mocking the Sabbath with guns and suchlike. Leave that sort of thing to the *papanaich* on Little Todday. It's their religion to break the Sabbath, poor heathen souls. Ah well, Mr Waggett, when we started this dreadful war on the Sabbath I said no good could come out of it."

George Campbell came in at that moment and his mother looked at her son with scorn. He was always uncomfortably self-conscious in uniform, and it was in an agony that he made a clumsy attempt to salute his Commanding Officer under the gaze of those blue glacial eyes.

"Goodness me, George, what's the matter with you? If you're wanting to scratch your head," said the old lady, "you'd be the better of taking that cap off your head and doing it honestly."

Like so many women who produce their first and only off-spring late in life, Mrs Campbell still treated her thirty-three-year-old son as a child of ten.

"All in order, Sergeant?" Captain Waggett asked sternly. He who was preparing to face the full weight of the German onslaught upon Britain was not going to be browbeaten by a disagreeable old woman.

"We had a little awkwardness with the Doctor at the Sròn Ruairidh road block, Captain."

"I'll go and make Mr Waggett a cup of tea, George, and don't you be telling him foolish tales," the old lady interrupted.

The commander of the Home Guard eyed her with austere disapproval.

"No, thank you, Mrs Campbell, I'm afraid I've no time for tea. Yes, Sergeant," he turned to ask, "what was the matter at Sròn Ruairidh?"

"I had your orders to hold up all cars and lorries."

"Quite."

"And I told the Doctor why we had the barbed wire across the road."

"Yes, and what did he say?" Waggett asked with an encouraging and protective smile.

The section leader of Garryboo blushed.

"It was very strong language he used."

"You mean he swore at you?"

"He swore at all of us, Mr Waggett. He was very insulting."

"But he didn't try to rush the road block?"

"No, he backed away from it and said he'd go by the other road to Snorvig. He'd been all afternoon and evening at a confinement with Bean Eoghain Chaluim at Knockdown, and I think he was wanting his tea."

"Did he complain about me? I mean was he at all personal?"

"He spoke very bitterly about you, Captain."

"George," interrupted the old lady, "that's enough of gossip."

"I'm sorry, Mrs Campbell, but I must insist on hearing what Dr Maclaren said about me."

"What he said was he didn't think that even you were quite such a clown as that," the schoolmaster gulped out in embarrassment.

"Quite such a clown as what?" asked Captain Waggett, with quiet dignity.

"I suppose he meant such a clown as to stop him on the road."

"Did you tell him the invasion had started?"

"I did indeed."

"And what did he say?"

"It was a word in Gaelic I wouldn't care to repeat in English, Captain."

"Indeed, no," the old lady put in. "Nor in Gaelic either."

"Oh well, we have more important things to worry about to-night than Dr Maclaren, Sergeant. You have your sentries posted along the coast?"

"Yes, Captain."

"And you'll relieve them every two hours night and day?"

"Yes, Captain."

"Where is your field-dressing post?"

The section leader looked embarrassed.

"I'm afraid I didn't think about that, Captain."

"Never mind. Perhaps it'll be better to use the school. Tell the women who volunteered for first-aid instruction to stand by through the night. And if they land in strength don't attempt the impossible. Communicate with me at once, and inform Lieutenant Beaton at Bobanish and Sergeant Macleod at Watasett. Then take as heavy a toll as you can of them while they're in the boats and fall back with your wounded, leaving any serious cases at the school. After that you'll retire up Ben Bustival and establish contact with Lieutenant Beaton's men on Sticla. The great thing to bear in mind is that the Home Guard is essentially a guerilla force. In our own hills we ought to be able to hold out for a long time."

"What will they do for hills on Todaidh Beag, Captain?" George Campbell asked.

"It is a problem. I had thought of evacuating the Little Todday platoon to Great Todday, and abandoning Little Todday to the enemy."

"I don't think the Todaidh Mór men would like to have the Todaidh Beag men over here," said George Campbell.

"Like it?" the old lady spluttered indignantly. "There wouldn't be a man left alive for the Germans to kill."

The fighting future of the Little Todday platoon was still undecided in Captain Waggett's mind when he left the men of Garryboo to their grim vigil and drove on to Bobanish.

At Sròn Ruairidh he was extremely gratified when the two men on guard at the road block advanced menacingly against his car. He was less gratified after he had put his head out of the window to felicitate them on their soldierly bearing when there was a bang and a bullet went past his nose.

"Steady on, men, it's Captain Waggett," he shouted as he hastily drew back from the window. "I say, you *must* challenge a car first," he expostulated when Angus MacCormac, a big crofter with a heavy grey moustache that would have been remarkable even among the *vieilles moustaches* of the Old Guard, came up to the door of the car.

"I'm very sorry if I scared you, Mr Waggett. The gun went off on me. Ay, indeed, one has to be careful with these rifles. They'd play anyone a dirty trick right enough."

"We'd be looking fine and foolish now if your pullet was after hitting Mr Wackett," observed the other guardian of the road block, a small man with sparse hair, a ragged moustache, a high voice, and a nose on him like Sròn Ruairidh itself.

"You certainly would, Sammy," the Commanding Officer agreed. "Never mind, all's well that ends well, but be more careful another time. Anything to report?"

"Nothing at all," said Angus MacCormac. "Mr Campbell . . ."

"Sergeant Campbell," Waggett corrected. "I want you to get into the habit of thinking of him as a soldier, not as a civilian. The Germans will seize any excuse to treat us as civilians with arms, and that means putting us up against a wall and shooting the lot of us."

"Oh well, well," Angus exclaimed. "Shoot anybody for not calling the schoolmaster sergeant? Oh well, they're hoolicans right enough . . . Sergeant Campbell . . ." the big crofter broke off to indulge himself in a hoarse chuckle at the prefix before he went on, "Sergeant Campbell had a bit of an argument with Dr Maclaren. . . ."

"Yes, he told me about it."

"The Doctor was very annoyed," said Angus.

"Och, he went off as fierce as a pull," Sammy MacCodrum confirmed. "He'd been with Bean Eoghain Chaluim all afternoon and evening and she with twins at the end of it all."

"Is it twins she's after having?" Angus exclaimed.

"Ay, and curls at that," Sammy added.

"Ah, poor soul, poor soul, what a calamity, and himself away at sea!" The big crofter sighed compassionately.

Captain Waggett broke into this duologue with a request to open the road block and let his car through. It took such a long time to remove the small thicket of barbed wire that in view of the possibility of having to rush reinforcements up at any moment the Commanding Officer ordered the block to be kept open.

"And if any car or lorry comes along you will stand in the middle of the road and challenge it. Make the driver dismount and show his national registration card."

"But we'll know who he is without a registration card," Angus MacCormac pointed out.

"I daresay you will," said the Commanding Officer. "But I've made a rule that while the state of emergency lasts everybody on the island is to carry his registration card."

"But what if he hasn't got his card?" Angus pressed.

"You must turn him back."

"It's very difficult to turn back a two-ton lorry," Sammy pointed out. "And if we took a shot at it we might hit it. A lorry's so big."

"No, I don't want any shooting," said Waggett. "There's been too much fuss in the papers lately about Home Guards shooting civilians. If the lorry won't stop, just make a note of who's driving it and I'll speak to him to-morrow."

Captain Waggett drove on to visit his second-in-command at Bobanish.

"I'm tremendously pleased with everybody's keenness, Mr Beaton. Angus MacCormac fired at me as I approached Sròn Ruairidh."

"Fired at you?" exclaimed the schoolmaster in shocked amazement.

"Yes, the bullet whizzed right past my nose."

"I hope you gave the silly fellow a good talking to, Captain."

"One can't be too severe when it's just keenness," Waggett commented, in a tone that was touched with the sentiment of the old veteran who was himself responsible for such keenness.

"You'll excuse me, Captain, but I'll be very severe indeed if any man in my section starts shooting at random like that," the schoolmaster insisted.

" Oh, of course I did warn him to be more cautious another time."

" I would think so indeed," said John Beaton, who had visions of his schoolchildren being fired at by precipitate Home Guards. "And are the men to remain on the watch all night, Captain?"

"Night and day until the emergency is over," his commanding officer replied, in the dreamy voice of one who sees himself as Busiris at the head of the Memphian chivalry. "And you can relieve the sentries along Loch Bob every two hours. But the men relieved are not to get out of uniform. They must be ready for the alarm at any moment. By the way, did you see anything of Dr Maclaren?"

"I believe I saw his car go by about an hour ago."

"I'm seriously thinking of putting him under arrest."

"Under arrest?" the schoolmaster echoed in astonishment. "But that would be rather high-handed, would it not, Captain? What about his patients?"

"Oh, I should allow him to go his rounds—with an armed guard, of course. However, I hope it won't be necessary. I hope he'll give up swearing at people who are only carrying out orders and trying to get on with the war. But I shan't hesitate to make an example of him if I think an example must be made."

In this resolve Captain Waggett found on his way back to Snorvig that he had been anticipated by Sergeant Norman Macleod who commanded the Watasett section, and was therefore in charge of the road block established where the road to Watasett branched off from the main road that ran right round the island.

Norman Macleod, a native of Great Todday, was an ardent young socialist who had been several times reported to the Director of Education for advocating communism during school hours, and when Waggett had given him the command of the Watasett section of the Home Guard a good many people had shaken their heads because they felt there was a risk of Norman Macleod's turning into a Todday Trotsky. He was a good-looking and attractive young man with rather long wavy hair whose influence over his pupils was magical, and the Director of Education was therefore unwilling to pay heed to stories about Macleod's communism so long as the reports of the Inspector were as favourable as they always were, and so long as the bursaries won by the Watasett boys and girls were as well deserved as they were.

"Anything to report, Sergeant Macleod?" Captain Waggett asked.

"I've got the Doctor locked up in the school?" replied

Norman Macleod, his brown eyes twinkling. "Och, he tried to rush the block and I wasn't having any. The Doctor's a fine fellow when he's had his dram, but he's a real bourgeois when he's blind sober. And he's blind sober this evening."

"Did he offer any resistance?"

"He put up a fine barrage of swearing. Och, he knows how to swear, drunk or sober. I'll always give him that. And he swore with a beautiful variety."

"I hope you didn't use force, Sergeant?"

"No, no. I just said to him, 'God knows I love you, Doctor dear, but God knows just as well I'll stick this bayonet in your guts if you don't come quietly along to the school.' A bhalaich, did I laugh? Oh boy, oh boy, I laughed."

"I hope he'll take it in good part," said the Commander of the Home Guard a little doubtfully.

"I don't know if he will. Ach, I wouldn't say he would. He's pretty mad just now."

"I suppose I'd better see him," said the Commander still more doubtfully. "I don't think we can keep him shut up all night. I think perhaps another time, Sergeant, it would be better to refer to me before you put anybody under arrest."

"But what was I to do, Captain? The man was determined to pay no attention to us—no attention at all."

"I'm not blaming you, Sergeant. As I shall tell Dr Maclaren. He's in one of the classrooms, you say?"

When a doctor has spent the whole of the afternoon and evening superintending the entry of twins into this world, when he has accomplished this task and turned homeward in his car with the thought of supper in his mind and the stiff whisky he intends to drink before supper starts, not to mention the several stiff whiskies he intends to drink afterwards, when he finds the road he had intended to take blocked by a thicket of barbed wire and two of his own patients levelling rifles at him, when his language has lacked enough punch to knock out even a George Campbell, when he has backed his car for over a hundred yards to find a place where he can turn without getting the wheels stuck in a bog, when he has motored on the vile road between Knockdown and Bobanish, when he has discovered another thicket of barbed wire between himself and those whiskies, and when finally he has been driven at the point of the bayonet into a classroom smelling of chalk, children, and

faded collections of wild flowers and there has been locked in
by a young man he had regarded as a feckless but amusing
and attractive example of contemporary youth, when all this
has befallen a hard-worked doctor, there is no reason to expect
he will be anything else than 'pretty mad'.

"I'm sorry, Doctor, you've landed yourself in this spot of
bother," said Captain Waggett. "But you shouldn't have
tried to rush the road block. However, we'll call it a day,
shall we, and forget about it?"

"You can call it a bloody year, you clown, but I'll not forget
about it."

"Please don't get abusive. Perhaps you didn't know we
were warned from Fort Augustus this evening to expect an
attempt by the enemy to land at any moment."

"Land on Todday? My god, do you think Hitler's as big
a playboy as yourself, Mr Waggett?"

"It's nothing to do with what I think. It's what Scottish
Command thinks. I'm sorry you've been inconvenienced, but
there is a war on, you know."

"Mr Waggett, as an emetic you'd make a bottle of ipecacu-
anha as mild as a glass of sherry," the Doctor declared with
slow emphasis.

"I thought you were a sportsman," said the Commanding
Officer regretfully.

"Not on any land you shoot over," the Doctor snapped back.

Captain Waggett turned on his heels. He was not going
to stay here and listen to the Snorvig House shooting and fishing being insulted.

As his commanding officer strode off to get into his car
Norman Macleod came into the classroom and looked quizzi-
cally at the Doctor.

"Doctor dear," he said, "Catriona's just after roasting a
brace of grouse. Come on in now and let you and me sit
down to them. And they're his own grouse." He indicated
with his thumb over his shoulder the owner, and chuckled.
" That's the cream of it. I killed them myself last week. And
look you now, I've a bottle of port wine which the captain of
the *Anna Maria* gave me"—this was one of the winter wrecks—
"and I've a bottle of the very whisky you like, and there's just
you and me to enjoy it. And if the Germans come, to hell
with them. I'll be twice the sergeant I am when we've put

that whisky away in a safe place."

"Well, I'll have a dram with you, Norman, to show there's no ill-feeling," said the Doctor. "But my own supper is waiting for me. And has been since before you started playing the giddy goat with that bayonet."

So the Doctor accompanied Norman Macleod into the sitting-room of the schoolhouse, and when he had had a dram the perfume of the grouse coming in from the kitchen where Catriona, Norman's pretty sister, was roasting them was so alluring that in the end the Doctor decided to give his own supper the go-by and stay with Norman.

"I hope they're not old birds," he said sharply.

"No, no, Doctor, would I be asking you to sit down and spoil a good appetite with old birds? I wish I had a sea-trout for you. I put the net down last night, but I didn't get one."

"You're a black poacher, Norman," said his guest. "Did you poach this whisky from Roderick?"

"I did and I didn't, Doctor. I gave Roderick a brace of grouse, and he gave me a bottle of whisky. Yes, yes, that was the way of it."

"And how do you justify your poaching? Is it a part of your infernal communism?"

"*A bhalaich*, no! I wouldn't mind bringing sport into politics, but to bring politics into sport, that would be a crime against nature altogether."

The Doctor poured himself out another dram, and then suddenly he leaned back in his chair and began to laugh heartily.

"Ah, wait a minute now, Doctor. Don't you be laughing too hard," said Norman, a little huffily. "You'll find it will be a different kind of a world altogether after this war."

"I wasn't laughing at your political opinions, Norman, though that doesn't mean I'm prepared to take them too seriously. I was laughing at myself for losing my temper a while back. Ah, here comes Catriona with the grouse."

The schoolmaster and the Doctor sat down at the table, and an hour later they were still exchanging stories across the remains of the grouse when from the direction of Little Todday came the sound of musketry.

"It's the Germans," the schoolmaster shouted in wild excitement. "Come on, Doctor. You're in the Home Guard yourself for the emergency. Oh well, I never thought we'd be able to have a crack at the Germans on these islands. Oh boy, oh boy, this is the grandest night of my life!"

The section leader of Watasett rushed up the slope to muster his men.

"Come on, boys, come on and get into the boat," he urged.

And while the men of Watasett, the Doctor with them, are pulling down Loch Sleeport toward the wider waters of the Coolish our attention must be turned to what had been happening on Little Todday after Archie MacRurie, more familiarly known as the Biffer, had brought to Kiltod the news that invasion was imminent.

Chapter 8

GOOD SHOOTING

THE origin of many of the nicknames on the two Toddays was obscure, for even the owners of them could not always be persuaded to reveal how they were acquired. There was no mystery about the way Archie MacRurie became known as the Biffer. It dated back to his schooldays when an English visitor, filled as some English visitors are with a desire to impose the slavery of sport upon a free community, instituted a boxing competition for the schoolchildren. Archie MacRurie was the performer who particularly attracted the attention of the English visitor and he used to encourage him from the ringside with cries of 'biff him, Archie, biff him'.

This injunction Archie never failed to obey. The ten-shilling prize he won kept himself and his defeated adversaries in sweets and cigarettes for two days: the nickname he won endured. Moreover, it preserved the 'B' of the Sasunnach who inspired it and was never corrupted to the Piffer, except in speech, for the Biffer himself who was proud of his nickname was accustomed to use it as his signature instead of Archie MacRurie. In fact it was difficult to persuade him that the Territorial Association which preoccupied itself with the records of the Home Guard would not prefer in the interests of historical accuracy Corporal Biffer to Corporal Archie MacRurie.

In private life the Biffer was a crofter a great deal more interested in lobster-fishing than agriculture. His little boat the *Kittiwake* was as much a feature of the rocky coast of Todaidh Mór as Sròn Ruairidh itself. At this date he was about fifty years old, with a nose and a chin on him like a lobster's claw and a fierce red countenance. He had four boys away in the mercantile marine, and another couple who would be in it as soon as they were old enough. He had plenty of daughters too, and a large placid wife.

The Biffer had thrown himself into the work of the Home Guard with enthusiasm and had adopted one of the Lewis guns as a household pet. To nobody could Captain Waggett have entrusted a more congenial task than to the Biffer when he chose him to bear the tidings of invasion to Todaidh Beag.

"What are you telling me?" Joseph Macroon gasped.

"I'm telling you what's what," said the Biffer imperiously. "Mr Waggett heard the news in a telegraph. 'Look out,' they told him, 'the Germans will be on the top of you in a few hours.'"

Joseph Macroon snatched from his head the conical red woollen cap, fell on his knees, crossed himself several times, and mumbled at a great pace three tremulous Aves.

"Where's Duncan Bàn?" the Biffer asked when Joseph had risen from his knees.

"He's away over the other end of the island just now. Will I send Kenny for him?"

"Ay, that's the very thing. I'll go along and tell Father James."

The Biffer felt sure that news such as his would win him a hefty dram at the Chapel House.

"Ay, and you'd better ask him to ring the Chapel bell," Joseph urged. "Do you think Hitler will be with them?"

"Ah, man, you're not wise. What would Hitler want with Todaidh Beag? It's Puckingham Balace he's wanting. Where's Kenny?"

Joseph went through to shout for his youngest son who presently appeared, his freckled face wreathed in a grin of seraphic happiness.

"It isn't true, Airchie?" he demanded, the grin fading in

anticipation of hearing that the Biffer had played a trick on his father.

"It's the truest thing that ever happened, *a Choinnich*."

"The Germans are really coming here?" the boy pressed.

"Yes, yes. They're on the way at this moment. You must run to Duncan Bàn and tell him he's to put every man to his post right away. I'm going along up to ask Father James to ring the bell and give the alarum."

Kenny's last apprehensions of a practical joke vanished at the tone of the Biffer's voice. He uttered a loud whoop of triumph.

"*Nach ist thu?*" growled his father, whose nerves were in no condition for such noises. "You're worse than the Germans."

But Kenny had rushed away for his bicycle before his father's rebuke was finished, and a moment later he could be heard through the open window telling the sublime news to Michael Gillies.

"Michael, Michael boy, the Germans are here."

"Where?"

"They're coming soon. I'm away to tell Duncan Bàn."

"What does your father say about that?" the handyman asked.

"He isn't at all pleased."

With another ear-piercing whoop of exultation the postmaster's youngest son mounted his bicycle and set out to spread the glorious news.

"Ach, I believe the children are all going mad," the postmaster ejaculated gloomily. "Just a lot of Germans themselves."

"Well, well, *matà*, I'll be getting along," said the Biffer who felt he required more exhilarating company than Joseph's.

"Ach, perhaps they won't come at all," said the postmaster when he went outside and surveyed the tranquil twilight deepening over Todaidh Beag.

"They'll come right enough. Why would Waggett be having a telegraph if they weren't coming?"

"*A bhobh bhobh*," Joseph groaned to himself, turning back indoors to consider where to hide his more precious possessions.

The parish priest had just reached the *Nunc Dimittis* of compline when his housekeeper brought him word of the Biffer's arrival.

"Bring him along, Kirstag," he boomed, and as the Biffer appeared in his doorway, "Roll right in, my boy," he invited. "What brings you to Todaidh Beag, Archie?"

"The Germans."

The priest laughed boisterously.

"*A Dhia, Dhia*, oh well, that's a good one. What brings you to Todaidh Beag? The Germans!"

"Och, it's no laughing matter, Father James. They're coming right enough."

The priest threw himself back in his armchair, patting his great chest in a paroxysm of mirth.

"Indeed it is true what I'm telling you," the Biffer insisted. "Mr Waggett had a telegraph to say they were coming."

Father Macalister was seized with another convulsion of merriment and rolled about in his chair, gasping "Waggett's had a telegraph. Oh, great sticks, what a beauty! He's had a telegraph from Hitler. *A Dhia na gràs*, that's the richest one I ever heard."

"Och, he didn't have a telegraph from Hitler," said the Biffer earnestly. "The telegraph came from Fort Augustus."

"From the Loch Ness monster, by all the holy crows," Father Macalister gurgled in an ecstasy of laughter.

"No, no, you mustn't take it as a fun, *a Mhaighstir Seumas*. It's the pure truth I'm after telling you. We're all to our action stations in Todaidh Mór and Mr Waggett sent me over to give the word here. Kenny Iosaiph is away on his bicycle to find Duncan Bàn. And look at me. I'm in my uniform, gassmask and all. Would I be coming to Todaidh Beag in my uniform and gassmask for a fun? Mr Waggett is away to Garryboo and Bobanish just now, but he'll be over here himself later. And will you give a ring on the church bell, because that's the signal agreed upon with the Government?"

During this long speech of the Biffer's Father Macalister recovered himself sufficiently from his spasms of mirth to comprehend that the imminence of invasion really had been signalled from the mainland.

A minute or two later the bell of the Chapel of Our Lady Star of the Sea and St Tod, which had been silent since Dunkirk, clanged out the alarm. And if the bell lacked the terrifying urgency of the tocsin that was not Father Macalister's fault, but due to the lightness of its metal. Anyway, it roused the four or five hundred dogs of Little Todday, who carried the alarm to the remotest croft in the island.

"Well, that's one in the eye for Lord Haw-Haw," Father Macalister avowed after five minutes of strenuous pulling.

"It's you that's a good bell-ringer, Father James," the Biffer observed admiringly. "I don't believe our own wee Minister could ring a bell so nice as that. It does anybody good to see a bell rung so nice. It's a pity Mr Waggett sent me off in such a hurry. I would have brought you a lobster. But don't you worry. I'll pick you out a beauty when we've beaten off those rascals of Germans."

"You'll come in, Archie, and take a dram," the priest told him.

"Ah, well, a dram is good right enough in times like these," the Biffer declared solemnly.

In the sitting-room of the Chapel House Father Macalister poured out for the Biffer a dram of such heftiness that for the moment he could not bring himself to disturb with his lips the abundant gold.

"Oh, well, well, that iss a dram," he declared spellbound. There was another pause of exquisite anticipation before he raised the glass. "*Slainte mhath! Slainte mhór*," he intoned reverently before he emptied it in one sublime gulp. Then he wiped his lips in the luxury of a remembered delight.

"That's beautiful stuff, Father James. That puts the heart into a man." The Biffer's eyes glowed. "Could you do with two lobsters, Father James?"

"Could you do with two drams, Archie?" the priest asked, picking up the bottle.

"No, no," the Biffer protested. "I'll be seeing two Germans for one, and maybe wasting my ammunition shooting at the wrong one. No, no, I must be getting back across to Snorvig. Mr Waggett may be waiting for me. Will I tell him to come up to your house when I bring him over?"

"It depends when he comes," said the priest. "The Germans aren't going to keep me out of my bed after one o'clock."

"There's just one thing I'd like to know, Father James, as between you and me . . ."

"And the dram," the priest chuckled.

"Is Duncan Bàn himself to-night?" the Biffer asked anxiously.

"Which self?"

"Ah, you know fine, Father James, which self I'm meaning."

"Don't you worry about Duncan. He'll not let the Home Guard down. Take it from me, my boy."

The dogs were still barking from one end of Little Todday to the other when the Biffer bade Father Macalister good-night and walked down to the minute harbour. The dew was heavy on the machair, and the scent of the late Hebridean hay sharply sweet in the last grey of the gloaming.

"Oh, well," the Biffer told Joseph Macroon when he reached the post-office, "the blaggarsts have picked a fine night for their invasion sure enough."

Joseph shuddered noisily.

"Brr! Don't be talking of it."

Away over at Duncan Macroon's croft Kenny had had a great deal of difficulty in persuading the commander of the Little Todday platoon that the island was in danger of being invaded by the enemy that very night.

When he arrived Duncan was sitting on a green knoll gazing across the rolling machair to where the ocean had turned from tarnished silver to lead in the twilight.

"Duncan! Duncan!" the boy called.

The bard who was in the throes of composition waved away the intrusive voice.

But Kenny refused to be silenced.

"The Biffer is after coming over with a message from Mr Waggett to say the Germans will be here any time now and will you have the Home Guard ready for them."

"Ah, to hell! How can I compose a song and you croaking at me like a hoody-crow? We had a parade last week and we had another parade the week before that. We can't be parading all the time with the harvest work."

"Ach, you and your parades! Do you want to see the Germans parading on the island?"

"I'd sooner see Gobbles swaggering about Todaidh Beag than hear that voice of yours when I'm trying to compose a song," Duncan Bàn retorted.

"What will I say if Mr Waggett comes over and you sitting here when the Home Guard ought to be gathered ready?"

"Listen! You'll just say another word till I'm after finishing this song, and I'll murder you."

At this moment, the ding-dong of the Chapel bell was heard across the island's green expanse, and a few seconds later the noise of barking dogs resounded from every direction.

"There you are now," said Kenny. "That's the Chapel bell ringing to give the alarum."

Duncan Bàn's incredulity was shaken.

"Dash it, there must be something the matter," he admitted.

"Amn't I after telling you it's the invasion?" Kenny demanded indignantly.

"Oh well, well, well, Kenny boy, I've thought all my life that the English were the stupidest craytures in the world, but if the Germans invade Todaidh Beag they're stupider than the English. They've spoilt a good song on me, that's one thing certain. So I may as well get myself into uniform and charge it up to Hitler."

The Biffer had long gone back to Snorvig when the Home Guard of Little Todday was marshalled to hear an address from their commander.

"Boys, the Germans are here at last. Or if they're not here they're somewhere in the neighbourhood. We don't know yet whether they'll have a try at us or not, but if they do, just let them have it."

There was a murmur of determined animosity in the ranks of the Home Guard.

"Now there's no use in all of us tiring ourselves walking about. We'll send out ten good men to prowl around for an hour while the rest of us stay here and have a *céilidh* in the hall. After that ten good men can go out and prowl around for another hour while the first bunch have a rest. And so on right through the night. Does that suit everybody?"

There was a murmur of approval, and the first batch of men was chosen.

"Now listen, you boys."

The selected boys not one of whom was under fifty and most of whom were a full sixty-five, listened.

"Don't go wandering around in a bunch. Scatter yourselves. Sergeant Stewart and Corporal Michael Joseph Macroon, it will be your business to keep yourselves scattered. Are you understanding me? Any man who sees a German must shoot at him right away and retire towards the hall where the rest of us will be having our *céilidh*. And that reminds me.

Run you up to Father James, Kenny boy, and ask him if we can have the key of the hall.   And you, Michael, it's no use for you to be wandering around with the first patrol.   You'll be wanted for a little piping to keep us all lively."

"Duncan, how will I know it iss a Cherman when I see the rascal?" one of the first patrol enquired, a long lean man with a trim square beard.

"Alan, *a bhalaich*," said Duncan Bàn reproachfully, "is it you that reads the *Sunday Post* must be asking what a German looks like?"

"Ah, but a man may look one way in a picture and a different way altogether when he's walking about as large as life," Alan objected.

"Well, I'll tell you, Alan.   If you see somebody and you can't see if it's somebody or not, shout at him 'Who is it going there?'   And if he doesn't say who is it going there, then, Alan boy, let him have it in the abdomen."

"Who's the abdomen?"

"The aptomen isn't a crayture, Alan," said Sergeant Stewart, a round sandy little man who bred the best cattle on Little Todday.   "The aptomen is a *stamac*.   Chust plaze right at him, that's what Tuncan is telling you."

So the patrol started to move away.

"Wait a minute, wait a minute," the platoon commander shouted.   "*A chlann an diabhoil*, do you think you will see the Germans between your two feet?   Don't you remember the War Office told you to walk about in an attitude of suspicious alertness with your rifle and your bayonet all ready in front of you not hanging on your shoulders, and your two eyes in the back of your head as well as in the front of your face?"

There had in fact been such advice tendered by some theorist of the War Office to Zonal Commanders of the Home Guard, who had passed it on to Sub-Zonal Commanders, who had passed it on to Battalion Commanders, who had passed it on to Company Commanders, who had passed it on to Platoon Commanders, who had passed it on to Section Commanders, who had tried to show their Sections by suiting the action to the word how to patrol in an attitude of suspicious alertness.

The first patrol moved off in an attitude of suspicious alert-ness to look for Germans and were presently scattered into separate units by Sergeant Stewart and Corporal Michael

Joseph Macroon, who was one of the island schoolmasters. It was not too soon, because the attitude of suspicious alertness in close formation meant that the leaders ran a risk of getting a jab in the back from a bayonet.

Meanwhile, the rest of the Little Todday platoon gathered in the hall to pass the vigil in piping, the telling of tales, and the singing of Gaelic songs.

Father Macalister, who could never resist a *céilidh* like this, came along from the Chapel House to enhance the proceedings.

"Good shooting, Duncan. A lovely and beautiful idea of yours," he declared, an expression on his large countenance of ineffable benignity. "And if the Germans come, my boys, you'll knock sparks out of them."

"We'll do that right enough," Duncan Bàn promised. "Come on now, Michael, give us a *pìobaireachd*."

The slim dreamy-eyed piper mounted the platform to stir the hearts of the warriors with strains heard above the clash of battles long ago.

It was nearing the hour when the first patrol was due back for the second patrol to take their place, and Alan Macdonald, the long lean crofter with the trim square beard who had asked Lieutenant Macroon how he should recognize a German, was skirting one of the little sandy beaches on the south-east coast of the island in a state of suspicious alertness which would have warmed the heart of that War Office mandarin who coined the phrase. If the suspicion was faintly tinged with superstition, the alertness lightly touched with alarm, it was not on account of the Germans but because Tràigh nam Marbh—the strand of the dead—by which he was walking had once upon a time been the strand from which dead Macroons had been embarked upon the boat that carried them to the ancient burial-place of the clan on the tiny island of Poppay. It was therefore naturally much frequented by ghosts of the departed who having so long ago lost any link with contemporary humanity had taken on the attributes and the appearance of *bòcain* or bógles.

Alan Macdonald whistled softly to himself the refrain of a catchy hymn to the Sacred Heart which the faithful of Little Todday often sang at Mass, gripped his rifle more firmly, and stepped forward on the turf above the haunted strand. Suddenly he saw straight ahead of him two luminous eyes, a luminous nose, and the outline of a large luminous face.

"*A Mhuire mhàthair*," he gasped, and crossing himself fell on his knees to mutter a desperate Ave. But the luminous eyes still regarded him. He crossed himself again and galloped through a Paternoster, three more Aves, and a Gloria. The apparition did not blench before the holy words.

"*A Dhia*, it cannot be a *bòcan*," Alan reflected. "No *bòcan* could stand his ground against that. It must be a Cherman."

The horror which had bedewed his forehead turned to the warmth of anger.

"Ah, you bustard of a Cherman," he shouted, as he fired into the luminous outline.

The sound of Alan's shot roused the nearest man in the patrol to action. He could not see anything to fire at. So he fired at the zenith. Three or four stirks that were lying down in the machair started to their feet and thudded wildly away. Other members of the patrol presumed that this was the enemy charging and fired shot after shot in their direction.

Over at the hall in Kiltod Father Macalister was singing to an enraptured audience when Joseph Macroon, his pallor accentuated by his red woollen cap, rushed into the hall, crying:

"They're here! They're here! The shooting has begun!"

And sure enough in the silence that this announcement caused the sound of musketry was distinctly audible.

"Great sticks alive!" ejaculated Father Macalister. "They are here! Come on my boys, give me a pike and we'll roll right over them."

"Don't lose your heads," Duncan Bàn implored, as the men of his platoon hurried from the hall to get to grips with the enemy. "Spread out to five paces and don't lose touch with one another. They're away to the south, the blackguards."

The platoon advanced cautiously over the machair in extended order. The shooting had died down for the nonce. Some ten minutes later the voice of Alan Macdonald was heard from the darkness ahead on the left challenging the reinforcements to advance another step.

"It's ourselves, Alan," shouted Duncan Bàn.

"Are you Chermans?"

"How the devil can we be Germans when we're ourselves?" Duncan shouted again. "But where are the Germans?"

"I don't know," Alan replied. "But I killed one dead back on Tràigh nam Marbh."

"Good shooting, Alan," boomed the voice of Father James. "Good shooting, *a bhalaich*."

And now the centre of the battle moved from land to sea. Above the motor of the Biffer's boat which was chugging along with Captain Waggett, who had been roused by the sound of firing, to direct the defence on Little Todday the commander of the Home Guard had heard the click-click of rowlocks to the southward.

"Biffer," he said, "I can hear an enemy landing-barge. Stop your engine."

The Biffer cut off the engine.

"Ay, Captain, you're right. It is them. Will I turn my Lewis gun on the blaggarsts?"

"Give them a burst," Captain Waggett ordered.

It was lucky that the Biffer was not yet such an adept with a Lewis gun as with a lobster creel. Otherwise, not a man of the Watasett section would have been left alive, not to mention Doctor Maclaren who was with them in the boat. As it was, the bullets of the Lewis gun ended their career harmlessly in the waters of the Coolish about a hundred yards astern.

"Who are you?" Sergeant Norman Macleod yelled from the Watasett boat. "Tell us who you are or we will shoot you to pieces."

"That's Norman Macleod's voice," said the Biffer. "My goodness, if it was not so tricky to fire my Lewis gun from a boat they would all have been dead by now."

"This is Captain Waggett in the *Kittiwake*," the Home Guard commander shouted. "Who are you?"

"This is the Watasett section. We heard firing on Todaidh Beag and are coming along with reinforcements," Norman shouted back.

"I'm steering for Kiltod," shouted Waggett. "We'll land there, and you can stand by for further orders."

"I wouldn't say they wouldn't shoot at us from Todaidh Beag," the Biffer demurred. "They'll be thinking we're Germans. And if we turn round and go back to Snorvig they'll be thinking we are Germans there, and the banker is a terrible good shot."

"But we can't stay here for the rest of the night," Waggett expostulated.

"I believe we'll have to," the Biffer told him. "We'll see better where we are in the morning."

"Start up your engine and I'll steer for Kiltod," the commander insisted.

So the Biffer started up his engine and Captain Waggett steered for Kiltod, until half a dozen shots from the shore persuaded him to change his mind.

"We'll have to go back to Snorvig," he exclaimed petulantly. "If the Little Todday platoon is in trouble they'll have to get out of it the best way they can."

"I wouldn't want to go against your orders, Captain," the Biffer said firmly. "But I won't take the *Kittiwake* back to Snorvig. You think the banker's a very quiet man, but when he starts firing he isn't at all so quiet. He's a pure terror. The best thing we can do is to get in touch with the boat from Watasett and follow them in up Loch Sleeport."

Captain Waggett considered this pusillanimous advice, but he accepted it because at any rate it provided him with the opportunity to give some orders, and after a good deal of ahoying he persuaded Norman Macleod to return to Watasett where on landing he had the mortification of seeing Dr Maclaren.

"Well, well, they fooled you just as they fooled us," the Doctor observed, a broad grin on his florid countenance.

"I don't understand," said the commander stiffly.

"Why, Norman and I thought for a time the Germans really had landed on Todaidh Beag."

"I'm not convinced that they haven't," Captain Waggett insisted sulkily.

"Ah, no, Captain," Norman Macleod protested. "We must apply a little dialectical materialism to the military situation. They were just shooting at one another on Todaidh Beag, the same as you and the Biffer were shooting at us. It's a pity too, because the Doctor and I were just in the right mood to obliterate a German Army Corps if the rascals had only given us the chance."

"I'm afraid I can't afford to indulge in theories," said the commander of the Home Guard with dignity. "I must get along to Snorvig and find out what really is happening."

"That's a good idea, Captain," Norman Macleod agreed. "There's a lot to be said for realism at a moment like this."

"I hope you won't scorn a lift back in my offending car, Mr Waggett?" the Doctor asked. "And perhaps you'll be good enough to accept that suggestion as an apology for having shown some heat a while back?"

Captain Waggett hesitated for a moment, and then yielding to the impulse of *noblesse oblige* he entered the offending car. Before it started he called out to Norman Macleod:

"The men must go back to their posts, Sergeant. The night isn't over yet, you know."

"I believe the best part of it is over," said Norman Macleod, with a wink over his shoulder at the Doctor.

In Snorvig Sergeant Thomson had nothing to report from Bobanish or Garryboo in the way of alarms.

"And what was the matter on Little Todday?" he asked.

"I haven't found out yet. It may be a false alarm of course."

"Imphm," Sergeant Thomson agreed.

"The Biffer and I were fired at in the *Kittiwake*."

"Is that so, Mr Waggett?"

"I was rather amused because when I wanted to come back to Snorvig the Biffer was afraid you'd fire at us."

"I did have both the Lewis guns trained on the harbour, but if you'd hailed us I *think* I would have recognized who it was. . . . Imphm, I *think* so."

While the commanding officer and the section leader were discussing the might-have-beens of the recent situation the chug-chug of a motor-boat was heard in the Coolish.

"That'll be the *Morning Star*," somebody said.

"Imphm, I believe it will be," Sergeant Thomson agreed.

It was the *Morning Star* bringing over Duncan Bàn to report on the events of the vigil up to date.

"Well, Mr Macroon?" the Commanding Officer asked, looking very stately.

"It isn't at all well, Captain. We thought we had the Germans and all we had was a barrel of rotten herrings on Tràigh nam Marbh. Father James had a good laugh at Alan Macdonald, but all the same he was pretty disappointed himself."

"But how on earth could Alan Macdonald mistake a barrel of rotten herrings for Germans?"

"Ach, poor Alan, it was easy enough," Duncan replied. "They were phosphorescent, and the eyes of them were glaring at him terribly. But he made a good shot for a man who had such fear on him. If that barrel of herrings had been a German, it's a dead German he would be just now. His bullet went right through as clean as a whistle."

"Then why did you start firing at me and the Biffer?" the commander asked.

"We heard firing in the Coolish, and how were we to know the *Kittiwake* was just another barrel of herrings?"

Chapter 9

THE SERGEANT-MAJOR

THE next morning a telegram came from Fort Augustus to say that G Company could relinquish its action stations and resume the humdrum of Home Guard existence.

For a while people in the two Toddays were rather disinclined to talk much about the alarm of invasion. There was a feeling the other islands would have a laugh against them over that barrel of herrings, and many went so far as to say the whole affair had been nothing more than another bit of Home Guard nonsense.

Presently, however, commercial travellers with permits for repeated journeys and an odd visitor or two who had managed to persuade the Military Permit Office that he had a valid reason for crossing the Minch brought startling tales of that invasion, which apparently had been a simultaneous attempt to land along the whole of the coasts of Britain west of Berwick-on-Tweed.

At one port in Aberdeenshire the number of German bodies floating in the sea had prevented the fishing fleet from leaving harbour, and similar stories from ports and seaside resorts everywhere proved that the enemy had suffered a cruel blow. Like the Russians in the First World War that Sargasso Sea of drowned Germans was considered splendid for public morale.

"I'm bound to say it does give me a good deal of satisfaction to think that the preparations I made that night were not just a waste of time," Paul Waggett said to his wife after he had heard the tale from Aberdeenshire.

He was feeling a little sore because he had been informed that the ringing of the church bell on Little Todday had failed to observe the rule in W.O.I. 566789/BC/4001, par. 2, sec. (iv), sub-sec. A, which laid down that no church bell was to be rung after the signal for action stations had been given unless more than four parachutists had been observed landing in one parish, and sub-sec. B which laid down that the observation of four parachutists in the air was not sufficient reason for ringing church bells. If two of the aforesaid parachutists landed in one parish and the other two landed in another parish, the bells in neither parish were to be rung. No exception to this rule would be tolerated without a signed authority from the senior military officer of field rank within two miles of the nearest parish. In no circumstances was an officer in the Home Guard to give such an authority. See W.O.I. 566320/BC/3089, par. 3, and W.O.I. 552688/XY/23, par. 4, sec. (iv).

"I suppose we shall muddle through as usual, Dolly," her husband sighed. "But I hope we're not going to have a repetition of Norway on the Toddays."

Fortunately for Paul Waggett's apprehensions the climate of the Hebrides in autumn and winter offers no encouragement to invaders, and the next six months went by disturbed only by an endless flow of equipment, the details of which for obvious reasons must remain a secret. The commander of G Company felt that he was entitled to a little sport, and the snipe and the woodcock were given the lesson he was unable to administer to the enemy. With spring, however, the invasion season set in again, and in order to give G Company the full benefit of the reams of paper instructions which had arrived every time the *Island Queen* was able to make the little harbour of Snorvig, a sergeant-instructor was sent over from the mainland to give the Home Guard of Great and Little Todday lessons in the art of war.

The trews of Sergeant-major Alfred Ernest Odd proclaimed him to be a Clanranald, but his appearance and his accent proclaimed him to be a Cockney.   He was in fact a Cockney, who had served for many years in the Queen's Fusiliers and had been transferred to the 40th Clanranalds, a mysterious battalion recruited largely in Nottingham.   Why a Highland battalion should have been recruited in Nottingham nobody knew, but as for so many unexplained mysteries at the War Office Mr Hore-Belisha was blamed.   This mysterious battalion was disbanded in the spring of 1941 and Sergeant-major Odd was attached as a P.S.I. (Permanent Sergeant Instructor) to the 8th Inverness-shire Home Guard.   Hence the arrival of this trim, genial, forty-three-year-old survivor of the First World War at Snorvig on a fine April afternoon.

"Sergeant-major Odd?" the commander of G Company enquired when the new arrival reported at Snorvig House.

"Yes, sir."

"Well, I shall be very glad of your help.   I suppose you know the Islands well?"

"No, sir.   This is the first island I was ever on.   Quite an experience for me."

"Not the first island," said Waggett, smiling instructively at his sergeant-instructor.   "You've just come from one island."

"That's right, sir.   I was forgetting I've spent the best part of my life on an island, as you might say."

"Are you a Gaelic speaker?"

"I beg pardon, sir?"

"Do you speak Gaelic?"

"Oh, you mean what some of 'em were jabbering on the boat.   No, sir.   And I don't think I ever would from what I heard of it.   What's the idea exactly of talking such a queer language?   Still, I'm bound to say they seemed to understand one another all right."

"You'll want to remember when you're giving them instruction to speak very clearly."

"But they do speak English, don't they, sir?"

"Oh yes, they speak English extremely well.   But they don't always catch what one's saying, and some of our military expressions are strange to them.   I don't want you to be too sharp with them at first.   Most of the Home Guard here are either crofters who have never been far from home or else they're old merchant seamen who have been all over the world but know nothing about soldiering."

"Yes, sir, Captain Grant told me I might find things a bit strange at first. Of course, Scotland itself was a bit strange at first."

"But you're a Clanranald, aren't you?"

"Yes, sir. But only by accident as you might say. I did all my military service with the Queen's Fusiliers. I was fetched out of retirement from my present job when the 40th Clanranalds were recruited in Nottingham and almost as soon as we came up to Scotland the battalion was disbanded, and Colonel Lindsay-Wolseley applied for me. I knew him in India after the last war. And that reminds me, sir, Colonel Wolseley said he hoped to pay you a visit next month."

"Well, we shall be very glad to see him. I suppose you'll agree with me, Sergeant-major, that the most useful training for out here will be in musketry and that sort of thing? I mean to say you'll find it difficult to get any kind of barrack-square standard."

"Oh, I shan't worry them with too much drill, sir. No, no, what we have to do is to make good gorillas of them."

"Well, that's what I've been trying to do. You know where you're staying?"

"Miss MacRurie's, I believe it is, sir."

"Miss Flora MacRurie, yes. There are a great many Miss MacRuries on the island. I think you'll find it very comfortable there. When you go over to Little Todday I shall arrange for you to stay with Mr Joseph Macroon, who is the postmaster and has the chief shop on the island."

A night or two later Captain Waggett slipped unobtrusively into the back of the Snorvig Hall to listen to C.S.M. Odd instructing the men of the Snorvig section in individual fieldcraft.

"Now first of all we have what is known as the Panther Crawl. This is a movement executed by day. Lie down on your stomach first. Then dig your chin well into the ground with a sort of corkscrew motion, and do the same with both toes. You don't want to show the enemy your heels when you're lying down. So, toes routing about all the time like porkers. Have you got that?"

"Porkers?" somebody murmured. "What's a porker at all?"

"I don't want to interrupt, Sergeant-major," the Commanding Officer spoke up from the back of the hall. "But wouldn't it be better if the men did the movement? I mean to say I think an ounce of practice is better than a pound of theory."

"As you please, sir," said the Instructor, the faintest suggestion of surprise at being interrupted colouring his tone.

"It'll be very difficult to dig the chin into the boards of this hall, Captain Waggett," Sergeant Thomson observed, eyeing the floor gloomily and distastefully.

"But Sergeant-major Odd will find it easier to explain what he wants if you're all in position," Captain Waggett replied firmly.

"Ah, well, down we go, boys," exclaimed the Biffer, suiting the action to the word. "*A Chruithear*, this floor is hard right enough. Panter Crawl it is, right enough. Anybody would need a pair of good pants for this crawl."

Half the section had followed the lead of the Biffer: the other half eyed the bank agent who was still upright.

Nobody in that hall knew what a mental effort it cost Andrew Thomson to lead the other half of his section floorward; but he achieved it, although, as he told his wife later on that evening, he was on the verge of resigning from the Home Guard on the spot.

"Now, I think, they're in a better position to follow out your instructions, Sergeant-major," said the Commanding Officer.

"Yes, sir," the Sergeant-major assented brusquely. Then he turned to his pupils. "Well, you've got to fancy you *can* dig your chin and toes in. Now stretch your arms out in front of your heads."

"The floor smells terrible strong of paraffin where I am," said one of several MacRuries, turning over on his side. "Would it be all the same to you, Sergeant, if I put myself somewhere else?"

"Permission granted," said the Instructor. "Move along to the right."

When the MacRurie had re-settled himself the Instructor continued.

"The object of your present position is to advance on the stomach without being observed by the enemy. What you want to do is to roll along from side to side, at the same time using your thighs to push you forward. Owing to the nature of the ground in which you find yourselves at present, the Panther Crawl is not practical. Therefore you will make use of what is called the Monkey Trot. Now then, all on the hands and knees. Clench your fists and go forward as fast as you can, dropping down flat on your stomachs every ten yards or so, and then after a short pause move on again. By the way, sir," the Instructor said to the Commanding Officer, "have you practised this movement?"

"I've not actually practised it, no," Captain Waggett admitted.

"The *Handbook* makes a great point about officers learning these movements as well as the men," the Instructor reminded him.

Sergeant Thomson on all-fours looked up with a glance of dour approval.

"I shan't have time to practise to-night, I'm afraid," said Captain Waggett in a voice of apparently deep regret. "In fact I'll have to be off now. I only looked in for a moment to see how things were going."

"Yes, sir," said the Instructor.

"Good night, Sergeant-major."

The Instructor saluted, and the Commanding Officer left the hall.

"Now then," the Instructor went on, "I think I'll give you a few hints on movement by night. You can stand up. The first movement by night is known as the Spirit Walk. What you've got to understand is that, when you're moving about at night, the most important thing to remember is to do it quietly. You want to lift the legs right up so as you don't make a noise even in long grass. The best way is to sweep one leg out in a semicircle and be sure where you put your foot down next. Don't lift the left leg till the right leg is safely down. If you try to lift both legs at once you'll fall right over, and that'll warn the enemy of your approach."

"*A Chruithear*," exclaimed the Biffer, "who can lift two legs at once?"

"That's just what I'm warning you not to do," said Sergeant-major Odd.

Snorvig, Garryboo, Watasett, and Bobanish had all been given instruction in fieldcraft when a week later the Instructor himself crossed over to spend a couple of nights on Little

Todday in imparting to Duncan Bàn's platoon the mysteries of the Panther Crawl, the Monkey Trot, and the Spirit Walk.

And upon Sergeant-major Alfred Ernest Odd Todaidh Beag cast a spell even as in the far distant past the seal-woman of Todaidh Beag had cast a spell upon the exiled son of Clan Donald and made him the progenitor of Clan Macroon.

On the third day of his stay the Sergeant-major crossed over to Snorvig and reported to Captain Waggett.

"Would you have any objection, sir, if I carried on at Little Todday for the rest of the week, and come back Monday morning? The platoon over there wants a lot of elementary instruction. Mind you, Mr Macroon has the makings of a really good platoon commander, but he has no military experience."

"No, of course, he was just too young to be in the last war; but for various reasons he was the only suitable man to command the Little Todday platoon."

"Oh, I haven't a word against him, sir. That's what I mean. It seems a pity not to take advantage of such good material."

"But if you spend the whole week on Little Todday," the Commanding Officer objected, "you'll have no time left for the Great Todday sections."

"My idea was, sir—you'll excuse me for mentioning it?—my idea was you might wire Colonel Lindsay-Wolseley for permission to keep me out here for another week. Or if you were to ask for another fortnight perhaps that would be even better, and then I could put in a few more days with the Little Todday platoon."

"Well, of course, two days hardly give you much opportunity, Sergeant-major."

"Just so, sir," said the Sergeant-major eagerly. "I do want to feel the Little Todday lot have had a fair chance. There's really wonderful material there."

"Do you think it's better material than there is on Great Todday?"

"Oh no, sir, I'm not suggesting that, but"—and here Sergeant-major Odd fixed Captain Waggett with his bright hazel eyes, the eyes rather of a keen young recruit than of a hard-bitten C.S.M. of forty-three—"but in the nature of things the Little Todday platoon won't have the advantage of your personal instruction the way the Home Guard can on this island."

"Well, of course, during the winter months it has been difficult," Captain Waggett admitted.

"So my idea was, sir—you'll excuse me for mentioning it —my idea was for me to go back anyway to Little Todday— I haven't checked over the stores and equipment yet—and perhaps if Colonel Wolseley was agreeable to me staying on another week out here you could send over word not to come back to Snorvig till the beginning of next week."

"Very well, Sergeant-major," the commander of G Company assented.

The Sergeant-major saluted and retired. The buoyancy of his bearing on the way back down to the harbour was remarked by the Biffer who was standing talking on the pier to the crew of the *Morning Star*.

"You're looking fine this morning, Sergeant. My goodness, I believe you're liking your stay here very well."

"Yes, the air's very bracing out in these islands."

"Ay, I believe it will be," the Biffer agreed. "Are you going back to Kiltod then?"

"I'm going back for to-night at any rate. Captain Waggett is asking for an extension so as I can get in some rifle practice over here next week."

"Ay, that's better than crawling about like panters on your chin. Will you do me an obligement, Sergeant? Will you take a couple of lobsters from me to Father Macalister?"

"Certainly I will."

"He's a very fine man, Father Macalister," said the Biffer, preparing the lobsters for transport.

"A very fine man indeed I should say," the Sergeant-major agreed cordially.

A few minutes later the *Morning Star* was chug-chugging across the calm water of the Coolish, bound for home.

"Father Macalister will be very glad to see those lobsters," Michael Gillies observed. "*Giomach* we say in Gaelic for a lobster."

"Gimlet?" the Sergeant-major repeated.

Two or three more efforts were demanded before Michael and young Kenny gave his pronunciation their approval.

"It's a tongue-twisting language right enough. Gimmack.

Gimmack. I must remember that. And what's girl?"

"*Caileag*," said Michael.

The Sergeant-major made a shot at this, the result of which was to throw the crew of the *Morning Star* into a gurgle of merriment.

"You said '*coilleag*'. That's a cockle," Kenny explained.

The Sergeant-major made another shot, and won another laugh.

"That's *cuileag*. That's a fly," said Kenny.

The Sergeant-major took a deep breath and tried to yet once more. His third effort earned him the loudest laugh of all.

"That's *caileach*," Michael controlled himself enough at last to explain.

"And what's that mean?"

"A cock fowl," Michael told him.

"And *cailleach* is an old woman," Kenny added.

"Do you mean to say that if I want to tell a girl in Garlic that she's a nice girl I've got to run the risk of telling her she's a cockle or an old woman? Talk about careless talk! You want to watch your tongue in these parts, and that's a fact. By the way, Kenny, how old is your sister Peggy?"

"Which Peigi?" the boy asked.

"What do you mean 'which Peggy'? Your sister Peggy."

"Four of his sisters are called Peigi," Michael explained.

"Four sisters all called Peggy?" the Sergeant-major gasped.

"Peigi Mhór, Peigi Bhàn, Peigi Bheag, and Peigi Ealasaid," Michael said.

"Peggy Four, Peggy Farn, Peggy Feck, and Peggy Allsuch," the Sergeant-major repeated in a daze. "Well, I understand why one of them's called Peggy Four, but what about Peggy One, Two, and Three?"

"Peigi Mhór means big Peggy, and Peigi Bhàn means light Peggy," Kenny explained.

"Because she has light hair," Michael put in.

"And Peigi Bheag means little Peggy and Peigi Ealasaid means Peigi Ealasaid," Kenny went on.

"Yes, but what does Allsuch mean? Not but what it isn't a good name for one of a bunch of Peggies."

"Ealasaid doesn't mean anything. It's just a name."

The Sergeant-major shook his head.

"Well, let's get this straight. You've got two sisters at home,

Kenny. One of them's called Kate Anne and the other's called Peggy. Is that right?"

"That's right. Peigi Mhór and Peigi Bhàn are away married, and Peigi Bheag is a school teacher away in Barra," Kenny related.

"So the Peggy who's at home is Peggy Allsuch?"

"It isn't Allsuch," said Michael. "It's Ealasaid."

"Yallasuch? Is that better?"

"It's a little better, but it isn't very good," said Michael sadly. "I knew an English girl once, and her name was May Williams. That's a strange name to be calling a girl. May! One of the months of June."

"No, no," the Sergeant-major corrected. "June is the next month to May."

"Well, it's very strange to be calling a girl for a month," Michael argued. "But the English are queer people, right enough."

"And how old is that sister Peggy of yours that's at home?" the Sergeant-major asked for the second time, turning to Kenny.

"Peigi Ealasaid? Och, I don't know. She'll be about twenty-two."

"Ay, she'll be about twenty-two," Michael corroborated. "I'm thirty-two myself."

"You'll be getting called up soon," said the Sergeant-major.

"Ay, that's right, I believe I will."

"Aren't you the lucky one, Michael!" Kenny exclaimed enviously. "If I went to sea like my brother Johnny, maybe I'd be away in two years, but I want to be an airman. But perhaps the war will go on for twenty years. Wouldn't that be splendid? They're terrible strong these Germans, you know."

"Twenty-two," said the Sergeant-major meditatively.

"Do you hear that, Michael? The war will go on for twenty-two years. Isn't that grand?" Kenny exulted.

And a quarter of an hour later when he caught sight of his father on the little pier of Kiltod he shouted:

"Sergeant-major Odd says the war will go on for another twenty-two years, *athair*."

"What are you telling me?" exclaimed Joseph Macroon, aghast. "Twenty-two years? *A Mhuire mhàthair*, what will become of us all at all at all? Is that true, Sergeant?"

But the Sergeant-major did not answer. He was looking beyond Joseph Macroon to where Peigi Ealasaid was standing by the door of the post-office—a tall slim girl with a wealth of dark-brown hair and deep-blue slanting eyes.

"He has his eye on you, Peggy, right enough," her younger sister laughed that night when the two of them were going to bed.

"Ach, don't be a clown, Kate Anne," Peigi Ealasaid scolded; but she looked at herself again in the glass a moment later with an added curiosity.

And up at the Chapel House Sergeant-major Odd was at that moment asking Father Macalister if there would be any objection to his coming to church next Sunday, he not being a Catholic.

"Roll right in, my boy," said the priest with as expansive a religious hospitality as that he had just been displaying over the lobsters sent over by the Biffer. "And you'll look after him, Duncan," he enjoined the commander of the platoon.

"Och, I'll put him into his seat, Father James, just the same as a good dog would put a sheep into a fank," Duncan Bàn promised.

"Of course it depends whether Colonel Wolseley agrees to me staying on for another week," the Sergeant-major added cautiously.

"He'll agree, my boy," said the priest with conviction. "He knows that the safety of the whole country depends on the Home Guard of Todaidh Beag."

Chapter 10

TÌR NAN ÒG

"MANY and fair are the long white beaches that stretch beside the western shores of the islands at the edge of the mighty Atlantic, but none is fairer than lovely Tràigh Swish of Little Todday. Philologists differ about the origin of the name. So let us fly backwards out of the prosaic present upon 'the viewless wings of poesy' and accept the

derivation from Suis, a Norse princess of lon'
legend relates, flung herself into the ocean fro
rock which marks the southern boundary o'
Alas, her love for a young bard of Todaidh Beag, as
Todday is called in the old sweet speech of the Gael, was
foredoomed.

"And while we are back in the faerie days of yester year
let us ponder awhile that grey rock which marks the northern
boundary of Tràigh Swish. Does it seem to resemble the
outline of a great seal and justify its name—Carraig an Ròin?
Some relate indeed that it is no mere likeness of a seal but
the petrified shape of the seal-woman herself from whom the
Macroons sprang. Who shall say? Upon this magical
morning of spring when the short sweet turf of the machair
is starred with multitudinous primroses, the morning-stars
of the Hebridean flora as they have been well called, we
yield our imagination to the influence of the season and are
willing to believe anything. We stand entranced midway
along Tràigh Swish and watch the placid ocean break gently
upon the sand to dabble it with tender kisses. We listen
to the sea-birds calling to one another as they wing their
way to their nesting grounds on the two guardian isles of
Poppay and Pillay. We gaze at the calm expanse of the
Atlantic and try to forget its winter fury of which the heaped-
up tangle along the base of the dunes reminds us. We are at
one with nature. We have the freedom of Tìr nan Òg—
the Land of Youth."

Thus has written Hector Hamish Mackay in *Faerie Lands
Forlorn*, and although Sergeant-major Odd had never read a
word of the topographer and never heard of Tìr nan Òg, he
was feeling on that Sunday afternoon at April's end the full
effect of the legendary Celtic paradise. In other words, he
did not feel a day older than twenty-five as he sat on a warm
hassock of sandy turf and gazed at Peigi Ealasaid sitting on
another hassock opposite him, the glistening sea behind her.

"To-morrow morning I'll be going back to Snorvig," he
sighed.

"It's a pity you can't be staying in Kiltod."

"Do *you* think it's a pity, Peggy?" he asked meaningly.

"They all think it's a pity. They all enjoyed their shooting
fine," she assured him.

"At the end of next week," he went on, "I'll be going back

to Fort Augustus. I don't know when I'll get a chance to be sent out here again."

"Have you enjoyed yourself here?"

"Have I enjoyed myself? Can't you see I've enjoyed myself? And don't you know *why* I've enjoyed myself?"

"Oh well, it has been beautiful weather right enough," she declared. "Indeed yes, really beautiful."

"There's been something more beautiful than the weather, and mind you, that's been good. I'm not saying a word against the weather. And *you* know what that little something is."

Peggy's deep-blue slanting eyes gazed into those of the Sergeant-major without, it seemed, the slightest notion of what that little something could be.

"Well, what is to be is to be, as the saying goes," he went on. "But if anybody had have said I was going to be knocked all of a heap instructing the Little Todday Home Guard I wouldn't have believed him. But there you are, Peggy, what is to be is to be."

"I don't understand what you're saying. It's a pity you can't talk the Gaelic."

"Ah, get along with you, you'd understand what I'm saying now whatever language I said it in."

"I wouldn't at all," she insisted, just too positively to be convincing.

"Well, if you're determined *not* to understand, I'm talking about you and I."

An eloquence of virginal wonderment such as Eve may have possessed before the Fall was Peggy's only reply.

"And what's more," the Sergeant-major insisted, "you know that's what I'm talking about."

"Why would you be talking about you and me?"

"And that you know quite well also."

She pouted.

"I think you're a very funny man."

"I'm in a very funny position," he told her.

And on this observation Sergeant-major Odd relapsed into a contemplative silence which the murmur of the ocean and the occasional chatter of a passing gull made more profound.

"Will you marry me, Peggy?" he broke the silence to ask suddenly.

"*A Mhuire mhàthair!*" she gasped.

"What's that mean?"

"You made me jump! What a thing to ask anybody!"

"I'm not asking *any*body. I'm asking *you*, Peggy Yallasich."
She laughed.

"Oh, don't look so crabbed, Sarchant Odd. I was laughing
the way you're saying 'Ealasaid'."

"Couldn't you call me Fred?" he asked earnestly.

"People would think I was terribly ignorant to be calling
you Fred. You're so old."

"That's torn it," he declared in disgust.

"Are you after tearing something?" she enquired solicitously.
"I'll sew it up for you when we reach home."

"Torn it in a manner of speaking. What I meant was I'm
not so old as all that. I'm only twenty years older than what
you are."

"You're twenty-one years older," she reminded him firmly.

"Oh, you worked it out like a sum, did you? Well, I suppose I ought to feel pleased it was worth your while. And
what's twenty-one years? Nothing, believe you me, when you
get past forty. As you'll find out one day for yourself."

"And you're a Protestant."

"Well, that doesn't worry *me*. So I don't see why it need
worry *you*."

"How many girls have you asked to marry you?"

"Oh, you think I make a habit of it, eh? That's just where
you're wrong, Peggy. Very wrong. I never asked any girl
to marry me before I met you. And in fact I made a very
particular point of not asking them."

"Just made love to them," she commented censoriously.

"And which you can't say I did to you," he pointed out.

There was a silence. The Sergeant-major appeared preoccupied with the cigarette he had lighted. Peigi Ealasaid
appeared equally preoccupied with a daisy-bracelet she was
making.

"Well, *will* you marry me?" he asked again at last, flinging
away the butt of the cigarette.

"It's a foolishness," she murmured, still intent upon the
daisy-bracelet.

"You don't love me, eh?"

"Who can love somebody in a few days?"

"I fell in love with you as soon as I saw you."

"You think you did."

"All right, I thought I did.   What does anybody do when he falls in love with a girl except think?   I've done it myself before now.   But I never thought I wanted to marry one yet. Do you like me, Peggy?"

"Yes, I like you very much.   I think you're very nice.   I wouldn't be going with you for a walk if I didn't think you were nice."

The Sergeant-major held up his hand in the gesture with which he was wont to signify to a squad of recruits that they had done all he required of them for the moment.

"Right, leave it at that for the present.   I haven't waited twenty years, as you might say, to find the girl I wanted to marry and then expect to rush it through in a week.   I'm going back to Snorvig to-morrow.   Then after a few days I'll be going back to Fort Augustus.   You'll settle down to think it over.   Next time I see you, and which I hope won't be so very long away, I'll ask you again.   Perhaps you'll say it's still too soon to make up your mind.   Right!"   The gesture with the uplifted hand was repeated.   "I'll go away again.   And you'll have some more time to make up your mind.   And so it'll go on until you give me my definite discharge or you sign me on for good.   What you've given me to-day is just the dismiss till the next parade.   That's the way I'm looking at it."

"You're terribly thrawn, are you not?"

"Say that in English."

"I'm after saying it in English."

" Well, you haven't caught up yet."

She shook her head in bewilderment.

"What's thrawn the Garlic for?" he pressed.

"Och, I don't know.   *Rag.*"

"Rack?   Here, something's going wrong.   What's thrawn in English?"

"Thrawn *is* English.   It means thrawn."

It was his turn to shake his head.

"Never heard of such a word in my life.   You've got it wrong.   What's it mean as well as thrawn?"

"What you are."

"But what am I ? "

"Who's being thrawn now?"

"Have a heart, Peggy Yallasich. How do I know what I'm being if I don't know what it is?"

"Were you never at school?"

"Certainly I went to school."

"A terrible queer kind of a school it must have been if you didn't learn what thrawn was."

"Give me another word for it in English."

She thought hard for a moment or two.

"Stubborn. Can you understand that English word?"

"Ah, stubborn's all right. That's good English, that is. So you think I'm stubborn, do you? Well, I reckon I am. And patient. I suppose you know what patient is? It means I can wait. And I'm going to wait for you, Peggy Yallasich. There's only one thing I would like to know. Is there anyone else?"

"Anyone else where?"

"Anyone else wanting to marry you?"

"Do you think everybody is like you?"

"I didn't say everybody. I said anybody."

"Goodness, what will you be asking next?"

"To give me a kiss."

"Isn't it you that's chicky! Fancy asking a girl such a thing like that," Peggy exclaimed primly. "If you want to be chicky you must be chicky in the Gaelic."

"So if I asked you in Garlic to give me a kiss, you'd give me one, eh?" the Sergeant-major murmured, twinkling.

"Perhaps I would, but you cannot be asking me, can you?" she trilled.

"Can't I? Poc me, Peggy Yallasich," he said triumphantly.

"Oh, well, *nach sibh tha carach!* Aren't you tricky!" she exclaimed, her deep-blue eyes opening wide amid a profuse blush. "Who was telling you that *pog* means kiss? And you pretending you didn't know. I would be ashamed to be so deceitful."

"Well, will you poc me?" he pressed.

"No, indeed I will not do such a thing."

But he kissed her, and he robbed her of her daisy-bracelet into the bargain. As he buttoned the flap of his pocket over the captured flowers he said:

"I'll write to you, Peggy. Will you write to me?"

"I won't say any more to you at all. You are too chicky.

And now we must be walking home."

"It seems a pity to waste such a lovely afternoon," the Sergeant-major sighed.

They sat silent for a while on their grassy hassocks, ocean-gazing.

"Well, life's a funny business," the Sergeant-major observed at last. "If anyone had have told me when Captain Grant gave me orders to proceed to Snorvig on duty that he was booking me for the best bit of pleasure I'd ever known I'd have laughed right out. I would really, Peggy. And when Captain Waggett said I would proceed to Kiltod in order to instruct the Home Guard, did I think I was going to learn the biggest lesson I ever had in my life? Not me. The Biffer they call him, don't they?" he went on meditatively. "Well, he gave me the biggest biff of my life when he pulled in alongside of the pier and I saw you looking down at me. I mean to say, 'Why?' People have quacked to me about love at first sight, and I've derided them. Derided them, I have, 'Yes, then you woke up,' I've said. I mean to say, I didn't believe it."

"I don't know why you think you like me," Peggy murmured. "It's very strange. Kate Anne said you liked me, and I was laughing at her."

"Did she? She's a very sensible girl, Kate Anne is. I've never had occasion before to look at any girl as a future sister-in-law, and so I haven't considered that question. But I'm going to be very fond of Kate Anne when she is my sister-in-law."

"Sarchant Odd, you really are a terrible man."

"Fred."

She tossed her dark-brown hair in an emphatic shake of the head.

"Come on, try it," he persuaded.

"No, no, I couldn't, please."

"Out here where nobody can hear you, only me. Come on, you couldn't have an easier name to say."

"Oh, just to keep you quiet then," she pouted. "Fred."

The smile with which the Sergeant-major received this monosyllable might have been called fatuous by anybody less in love than himself, and that such a smile should make Peigi Ealasaid blush did not suggest a complete imperviousness to the emotion of her suitor.

Certainly the Sergeant-major himself was by no means

pessimistic about the future. That night he sat late with Joseph Macroon in his parlour over a whisky that the postmaster of Kiltod did not produce for every guest.

"It's a strange thing when you come to think of it, Mr Macroon, that I never got married."

"Ah well, you may be happier for it. I lost my own wife two years ago last February, God rest her soul," Joseph said, crossing himself. "And I miss her terribly. Daughters are just an expense. Just not doing anything so well as their mother, and wanting twice as many clothes. Reading too in bed. What they cost me in paraffin before the black-out. Och, it's a good thing, the black-out, right enough."

"Well, I lost my dad when I was only a nipper, but I've had a wonderful mother, Mr Macroon."

"Has she any daughters?"

"No, I'm her only child."

"Look at that now. No daughters. There's a lucky woman." Joseph stretched across for the Sergeant-major's glass to pour him another dram.

"I don't know so much about that," said the guest. "I think she'd have liked to have a daughter. She has quite a nice little business in Nottingham where we moved from London. Tobacco, sweets, newspapers, and lodgers. Yes, she's often said to me she wishes I'd find a nice girl and marry and settle down. Well, she's getting on now. She'll be seventy next year. Yes, yes, by the time the war's over I'd like to be married. When a man gets on to forty-three he ought to be thinking seriously about getting married, and that's a fact. Well, to-morrow I'll be leaving you all in Little Todday."

"Ay, it's a pity you have to be away so soon. Duncan Bàn says you've taught them a lot. It's a pity you haven't the Gaelic."

"Yes, I've only managed to pick up a word here and there. And that reminds me, what's 'I love you', again? I never quite get my tongue round it."

"I love you? That's easy. *Tha gaoil agam ort.*"

"Hah, girl, ackamorst. Queer isn't it that girl should come into it in both languages?"

Joseph Macroon looked blank for a moment. Then he brightened.

"Ah; but we say *gaoil* for 'love'. We don't say *gaoil* for 'girl'."

"Still and all, one thing leads to the other, as you might say. Yes, I'm sorry to be leaving you all. However, perhaps I'll be back pretty soon. There's no doubt the Home Guard out here wants a lot of instruction."

"I believe they will."

"Yes, I've enjoyed my stay on Little Todday," said the Sergeant-major. "There's something about the air."

"Beautiful air, right enough. And plenty of it."

"Not too much for me," said the Sergeant-major firmly. "I like air, I do."

Chapter 11

THE BRIGADIER AND THE COLONEL

SERGEANT-MAJOR ODD returned to Snorvig full of enthusiastic optimism about the splendid military material on Little Todday of which, granted the opportunity, he confidently predicted he could weave as fine a platoon as any in the battálion.

"But I must have time, sir," he pointed out to Captain Waggett on the afternoon of his departure for the mainland.

"Well, I have allowed you more time with the Little Todday platoon in proportion to what you have given any of the other sections. Mr Beaton was inclined to think Bobanish had been rather neglected."

"In a manner that's true, sir. But the Bobanish platoon, and that includes the Watasett section, have the advantage of two good men in Lieutenant Beaton and Sergeant Macleod. And the Snorvig platoon with the Garryboo section have the advantage of your personal supervision, sir, not to mention Sergeant Thomson who's as good an N.C.O. as anybody could want."

"Sergeant Campbell at Garryboo isn't quite so good," said the Commanding Officer.

"Sergeant Campbell's all right, sir, as long as his mother doesn't interfere with him. But it's awkward for any N.C.O. if he's fetched away from a parade like a schoolboy. It's subversive to good discipline. I think it wouldn't do any harm, sir, if you spoke to the old lady about it."

"Mrs Campbell is rather a difficult woman," Captain Waggett observed. "She was once the factor's wife and so got used to having everything her own way."

"You're telling me, sir. Still, I think it would help if you put in a word. She's bound to pay attention to *you*. I wonder whether Colonel Wolseley'll send me out here again."

"I shall write and tell him what excellent work you have done, Sergeant-major, and I hope it won't be too long before he can spare you. Where do you think you'll be sent when you get back to Fort Augustus?"

"There was talk before I came away about me going to the Glenbogle company. And in fact Major MacDonald was creating about me coming here before I went to him."

"Ben Nevis?"

"That's right, sir. Queer notion, isn't it, calling anybody after a mountain? But they've got a lot of funny ways in Scotland."

"Well," Captain Waggett sighed, with a sentimental thought of Snorvig House, and the shooting and the fishing of which he was laird, "if I weren't an Englishman I'd sooner be a Scotsman than any other nation on earth."

"Oh, I'm not saying a word against Scotland, sir. And in fact I'm very sorry the shortage of cloth kept them from putting the 40th Clanranalds into kilts. I've always had a notion to wear a kilt ever since I went to a fancy-dress ball once as Bruce and the Spider. Well, sir, I mustn't waste any more of your time. The boat will be in presently. I hope it won't be too long before I'm back. I do want to get at that Little Todday platoon again. And of course the other two platoons as well," the Instructor added quickly.

"Good-bye, Sergeant-major. You'll remind Captain Grant about that cement we want for pill-boxes, won't you?"

"Yes, sir, I'll remind him all right. But I wouldn't count on it if I was you."

Captain Waggett smiled the tired smile of a thwarted Napoleon.

"I'm counting on nothing, Sergeant-major," he replied. "If the two Toddays are lost to the enemy because we have no cement to make pill-boxes I can't be blamed. Well, I mustn't keep you any longer."

The Sergeant-major saluted and retired.

It happened that when he reported at battalion headquarters Major MacDonald of Ben Nevis, the commander of C Company, had just driven over to Fort Augustus from Glenbogle and was present in Colonel Lindsay-Wolseley's office to hear the account the instructor gave of the Home Guard on the two Toddays.

"And if I may say so, sir," Sergeant-major Odd declared warmly, "I don't believe there's a company in the battalion would give a better return for time and trouble than G Company."

"I'm very glad to hear what you say, Sergeant-major," said the Colonel of the 8th Battalion of the Inverness-shire Home Guard, a neat man with an almost white moustache and a complexion tanned a yellowish-brown by years of service in India. "That's very encouraging, isn't it, Ben Nevis? I was afraid they might find it hard to pick up the job of soldiering out in those smaller islands, though I know the 2nd Battalion is making a good job of it with the larger ones."

"Pick up soldiering?" the Chieftain exploded, his great beak aglow. "They'll pick up anything in the islands. They picked up one of C Company's boots last autumn."

"I don't think we can reopen that boot correspondence, Ben Nevis," said the Colonel quickly.

"You know my views on that left-footed boot, Lindsay-Wolseley," the Chieftain barked.

"I do indeed," the Colonel replied drily.

The Sergeant-major, who saw that not even his presence would act much longer as an effective cork for the Chieftain's bottled-up wrath, asked if the Colonel required anything more.

"No, I'll go into details later, Sergeant-major."

As the Sergeant-major was closing the office door behind him the grenade of Mac 'ic Eachainn's indignation burst.

"Now look here, Lindsay-Wolseley, when I agreed to raise a company for the 8th Battalion I did not agree to let every Tom, Dick, or Harry defy me because the sea happened to be between him and me. You know perfectly well there's not another company commander in Wester Inverness who would have dared to treat me like this Cockney interloper on Todday. And I won't . . ."

"I say, Ben Nevis," Colonel Wolseley interrupted, "you

really must not talk about another company commander like that—even when there's nobody present except our two selves. This boot question is a difficulty we all have to contend with. The battalion reserve is short by 300 pairs, the quartermaster tells me. And every company shares in the responsibility."

"That's no excuse for this fellow Wuggins calmly appropriating a left-footed boot belonging to my company," the Chieftain maintained.

"His name is not Wuggins. His name is Waggett," said the Colonel a little irritably.

"What's the difference?" the Chieftain demanded. "I never heard such finickin' tommy-rot."

"Would you like Waggett to call you Ben Wyvis?"

"I shouldn't mind at all. I should think the fellah was an even bigger ass than I think he is now. You never saw the letter he wrote to MacIsaac. I never read such a piece of pompous drivel in my life."

"Well, I'm going over to Todday as soon as I can, and I'll try to find out where the misunderstanding has arisen."

"There's no misunderstanding about it," the Chieftain spluttered. "It's a piece of thieving by those confounded islanders. They've been thieving for years. Several of my forerunners have had to take drastic action against them. I think it was my great-great-great-great-great-grandfather who led a punitive expedition against Snorvig and hanged Mac-Rurie of Todday in his own kitchen chimney. Yes, by Jove, and smoked him like a ham."

"Well, you can't smoke poor Waggett like a ham, Ben Nevis."

The Chieftain snorted. He was evidently by no means convinced he could not.

"By the way, Wolseley, are you going to let me have that P.S.I. next week?"

"He must go to Bottley first. After that you shall have him."

"Because MacIsaac's very busy just now. He can't spend the whole of his time running about looking for missing rifles."

"Oh, you haven't found those five rifles that were missing?" the Colonel asked. "No rifles are missing on either Great or Little Todday," he added drily.

"There are no stags there," said Ben Nevis. "If there were, there wouldn't be a rifle left in either of the islands. At least there'd be no sign of them."

"I hope those Glenbogle rifles will turn up," said the Colonel. "Otherwise, I'm afraid it may mean a court of enquiry. Beamish is very angry about it."

"I know. He wrote me a ridiculous personal letter."

"He wasn't at all pleased by the reply he had from you."

"I don't suppose he was. I didn't intend it to be a *billet-doux*."

Mac 'ic Eachainn gave a scornful guffaw.

"He *is* the Western Sub-Stratum Commander you know. *And* a Brigadier," Colonel Wolseley pointed out.

"Look here, Wolseley, you've been living with us up here long enough to know that that kind of thing cuts no ice in the West. We didn't form the 8th Battalion of the Inverness-shire Home Guard to be messed about by some confounded fellow from Dorset or wherever it is he comes from. And Hugh Cameron agrees with me. What between boots and brigadiers, if it weren't for the wrong impression it might give I'd turn in my hand. I mean to say, one expects a modicum of gentlemanly common sense even from a professional soldier."

"Have you heard from Hector lately?" Colonel Wolseley asked. Captain Hector MacDonald Yr. of Ben Nevis had been taken prisoner at St Valéry, and the Colonel's enquiry was intended to administer a rebuke to Ben Nevis for his remark about professional soldiers and at the same time to direct the conversation away from Brigadier Beamish.

"He's been moved from one Off-lag to another Off-lag, but he seems fairly cheerful. Don't know how he manages it, poor lad. If I were shut up in an Off-lag I think I should burst."

It was about a fortnight after this conversation that Colonel Lindsay-Wolseley sent the following telegram to Captain Paul Waggett:

O.C. G Company Snorvig
    I propose to visit Todday next Tuesday with Brigadier Beamish stop please arrange transport and necessary accommodation for two nights stop you may be able to arrange an exercise

                                              Lindsay Wolseley

"The Western Sub-Stratum Commander and Colonel

Lindsay-Wolseley are coming over on Tuesday for a couple of nights, Dolly," Captain Waggett told his wife. "We must ask them to stay with us, of course."

"Of course, dear," she agreed, with as little dubiety in her voice as a loyal wife whose household staff had all departed to anticipate conscription into the A.T.S. by becoming conductresses of the Glasgow trams could achieve.

"You won't find it too much for you?" he enquired, without the slightest fear that she would.

"Oh no, dear. I shall manage somehow," she promised brightly.

"I think the Brigadier would like to see a night attack," Captain Waggett sighed dreamily. "And of course I shall have a guard of honour drawn up on the pier when the *Island Queen* arrives. On Wednesday we'll inspect the various sections. Then on Wednesday night Great Todday will attack Little Todday. Or *vice versa*. And on Thursday morning they might like some fishing on Loch Skinny. I'm afraid that's the only sport I can offer them this month. There might be a salmon in one of the pools of the Skinny."

"Yes, dear," said Mrs Waggett in the tone of voice in which a mother tells her children that Santa Claus might be caught in the act of coming into their bedroom down the chimney. For five years now her husband had been putting forward the theory that a salmon might be found in one of the pools of the minute stream fed by Loch Skinny. It never had been.

On Tuesday afternoon the Snorvig section of G Company was drawn up on the pier to present arms as Brigadier Beamish and Colonel Lindsay-Wolseley walked down the gangway of the *Island Queen*.

"Very creditable. Very creditable indeed, Waggett," his colonel assured him. "I think the Brigadier's very pleased. Yes, he's going to speak to the men."

Brigadier Beamish, a large blond man, took a deep draught of Atlantic air and began:

"I'm very pleased to see such a smart turn-out by the Todday Home Guard. It's very—er—gratifying to see such a fine —er—spirit. Colonel Lindsay-Wolseley has—er—told me of the fine—er—spirit you've shown since you—er—came forward—er—at a moment of crisis just a year ago to defend your own island and your own homes against the Hun. I think if the enemy ventures to attack Great Todday he'll meet with a very—er—warm reception."

"Ay, they'll get that right enough," the Biffer observed from the ranks. At this the other Corporal Archie MacRurie, who was standing behind the Biffer, dug him in the back to warn him that Sergeant Thomson had frowned at the interruption. Whereupon the Biffer turned round and hotly asked his namesake in Gaelic what he thought he was doing.

"Silence, men," Captain Waggett rapped out, and several of the volunteers turned on the two corporals with loud 'istibhs'.

"I know that you have given up a lot of your leisure time to your military duties," the Brigadier continued. "And your soldierly bearing reflects great credit on you all. I understand I shall soon be given an opportunity to see you in—er—what is after all the—er—the vital, I say vital rôle of the Home Guard —er—aggressive action in defence of your island homes. I'm looking forward to it very much."

The Brigadier nodded with a benevolent smile, and turned away to accompany his host up to Snorvig House.

"You must have done a lot of hard work, Captain Waggett," the Brigadier commented graciously.

"I've done what I could, sir."

"Well, I congratulate you. I think Captain Waggett is to be congratulated, don't you, Wolseley?"

"Very much so," said the Colonel.

"I must apologize, sir, for the interruption when you were speaking to the men," said Waggett.

"Oh, I liked it," the Brigadier declared benevolently. "After all, these chaps are doing a jolly fine job. Don't you think so, Wolseley?"

"Jolly fine job," the Colonel agreed.

"Yes, indeed, by Jove, a jolly fine job," the Brigadier repeated emphatically. "I say, Waggett, I hope we're not being a nuisance, camping ourselves on you like this, what?"

"On the contrary, sir, it's a pleasure."

"Well, it's very good of you to say so, isn't it, Wolseley?"

"Very good indeed," the Colonel murmured.

The Brigadier stopped in his stride and gazed round him at Snorvig.

"Now what do the people *do* here, Waggett?" he asked.

And for the rest of the way up to Snorvig House Waggett held forth to Brigadier Beamish on Hebridean economy.

"Well, I see you know all about it," said the Brigadier. "You're not a native, though, are you?"

"No, sir, I've only been living here for the last seven years. I'm very keen on sport, and it just suits me."

"Quite," the Brigadier agreed. "Is the fishing good?"

"Very very good," the host replied in that tone of dreamy sentiment he kept for sport. "I thought you might like to have a try for a salmon on Thursday. It's rather early of course, but we might have luck."

"That's very kind of you, Waggett," said the Brigadier warmly. "I think we ought to take advantage of that invitation, don't you, Wolseley?"

Colonel Lindsay-Wolseley was an authority on salmon fishing, and he was not prepared to believe in the Todday salmon. However, he decided that this projected expedition would keep the Brigadier quiet until it was time to sail and he therefore applauded the notion.

Tea at Snorvig House was graced by the presence of the Minister and his wife, and the cakes produced by Mrs Waggett made the Brigadier's light-blue eyes bulge.

"I know it's very rude to make remarks about food," he said. "But I really must compliment you on this cake, Mrs Waggett. I suppose you're able to get plenty of eggs?"

"We get as many as we can," Mrs Waggett replied simply. "But they're not so easy to get this year as last year, are they, Mrs Morrison?"

"No, I think the people are eating more eggs themselves with the difficulty of getting tins," said the Minister's wife. "But we mustn't complain."

"Oh, indeed no," her husband added earnestly. "The Ministry of Food has treated us very well."

"I haven't eaten such a good cake since I don't know when," the Brigadier declared. "Do you find you can get plenty of butter?"

"My husband manages to collect a certain amount here and in Little Todday," the hostess informed him.

"By Jove, if I lose my job in the Western Sub-Stratum Command," the Brigadier said merrily, "I think I shall apply to be one of your subalterns in the Home Guard, Waggett. What?"

Everybody except Colonel Lindsay-Wolseley laughed heartily at this capital joke, and none more heartily than Brigadier Beamish himself. It was not because the Colonel lacked a sense of humour that he failed to laugh. It was because he had heard the Brigadier make this kind of joke so often before.

The next morning was spent in interrupting the studies of the three schools of Garryboo, Bobanish, and Watasett in order that Sergeant Campbell, Lieutenant Beaton, and Sergeant Macleod might have the privilege of being asked questions which the Brigadier hoped might suggest the passionate interest that Scottish Command took in the military preparedness of Great Todday to deal with the enemy. At this date road blocks were going out of fashion on account of the inconvenience they had caused to the defenders of Britain, and as Hitler had not started to invade Russia the scorched-earth policy had not yet captivated the military imagination.

Hence there was not much to talk about except parachutists and the niceties of guerilla warfare and the need of being in a permanent condition of suspicious alertness.

"The idea of suspicious alertness is that a fellow never goes slacking around with his rifle slung over his shoulder," the Brigadier explained. "He must always be ready to jab his bayonet into anything he sees, and carry his rifle accordingly. The people at the top are tremendously keen on suspicious alertness."

After lunch the visitors embarked in the *Kittiwake* to inspect the Home Guard of Little Todday.

"Odd was particularly enthusiastic about your platoon there, Waggett," the Colonel observed.

"You'll find them better in the field than on the parade-ground, sir," the commander of G Company told him. "However, I hope they'll be able to manage the guard of honour."

As the *Kittiwake* chug-chugged into Kiltod about two dozen warriors of the Little Todday platoon could be seen drawn up on the pier, and the voice of Lieutenant Macroon was heard on a note of desperate entreaty giving them the order to present arms.

"Present arms! Don't you hear what I'm telling you? Will you present arms?"

There followed a voluble outburst of infuriated Gaelic from the platoon commander.

"I suppose you're pretty fluent in Gaelic by now, Waggett, what?" the Brigadier asked.

"I don't talk it much, sir, but I get the drift of it, you know," Waggett replied.

"What's that subaltern of yours saying now?" the Colonel asked. "He sounds as if he's using rather violent language."

"There seems to be some kind of a hitch," said Waggett nervously as he jumped out of the boat and offered a hand to the Brigadier on the slippery step.

The hitch was that hardly two men of the Little Todday platoon could agree what was the way to present arms and nobody was willing to be exposed in front of the rest as a blunderer. So in spite of Duncan Bàn's desperate entreaty to present arms the platoon remained obstinately at attention while the Brigadier, the Colonel, and the Company Commander were coming up the steps.

"*A chlann an diabhoil*, will you be pressenting your arms," Duncan Bàn urged. "What are you afraid of? Do you think the man will eat you?"

Something in Duncan's voice touched a chord in Alan Macdonald's heart, and he took two paces back out of the line in order to give himself freedom for the complicated movement. He had forgotten how near he was already standing to the edge of the pier, and so he stepped into space and landed with a loud splash in the water of the harbour.

There was plenty of laughter at the accident, but behind their laughter the men of Little Todday were inclined to resent the presence of the Biffer as an eyewitness. They did not enjoy the notion of providing a good story to divert the men of Great Todday, and they knew that Alan Macdonald's misadventure would lose nothing of its absurdity when the time came for the Biffer to relate it on the other side of the Coolish. Therefore when it was decided Little Todday should attack Great Todday that evening for the entertainment of Brigadier Beamish and Colonel Lindsay-Wolseley, the men of Little Todday rejoiced. They felt in a thoroughly aggressive mood.

"Zero hour will be nine o'clock," Captain Waggett informed Lieutenant Macroon. "Perhaps in the course of the afternoon you'll give me an idea of what you're going to do. Brigadier

Beamish and Colonel Wolseley will want to see as much as they can of the exercise. Of course, the Great Todday platoons will have to know where you will attack, but I shall take no active part in the exercise myself. The problem is the umpires. I was saying, sir, to Mr Macroon that our trouble here is umpires," he added, turning to the Colonel.

"What about the Doctor we met? Wouldn't he do for one?" the Colonel asked.

Captain Waggett shook his head and sniffed a larger air.

"Quite impossible I'm afraid, sir. He's had no military experience of any kind, and unfortunately he believes he has. And Mr Mackinnon, the headmaster of Snorvig school, is impossible too."

"I don't see why we should bother about umpires, Colonel," said the Brigadier. "You and I will be able to judge how the exercise goes. Mr Macroon is to let Captain Waggett know where he's coming and we shall see how quickly and effectively the defenders get to their positions. I assume it's just a simple exercise to demonstrate the defence of a portion of the coast against a hostile landing."

But Brigadier Beamish was wrong. Duncan Bàn had no intention of allowing it to be quite such a simple matter as all that.

When the visitors had departed, the commander of the Little Todday platoon went up to the Chapel House to tell Father Macalister of the way Alan Macdonald had exposed Todaidh Beag to the ridicule of Todaidh Mór by the way he had stepped backwards off the pier into the harbour in an effort to present arms. The priest laughed uproariously over the accident.

"Oh, well, poor Alan," he chuckled. "He'll be furious at himself, sure enough. Did the Brigadier enjoy a good laugh?"

"We all enjoyed a good laugh," Duncan replied. "But the man who laughed loudest was Archie MacRurie, and that's what I didn't like. He'll have made a good story of it over in Snorvig by now, Father."

"You may depend upon that, Duncan. The Biffer will have made a beauty, oh, a beauty, my boy."

"It's giving them the chance to laugh at us, and I don't like that at all, Father James."

"Ay, it'll be disagreeable for you, Duncan, right enough,

next time you go up to the hotel and Roderick asks whether you present arms with your legs in Todaidh Beag."

The priest laughed again; but Duncan scowled.

"And you were so beautifully sober yourself, Duncan," Father Macalister added.

"Oh, Alan was sober too, Father. Don't you be thinking he'd had a dram. No, no, no. It was pure good nature made him step back like that, because he was wanting to set an example and pressent arms the way Sergeant-major Odd had been teaching them all."

"Ah, well, Duncan, it can't be helped, and what can't be helped, well, you know what you have to do."

"But I've thought of a way to make them look a bit foolish in Todaidh Mór, Father."

"You have?"

"We're supposed to attack them to-night to show what we can do."

"Good shooting," the priest ejaculated, with warm approval.

"And I'm to send across and let Mr Waggett know where we're coming at nine o'clock.

"That's very kind of you, Duncan. I hope Hitler will send you a picture-postcard to say the same."

"Well, I was thinking I'd say we would attack them up Loch Sleeport and make a try to capture Watasett School."

"Good enough."

"It's lovely and calm this afternoon on the west," Duncan went on in meditative tones.

"Ay, it's calm."

"And no sign of a change in the weather."

"None at all."

"Well, I was thinking I'd tell the Dot to take the *St Tod* round to Bàgh Mhic Ròin."

The *St Tod* was a sizable fishing-boat with an auxiliary motor owned by Donald Macroon generally known as the Dot. Father Macalister used to call his boat the *St Dot*, and Donald himself, a small swarthy taciturn man, never failed to chuckle deeply at the priest's joke.

"What's the idea of doing that, Duncan?"

"I was thinking the *St Tod* could lie there safely till it was time to land the Todaidh Beag Expeditionary Force."

"To land in Loch Sleeport?" the priest exclaimed, for the

bay from which Duncan was proposing to sail was at the north-west end of Little Todday, and as far away as could be achieved from Watasett.

"No," he told Father Macalister, with a triumphant smile, "to land at Garryboo. There won't be anybody there."

"Mrs Campbell will be there," the priest reminded him.

"But she's not a Home Guard, Father."

"*A dhuine dhuine*, she's the fiercest Home Guard in all the islands from Islay up to Lewis."

"I'll send Jockey Stewart with half a dozen men in the *Kittiwake* to Loch Sleeport because Mr Waggett is sending over the *Kittiwake* and if we said we didn't want it he'd be suspicious. And I'll send two or three men in the *Morning Star* in the same direction. But the main attack will be made at Garryboo, and I'm not going to say a word to anybody about that. I'm just going to give them a good lesson in Todaidh Mór not to laugh at us because Alan Macdonald . . ."

"Presented legs instead of presenting arms," the priest put in quickly.

"Ah well, Father, I hope those rascals in Todaidh Mór will have a good lesson to-night not to laugh at Alan Macdonald."

"You'll do your best, Duncan."

"I'll do that, Father, right enough," the platoon commander promised fervidly.

Chapter 12

LITTLE TODDAY ON THE WARPATH

AT six o'clock the following message reached Captain Waggett at Snorvig House:

From Lieutenant Macroon

To Captain Waggett of the Home Guard.

Dear Sir,
    The attack will be made on Watasett School any time after nine o'clock.

Yours till Doomsday,

Duncan Bàn

"That will give us time to sit comfortably over some rather good port I was lucky enough to get hold of before the war," Captain Waggett announced to his guests, with a connoisseur's relief. Then he went to the telephone:

"I want Mr Beaton at Bobanish," he told the operator. "Hello, is that you, Mr Beaton? I want your platoon to cover the left bank of Loch Sleeport. The attack by Number Three Platoon from Little Todday is likely to develop in that sector. You are authorized to send a lorry for the Garryboo Section. Will you let Sergeant Campbell know. The Snorvig Section of Number One Platoon will hold the right bank of Loch Sleeport and the Watasett Section will hold the school, which will probably be the main objective of the attackers. Brigadier Beamish and Colonel Lindsay-Wolseley will be watching our little exercise, and as I shall be with them you will take command of the defences . . . there's no need for you to feel the slightest anxiety, Mr Beaton. I have complete confidence in you, and I shall be disappointed if you do not completely wipe out the attacking force before a man gets ashore. Of course, as it looks like being such a calm evening, the attackers may land lower down the Loch, but if you place your men well I don't see how they can get very far . . . no, they need not bring their respirators, and don't forget they will wear bonnets. Number Three Platoon will be wearing steel helmets . . . if you're in any difficulty don't hesitate to ring me up. I'm always available for advice. You'd better have your men at their action stations by half-past eight at the latest."

Captain Waggett hung up the receiver.

"I try to delegate as much responsibility as I can to my subalterns," he observed to the Brigadier and the Colonel. "It will make things easier if anything should ever happen to me. And out in the Islands it's essential to get people into the habit of accepting responsibility. I've learnt that since I came to Snorvig."

At dinner the host expanded under the good cheer he and his wife were offering their guests. Conversation soon became a monologue, and Mrs Waggett was hard put to it to see that the Brigadier and the Colonel wanted for nothing without relaxing the expression of enraptured attention her husband demanded for his tales. For a time he lectured them on military matters, for he never made the mistake of allowing professionals to know as much about their own job as he did. Then he turned to sport:

"I hope we shall find a salmon to-morrow. It's early of course. I wish you could be here for the Twelfth. I couldn't give you a drive. We haven't enough birds to make it worth while putting up butts. But if you like shooting over dogs you'll enjoy it as much here as anywhere. When I go to the mainland and see some of the most famous sporting properties in Scotland I don't envy any of them. I always say I wouldn't exchange any of them for my little shooting and fishing on the two Toddays." His voice grew dreamy. "An occasional salmon, a few brace of grouse, any amount of snipe and plover, a few cock, and of course wonderful for geese. Really wonderful! I believe Pillay, the small island north-west of Little Todday, is the best ground for barnacle geese anywhere in the country, and of course we get grey lag right through the winter on the west side of Little Todday and at Garryboo. I often think I should like to see a few head of deer on our Great Todday bens, but one can't have everything," he sighed, with a generous recognition of Providence's limitations.

"Do you find the people poach much?" Colonel Lindsay-Wolseley asked.

"Well, of course, when I came here Snorvig House had been untenanted for several years and the people had got into the habit of thinking the shooting and fishing belonged to them. However, gradually I've cured them of that idea, and poaching now is at a discount. The people have learnt to appreciate the advantage of having a resident laird."

"I didn't realize you owned the whole island," said the Colonel. "I thought it was Department land."

"So it is. I only own Snorvig House itself. I rent the shooting and fishing from the Department of Agriculture. But it's the equivalent of being laird. In fact I often laugh and say I have all the advantages of a laird and none of the disadvantages. I'm very strict with tourists. Of course, since we were made a protected area by the War Office we haven't been bothered so much with them. Frankly, I used to regard tourists as a pest. I made a habit of going down to the boat every time she called and warning any tourists I saw with rods that the fishing here was strictly preserved. One thing I miss on the islands, of course, is hunting."

"You went in for hunting, did you?" the Brigadier asked, and being a naturally courteous man, wondered the moment he had asked the question if the surprise he felt had been perceptible in his voice. He need not have worried. It took more than a faint inflection of astonishment to pierce the armour of his host's self-confidence.

"Yes, I used to hunt every winter with . . ." the host was on the verge of saying "the Pytchley and the Quorn", but a sudden doubt whether Brigadier Beamish might not have hunted with the Pytchley and the Quorn made him substitute "one pack or another". "But it was difficult when I was in business to get all the hunting I should have liked. One's partners, you know." He smiled waggishly. "Another thing I miss here is good bridge. I've tried to teach one or two of my neighbours contract, but they're rather inclined to think they know as much about the game as I do, although I taught them. It's the same about everything. I've tried to show them how to get the most out of their land, but they won't listen to me. They prefer to carry on in the way of their ancestors. It's useless to point out that agricultural methods which were no doubt the only ones possible a hundred years ago are hopelessly out of date now. I offered the Department to give lectures in the winter on soil fertilization and all that sort of thing, you know; but they didn't accept my offer. Riddled with red tape, of course," he sighed. "Absolutely riddled with it."

This was one of Mrs Waggett's cues.

"Tell Brigadier Beamish and Colonel Lindsay-Wolseley the story about the bull, Paul."

"Oh, it's just a little example of what can happen through red tape," said the host. "Do fill up your glasses. I know they say any port in a storm, but I do think this is rather an unusual wine."

"Most unusual," the Brigadier agreed. "But no more for me, thanks. Wolseley?"

"No thanks. We mustn't forget the time, Waggett."

"Oh; there's plenty of time," the host decided inexorably. "Well, I won't bore you with a long dissertation on the cattle-breeding problem out here," he continued. "But the point is that the people of Great Todday, unlike the people of Little Todday, are more interested in sheep than cattle, and so the various townships were putting up with any bulls the Department chose to send them. Well, one year a most ridiculous animal was sent to Snorvig. A Polled Angus. It used to wander about the road, mooing plaintively all day, and the children spent half their time throwing pebbles at it. Well, of course I saw a beast like that would lower the whole standard of the island cattle; so I imported a bull myself with the idea of helping. It was a Hereford. Admittedly it was an experiment, because nobody as far as I know has ever tried Herefords in the Islands. I charged a fee for its services, quite a small fee, and yet not a cow was sent to this really splendid bull. Apparently they didn't like its white face. They're still very superstitious out here, which I don't object to so long as it doesn't override common sense. And then the Department officials complained that I was not entitled to keep a bull at Snorvig House. Of course, they were annoyed at my animal being so much better than theirs. Petty minds riddled with red tape. Then my bull got restive one day. Poor brute, I suppose, not to mince words, he was suffering from sex starvation. Somehow he broke out of the byre where I kept him and went walking off down the road to the harbour. There was a lot of quite unnecessary excitement. Women started rushing indoors and screaming to their children to come in. All perfectly unnecessary of course, and very irritating for the bull. I was away fishing on Loch Skinny at the time, or of course I should have just gone out quite quietly and led the poor brute back to his stall. Unluckily, as it happened, the Scottish Nationalist candidate for Wester Inverness was visiting the island, and he had a habit of always walking about twenty yards in front of his wife and turning round from time to time to tell her to walk a little faster. Well, he turned round as usual this day to tell her to hurry, and she was up in the air."

"Up in the air?" the Brigadier exclaimed. "You don't mean literally?"

"It was my bull," said Waggett. "He'd come quietly up behind her and tossed her right up in the air. She came down in a garden beside the road."

"Good god!" the Brigadier gasped.

"Oh, she wasn't at all hurt. A few light bruises, that's all; but I had rather an unpleasant argument with the candidate, who is a most objectionable type of Sinn Feiner and talked of sueing me for damages. However, in the end I had to send the bull away, and so red tape scored."

"I suppose red tape would exasperate a bull," the Colonel observed drily. "But look here, Waggett, oughtn't we to be getting along to the scene of action? We mustn't be late."

"You're sure you won't have another glass of port?" the host pressed.

"No thanks indeed. I've drunk quite enough," both guests declared simultaneously.

"Then, I'll run you along to Watasett in the car."

"There was one thing I wanted to ask you, Waggett," the Colonel said. "You remember that correspondence with Ben Nevis about a missing boot?"

Captain Wagget stiffened.

"I am satisfied that C Company owes us a right-footed boot," he said coldly. "And if I send them the left-footed boot we have retained here pending the completion of the enquiry we shall be short of a pair, which will involve another long correspondence, sir."

"We don't want that," said the Colonel hastily. "But Ben Nevis spoke to me about this boot the other day, and I was hoping that perhaps the missing boot had turned up. Meanwhile, I sent him another pair a long time ago, so the matter had better rest."

"That boot business again, eh?" the Brigadier turned to enquire. "I asked for a thousand reserve pairs for Western Sub-Stratum, but they wouldn't hear of it. You've had trouble with boots, eh, Waggett?"

"Only with C Company, sir, over a right-footed boot of ours they failed to return."

"Well, there's an order just come in that in future battalion commanders are to impress on all their company commanders the vital necessity, in view of saving shipping space, that they should make themselves personally responsible for the maintenance of all boots issued to them. I expect you'll be sending that round next week, Wolseley."

"I expect I shall," said the Colonel gloomily.

It was exactly nine o'clock when Captain Waggett's Austin stopped at the Watasett schoolhouse.

"Any sign of the enemy, Mr Beaton?" the company commander asked.

"No, no, Captain. No sign of them yet at all. Ah, I don't think Duncan Macroon will move before dark. He's a foxy fellow. It's early yet by the real time," the schoolmaster of Bobanish said. "But the men are all in position on both sides of the loch. And Mr Macleod has put all in order up here, though I don't think they'll ever get as far as the school."

"Still, Duncan is a foxy fellow right enough," Sergeant Norman Macleod agreed. "You'll never know just where to have him. And that's the truth I'm telling you."

And indeed Norman Macleod was speaking the truth. At that very moment over in Kiltod harbour the Biffer was asking what Duncan Bàn thought he was doing to keep them waiting like this.

"We'll lose the tide and never reach Watasett at all if we don't make a start pretty soon," he warned.

"Duncan isn't coming at all," Sergeant Stewart informed the transport. "We're all here."

"Where's Duncan then? Drying the clothes on Alan Macdonald?"

The members of the Little Todday platoon chosen for the Loch Sleeport diversion scowled. They saw Alan Macdonald's mishap earlier in the day passing into the proverbial lore of the rival island.

"Duncan's where he has a mind to be," said Sergeant Stewart.

"Ay, just where he has a mind to be," the others echoed mysteriously.

Macroon's Bay or Bàgh Mhic Ròin was an inlet on the north-west coast of the island where according to legend the seal-woman had first met the exiled son of Clan Donald who was to make her his bride. It could be used as a haven only when the Atlantic was as calm as it was on this May evening on which the Brigadier and the Colonel were to be entertained with a simple little exercise. Here Donald's sizable fishing-boat the *St Tod* had been waiting since half-tide, and here at eight o'clock Duncan Bàn and twenty stalwarts of Todaidh Beag embarked upon it. Michael Gillies the piper was with them, in spite of a protest from Joseph Macroon, who by no means liked the idea of leaving the *Morning Star*'s marine future in the hands of his son Kenny. However, Duncan insisted that a piper was necessary to his purpose and Michael was conscribed.

The westering sun gilded the undulating machair of Todaidh Beag dotted with grazing stirks. Downy feathers of sea-birds floated upon the tranquil water, a sure sign of fine weather. The *St Tod* moved on a northerly course at about three knots. The piper up in the bows played his tunes. Seated astern beside the Dot, who held the tiller, Duncan Bàn dispensed twenty-three drams from two bottles of whisky and wound up by drinking the twenty-fourth and last himself.

"Well, this is good, boys," he declared, beaming at them.

"*Tha gu dearbh.* It's good right enough," the boys agreed in an appreciative chorus of satisfaction.

"This is going to take the gold off the gingerbread for Clann Ruairidh," Duncan affirmed.

"Do you not think they'll be seeing us as we come round the north end of Todaidh Beag?" asked Alan Macdonald, giving a monitory tug at his beard.

"Even if they are seeing us, who's to know it's us ourselves?"

There was a murmur of agreement.

"Ay, they'll just be thinking it's Donald going to set his lines," said one of the Expeditionary Force, half of whom were Macroons on both sides and the other half Macroons on one side. They were all crofters. Duncan Bàn had sent the Little Todday schoolmasters with the conventional attackers. He wished to avoid any intellectual jibbing at the morality of his tactics.

"My word, these hellimets are terrible hot," exclaimed somebody.

"Ay, and they're terrible heavy too," observed somebody else.

"The *cailleach* was using mine to feet the hence. I was after finding it chust as I had to come away. '*A Dhia,* woman,' I sayed to her, 'what the deffil are you doing feeting the hence with my Home Card hellimet?'" Thus spoke another.

"Why wouldn't we be wearing our bonnets?" asked Alan Macdonald. "*A dhuine dhuine,* it was pretty lucky I was wearing my bonnet when I went over the edge this afternoon. I believe I would have been drowned dead right enough with this *poit-mhùin* on the head of me."

"The Todaidh Mór crowd are wearing bonnets," Duncan

Bàn explained. "That's why we have to wear our steel helmets."

"There you are now," said Alan, "and isn't that always the way of it? All the roads, all the piers, all the schools, all the everythings for Todaidh Mór. And now it's they must be wearing bonnets and we must be wearing these *poitean-mhùin.* They're greedy right enough. *Co dha bhios MacRuairidh gu math, mur bi e dha fhéin?*" [1]

There was a murmur of hearty agreement with this Macroon proverb directed against their old enemies on the other side of the Coolish.

"It was Waggett's orders," the platoon commander reminded them.

"Ay, it would be Wackett right enough. He's chock full of no sense," a voice testified.

"But it's my own orders you would all bring your gas-masks. Have you brought them?"

"What would we be wanting our gass-masks for?" somebody asked.

"Just all put them on right away, and you'll see," Duncan replied.

So the respirators were produced and donned.

At the sight of his passengers even the taciturnity of the Dot was stung into speech, as he sent a small torrent of nicotine-brown spit over the side into the Atlantic.

"*A Dhia*, what a cargo, what a cargo!" he commented.

"Can you breathe, all of you?" Duncan Bàn asked.

A muffled bark seemed to indicate that they all could.

"Very well then, you can take them off again. *A bhalaich*," Duncan ejaculated happily, "you'll put fear on them in Garryboo without a doubt when you go running up from the shore like a waggon-load of monkeys. Gorilla tactics? Gorilla tactics it is. Oh, boys, I'm proud of you. I never saw an uglier-looking crowd even in Glasgow. Oh, my god, boys, you'd frighten the devil out of hell, and that's the truth I'm telling you."

The *St Tod* rounded the northerly point of Todaidh Beag and steered north-east toward the unsuspecting inhabitants of Garryboo, whose Home Guards under Sergeant Campbell were away at the other end of the island keyed up by the news that

[1] 'To whom else will MacRurie be good if not to himself?'

the Little Todday flotilla was steering down the Coolish for Loch Sleeport.

It was verging on twilight when the *St Tod* came alongside the low rocky promontory of Garryboo, which afforded a landing only when the tide was fairly high and the Atlantic was absolutely calm, a combination seldom attainable. Above this promontory the land rose in a gentle slope which gave good arable and grazing ground to the crofters of Garryboo, whose houses were clustered together about a mile inland, below the main road round the island. On the other side of the road was a wide stretch of level bog where the peats were cut, above which towered the rocky bastions of Ben Bustival.

As soon as the Little Todday men had scrambled ashore the *St Tod* put out to sea with the intention of proceeding southward into the Coolish as far as Snorvig, where the Dot was to wait until the raiding party reached the harbour and were ready to be transported to their own island again.

"I don't know how long we'll be, Donald, but you'll just wait for us," Duncan shouted to the skipper of the *St Tod*. "Now, boys, up we go and see what they can do to us in Garryboo."

Two daughters of Sammy MacCodrum, himself away over at Watasett with the rest of the Garryboo section, had been sent down to bring up a big plank which their father had marked for himself when beachcombing early that morning. They were half-way back with it when Annag, the younger of the two children, turned her head to see not one *bòcan* but twenty-one *bòcain* coming up from the sea in the twilight.

"*A Thighearna bheannaichte!*" she shrieked to her sister, aged fourteen. "Look, Morag, look what's coming!"

Morag looked, and then screamed louder than her sister. The two girls dropped the plank and ran, sobbing with terror, to gain the shelter of their home.

Bean Shomhairle, the wife of Samuel or Somhairle MacCodrum, was a tall fair-haired woman with a temper, and the sudden irruption of two screaming daughters into her kitchen just as she was simultaneously trying to prevent a smaller daughter teasing a still smaller daughter who had been charged with the temporary supervision of an even smaller son, to bake pancakes, and to pour herself out a much-needed cup of tea, brought that temper to the boil.

"*Istibh! Istibh!* Do you both want me to take the belt to you, the noise you are making?"

"They're coming to kill us," Annag wailed.

"Who's coming to kill you? Don't be talking like an *amadan*. I'll murder the pair of you myself in a minute."

"It's true, mother," Morag insisted. "They came up out of the sea and chased us from the beach and we had to drop the plank and run for our lives."

"What came up from the beach?" Bean Shomhairle demanded in exasperation.

"A terrible crowd of *bòcain* with faces on them like Sahtan," Morag replied.

"Like monsters," Annag moaned in support of her sister.

"Like wolfs," Morag qualified, with a shudder.

"They were water-horses," Annag declared, in a sudden horrific revelation.

"Oh, yes, yes, that's just what they were—water-horses, water-horses!" Morag screamed again. "Come to eat us."

By this time the two smaller daughters and the three-year-old son were screaming too.

"They'll eat us, they'll eat us," Annag sobbed. "Oh, what will we do?"

And all five children yelled louder than ever.

The mother, maddened by the din and seeing two pancakes already spoilt, went for the redoubtable belt which hung on the wall between a picture of Belshazzar's Feast and the calendar distributed annually by the manufacturers of a popular sheep-dip.

At that moment the kitchen door opened and round it appeared the head of wolf or monster or water-horse or perhaps of Satan himself.

"Oh, God Almighty, it's the Day of Judgment!" Annag screamed in an ecstasy of terror. "And they're after coming to take us down to Hell."

"What are you, for God's sake?" Bean Shomhairle asked, quavering lamentably for so usually bold a woman.

"You're all dead in this house," an unnatural voice woofed. "Every man and woman alive in this house iss dead. And if anybody who's dead comes out of this house he'll be taken prissoner."

The face then withdrew, closing the door behind it.

Similar scenes were taking place in all the houses of the township, and the theoretical massacre was presently complete. Garryboo had been obliterated from the map of Europe. While the bloodthirsty work was in progress Michael Gillies had marched up and down playing a wild pibroch to drown the cries of the victims.

"Well, that's pretty good, boys," said Duncan Bàn to his platoon when they had left the theoretically smoking ruins of Garryboo behind them and were near the main road, drinking in with relief draughts of fresh air after the respirators had been taken off. "There's not a living crayture left in the place."

"Except the schoolmaster's mother," said one.

"*A Dhia*, that's right," Duncan admitted. "We forgot all about Mrs Campbell. I'll go and kill her myself, I will. She got me a terrible strapping once when she was the factor's wife and caught me eating her currants after my grandmother sent me over to Snorvig to pay the feu of the croft."

Duncan Bàn put on his respirator and went across to the schoolhouse, himself a mischievous boy again. He knocked at the door, which was opened by the old lady.

"You're back early, George," she said. "I wasn't expecting you so soon. It's a good job. There's too much of your time being wasted on this Home Guard nonsense."

"You're dead," Duncan woofed at her.

"George," said the old lady sternly, "you've been drinking. Take that gas-mask off at once. Do you think you'll hide the breath of you with that? Take it off, I say, disgracing your poor father's memory like that. Wait you till I tell the Minister about you. Home Guard exercise indeed! Just drinking away at the bar in Snorvig and mocking the Lord."

"You're dead, Mrs Campbell," Duncan woofed at her again. "You and everybody at Garryboo is dead this night. The Germans have killed you all."

"That's not George," said the old lady sharply. "Who is it? Is it you, Angus MacCormac? Be off, you trash. I'll put the policeman on to your tracks, rascal that you are. Was it you skirling away like that just now? Home Guards indeed! Fine homes we would all be having if you were to be guarding them."

With this the old lady slammed the door and turned the key in the lock.

"Is she dead, Duncan?" Alan Macdonald asked him when the platoon commander rejoined his men.

"If she is," Duncan replied, "it's she that'll have the keys of Heaven by now and it'll be pretty difficult to slip in past her."

"Did you put fear on her?" somebody else asked.

"Fear on her? Did I put fear on her?" Duncan exclaimed. "Man, if the Devil himself came to fetch her she'd twist the tail of him like an old ram. But come on, boys, we've some miles yet to go before we're in Snorvig. Pipe us along for a bit of the road, Michael."

Over in Watasett the exercise had proceeded on prosaic lines compared with the poetry of the assault on Garryboo and its obliteration from the map of Europe. The attackers had advanced painfully along both sides of Loch Sleeport only to be informed at Watasett that they had been dead from the moment they stepped ashore.

"*A Dhia,*" Sergeant Stewart grumbled, "if we'd known we wass all dead we wouldn't have been crawling on our stamacs for a mile. I never heard of anybody who was a speerut crawling on his stamac."

"But where's Lieutenant Macroon?" the company commander asked in surprise.

"I just don't know where he is," Jockey Stewart cautiously replied.

"It's a very disappointing turn-out altogether for Little Todday," Captain Waggett went on petulantly. "And I particularly wanted Brigadier Beamish and Colonel Lindsay-Wolseley to see a good show. It's very disappointing indeed. You were hopelessly outnumbered."

"Ay, we wass outnumbered right enough," Sergeant Stewart agreed.

"I don't know if you'd like to say a word to the men, sir?" Waggett asked the Brigadier. "If you would, they could muster in the schoolroom. I think they'd appreciate it, if it's not too much trouble for you."

"Not at all, Waggett, not at all. If you'll get them together I'll certainly speak to them."

At that moment Norman Macleod came along to ask George Campbell to speak to his mother on the telephone. Presently George came away from the instrument looking rather shaken.

"What's the matter, Sergeant?" his commanding officer

enquired solicitously. "I hope you've not had bad news."

"Something very strange has been happening. I can't make it out at all. My mother says Angus MacCormac came along to the schoolhouse wearing a respirator and very much the worse for drink. But Angus MacCormac is here."

"Do you think somebody has been playing a joke on Mrs Campbell?" Waggett asked.

George Campbell shook his head.

"I never heard of anybody playing a joke on my mother in all my life," he declared firmly. "It's very strange indeed. My mother was a bit angry. I can't make it out at all."

"Well, you'll have to make enquiries when you get back," said Waggett. "It won't do to have people thinking they can play practical jokes with our respirators. It's a serious business interfering with Government property, especially in war-time."

"I fully realize that, Captain. It's very worrying," George Campbell muttered.

"But we mustn't keep the Brigadier waiting. He has kindly consented to speak to us," Waggett said, moving in the direction of the schoolroom, to take his stand on the left of the Brigadier while Colonel Lindsay-Wolseley stood on his right.

"I think it was a very—er—instructive little exercise. The disposition of the defending forces struck me as very—er—carefully thought out. Here and there perhaps there was a tendency to bunch. You mustn't bunch. You must watch that bunching all the time."

"Who wass punching?" somebody asked in an audible whisper. "I didn't see anybody punching anybody."

"I'm afraid I didn't make myself perfectly clear," the Brigadier went on tolerantly. "Bunching occurs when men get too close together. It's not a bad rule to keep ten paces apart, and it's up to the sub-section leaders to keep their sub-sections from bunching. I remember when I first went to Sandhurst extended order was the absolute rule. We'd learnt that lesson in South Africa. However, in the last war we forgot all about it, and now we are beginning to learn it all over again. So don't bunch. I noticed a certain amount of bunching, too, among the attackers when they first landed. Naturally there must be some bunching while you're still in the landing-barges, but the moment you've debarged then you must debunch as quickly as you possibly can. Of course, the attackers were rather outnumbered this evening, and I'm afraid any amount of debunching wouldn't have carried them very far against that strong defensive position. But I don't think you chaps from Little Todday should feel too much discouraged by the verdict to-night. After all—ha-ha—one of the advantages of a sham fight is that you do live to fight another day."

The Brigadier tittered. Captain Waggett smirked. The Colonel twisted his face into a painful smile. The warriors stared solemnly at the Brigadier. Neither the titter nor the smirk nor the painful smile convinced them that it would be good manners to presume the Brigadier was making a little joke.

"Well, I don't think I've very much more to say to you. Keep up your keenness. You're doing a grand job of work and we're all very proud of our Home Guard. I've enjoyed very much seeing you in action, so to speak, and I look forward to—er—visiting you again before the summer is over. And don't forget what I said about bunching, will you?"

The Brigadier had hardly finished his encouraging oration when Catriona, Norman Macleod's pretty sister, appeared in the door of the schoolroom and made signals for her brother to come at once.

"It's the telephone," she told him in a flutter. "They're saying the Germans are in Snorvig."

"Captain, will you go to the telephone, please?" Norman called out. "They're after playing some kind of a trick on Catriona, and it would be just as well if you were to give them a good fright."

So Waggett went along to the schoolhouse and picked up the receiver.

"Captain Waggett speaking . . . what? . . . what's that? . . . . . . who said so? . . . came charging through Snorvig in a lorry and they're now up at the hotel? . . . whose lorry was it? . . . Donald Ian's. . . . Was Donald Ian driving it? . . . a German was driving it? . . . it must be a mistake . . . anyway I'll come along and investigate."

The Commanding Officer hung up the receiver and walked back pensively to the schoolroom, where he called the bank agent aside.

"Sergeant Thomson, I've just had a rather peculiar message from Donald MacRurie."

"The postmaster?"

"Yes. Has he been at all strange lately?"

"I don't think so, Mr Waggett."

"Well, either he's gone mad or the Germans are in Snorvig."

It was not an easy matter to startle Andrew Thomson. His short stocky form and square dark face were as impenetrable as once upon a time the heart of Midlothian itself. Yet his scrubby black moustache and his bushy black eyebrows twitched perceptibly at this statement by Captain Waggett.

"Does Donald MacRurie himself say the Germans are in Snorvig?"

"He's positive they are."

"I've never known him the worse for drink. Never," Sergeant Thomson affirmed.

"Anything the matter?" the Colonel enquired.

His company commander gave him the news.

"Rubbish," said the Colonel emphatically. "Somebody's pulling your leg, Waggett. What on earth would Germans be doing on Great or Little Todday? I mean to say, of course, we've got to be prepared for anything," he added quickly, for he did not want G Company to resign in a body and deprive the 8th Battalion of the pleasure of being a thorn in the side of the 2nd Battalion by having a company in the Islands.

"Well, sir, I can't believe the story myself," Waggett agreed. "But if by any chance the Germans have captured Snorvig we should look rather foolish if we did nothing about it."

Catriona came back to say that Roderick MacRurie at the hotel was on the telephone now and wanted to speak urgently to Captain Waggett.

"We may get some definite information at last," he said to his colonel as he hurried away.

"Hullo? Yes, yes . . . Captain Waggett speaking . . . yes . . . drinking you dry at the hotel? . . . but are you sure they are Germans? . . . they snorted at you like Pekes? . . . oh, pigs . . . I see, yes . . . and you couldn't understand what they were saying . . . how did you know they wanted drink? . . . oh, they broke into the bar and barricaded themselves in . . . they're in the bar now, then? . . . where's the constable? . . . went to call out the civil defence people . . . ridiculous! What can they do with a stirrup-pump and a few buckets of sand against a German raid? . . . well, I'll come along at once with the Home Guard."

But when the Home Guard arrived at the hotel Duncan Macroon and his twenty stalwarts had already been piped on board the *St Tod*, and from the Coolish was heard the skirl of the mocking Macroon pibroch, *A Crooked Nose for MacRurie*. Todaidh Mór would hardly dare now to laugh at the way Todaidh Beag presented arms.

"I'm afraid you'll feel that G Company lacks discipline, sir," Waggett said to his colonel. "Do you think I ought to reduce Lieutenant Macroon to the ranks?"

"Oh, it was rather a sporting effort," the Brigadier laughed. "And apparently they paid for the beer they drank before they went back."

"Well, it's very good of you to overlook the whole business, sir," said Waggett. "I do hope we'll get a salmon to-morrow in the Skinny."

"Yes, I'm looking forward to my day's fishing," said the Brigadier heartily.

"I hope your salmon won't be a German," Colonel Wolseley observed.

Waggett's nose detected a bad smell beneath it. He did not think it was quite the thing to make jokes about salmon.

Chapter 13

GLENBOGLE

THERE were moments when the Lady of Ben Nevis in the chintz privacy of what was still called the Yellow Drawing-room at Glenbogle Castle used to wonder whether she did not feel the strain of war more acutely as the wife of a company commander in the 8th Battalion of the Inverness-shire Home Guard than as the mother of five children serving their country. Her eldest boy Hector had been a prisoner in Germany since St Valéry. Murdoch was commanding a destroyer in the Mediterranean. Iain was a Pilot Officer in a bomber squadron of the R.A.F. The hefty Catriona was an officer in the Wrens. The still heftier Mary was a sergeant in the Waafs. She was worried about all of them; but she was not a spectator of the risks they ran on active service. She did not see Hector losing his temper with a spigot mortar. She did not see Murdoch mixing a Molotov cocktail in the gunroom of the Castle. She did not see Iain puffing into the barrel of a jammed Lewis gun. She did not see Catriona instructing Sergeant Toker the butler to keep his finger on the pin of a grenade. She did not see Mary bobbing up from behind a target to bellow incomprehensible directions to Corporal Kenny Macdonald the blacksmith about sighting his rifle properly.

"I do wish Donald wouldn't be quite so energetic," she would complain to Mr Fletcher, the venerable Episcopalian divine who was Mac 'ic Eachainn's private chaplain. "I wish he would leave more to Major MacIsaac, who had so much experience in the last war."

"But Ben Nevis *is* very energetic, Mrs MacDonald. A wonderful example of vigour. And he enjoys it," the Chaplain would reply.

"Oh, I know he enjoys it," Mrs MacDonald's deep contralto would boom majestically. "But I must say I shall be relieved when this Home Guard business comes to an end."

It was about a week after the visit of Brigadier Beamish and Colonel Lindsay-Wolseley to the Islands that the Chieftain came surging into his wife's room, waving a piece of paper.

"Listen to this, Trixie, will you listen to this preposterous communication I've just had from Fort Augustus. I'll leave out all the idiotic numbers and letters and dates. Just listen to this. It's sent to all company commanders of the 8th Battalion:

Owing to the very serious shortage of boots and the impossibility of replenishing the already depleted battalion reserve of boots, Company Commanders in future will assume personal responsibility for the maintenance, upkeep, and repair of all boots issued to them.

A. No N.C.O. or Volunteer on being transferred from one Home Guard Company to another will be allowed to take with him the boots issued to him in the Company to which he originally belonged.

B. Every N.C.O. and Volunteer struck off the roll of a company either for ill health or any other cause must return his boots to the Company Commander, who will take steps to put them in a serviceable condition for reissue.

G. B. Grant
Captain and Adjutant

"Does that nincompoop Lindsay-Wolseley think all his company commanders are cobblers?" the Chieftain demanded.

"I don't suppose so, Donald. Why should he think they are cobblers?"

"Because he is such a nincompoop, that's why," the Chieftain barked. "I suppose he imagines I'm going to sit cross-legged on a bench with an awl or whatever the thing's called and start soling the heels of Toker's boots. It's the most preposterous communication I've had yet. And that's saying a lot. And only the other day Lindsay-Wolseley had the impudence to tell me he wouldn't support me in trying to recover that boot which was stolen from us by that confounded Cockney who commands G Company. Waggett his name is. He wrote a most insolent letter to MacIsaac after his own idiotic quartermaster fellow got into a wooden-headed muddle about those boots."

"Yes, Donald, I remember how annoyed you were at the time. But that was last year. Surely . . ."

"I don't care whether it was twenty years ago," the Chieftain exploded. "I don't forget that kind of thing. The Mac-Donalds of Ben Nevis never forget. I haven't forgotten yet the cowardly way in which Lindsay-Wolseley behaved when I had that trouble with those hikers on Drumcockie before the war."

"But I like Colonel Wolseley, Donald. I think he's such a sensible cool-headed man."

"I like him when he doesn't behave like a nincompoop, but it's monstrous to try and turn people like myself and Bertie Bottley and Hugh Cameron into cobblers. These fellows who've served a long time in India get into their heads that they can order anybody to do anything. Wallahs, and all that kind of nonsense. Anyway, if Lindsay-Wolseley thinks I'm going to let that bounder over in Great Todday keep that boot he's stolen from us, he's mistaken."

"Donald, Donald, please don't excite yourself so much," his wife urged placidly.

"I'm not in the least excited, Trixie. I'm simply in a boiling rage over the old-maidish way battalion headquarters is run. I believe the monks at Fort Augustus would make a better job of it. But what can you expect from a lot of duffers who don't believe in the Loch Ness monster?"

Fortunately at this moment the soothing presence of Toker suddenly permeated the room.

"Sergeant-major Odd, sir, has reported to you for duty and would like to know if you wish to see him."

"Is that the Sergeant-instructor?"

"I believe so, sir."

"I'll see him, yes. Where is he?"

"He's in the Great Hall, sir."

"I'll come down."

"Very good, sir."

The butler had reached the door of the Yellow Drawing-room when he was stopped by a loud 'Toker'!"

"Sir?"

"Can you mend boots?"

"I have never attempted such an experiment so far, sir."

"Well, you'd better get some lessons from old Willie Fraser in Kenspeckle. We're all to become cobblers in the Home Guard now."

"I will consult Mr Fraser at the first opportunity, sir."

"Extraordinary fellow, Toker," the Chieftain observed to his Lady when the butler had retired. "I believe he jolly soon would learn how to mend boots."

"I'm quite sure he would, Donald."

The Chieftain went down to the Great Hall where he found Sergeant-major Odd gazing with interest at the Lochaber axes and muzzle-loaders and stags' heads and portraits of bygone Ben Nevis lairds.

"Good morning, Sergeant-major."

The Instructor clicked his heels.

"I see you're looking at our old armoury, what? When I raised the Glenbogle Company I armed them with those muzzle-loaders and Lochaber axes. And if Hitler had come over in June 1940 we should have been about the only L.D.V.s in the whole country capable of offering the slightest resistance."

"Anybody could give anybody a bit of a nasty bang with one of those long-handled hatchets, sir."

"I should think you could. An ancestor of mine—the ninth of Ben Nevis—cut a Macintosh clean in half with one of those axes at one stroke."

The Sergeant-major, who thought the commander of G

Company was referring to a waterproof, seemed less impressed than he should have been.

"Have you done anything with those pikes they issued, sir?"

"I handed them over to the salvage collectors in the last drive for scrap. They were very pleased with them. They liked them much better than railings. Well, I'm glad you're here at last, Sergeant-major. I think you'll find my men in fairly good trim."

"I'm sure I shall, sir."

"They're a bit ragged by Loch Hoch side and in Strathdun; Mr Munro the Minister made a fuss about their parading on Sunday. They will read all these tales about Elijah and Jeremiah and Samuel and what not, and then they think they are Elijah and Jeremiah and Samuel and what not, if you know what I mean. I asked Mr Munro what he'd do if Hitler walked into his church in the middle of the sermon. I thought I rather had him there, what? But in Glenbogle itself, where I will not have any nonsense about Sunday, we are pretty smart, I think. And in Kenspeckle too. I'm very pleased indeed with the Kenspeckle platoon. You'll find young Macdonald at the post-office who commands them a very keen fellow. Of course, I've had trouble with the Post Office people in Glasgow. They seem to think their idiotic regulations are more important than the needs of the military situation. Yes, I cut off the telephone for a few hours when Captain Cameron of Kilwhillie was invading us one Saturday afternoon, and the Post Office bigwigs made a ridiculous how-d'ye-do about it. Some Bolshie fellow down in Kenspeckle got our dunderheaded Labour member to ask a question about it in Parliament. And now the latest piece of War Office nincompoopery is this boot business. Have you seen this communication the Adjutant has just circulated to all company commanders?"

"Which one is that, sir?"

"About making company commanders personally responsible for mending the boots of the men under their command? They'll be asking us to darn their pants next."

"I've not seen that instruction yet, sir. It hadn't reached Sir Hubert Bottley when I came away from Cloy."

The Chieftain plunged his hand into the pocket of his doublet and produced the offending piece of tissue paper.

"Read that, Sergeant-major."

"I don't think it means you've actually got to mend the boots personally, sir," said the Sergeant-major when he had digested the communication. "I think it only puts on you the responsibility for seeing the men's boots are in good repair and if not getting them repaired by a shoemaker."

"But I can't go sniffing round on my hands and knees to see if some fellow's got a hole in his sole."

"The sub-section leaders could do that, sir, if it had to be done," the Sergeant-major pointed out.

"Well, you must talk to Major MacIsaac about it. He's my Chamberlain, and he's second-in-command of the company. The disgraceful thing is that, although they're quite ready to turn a company commander into a shoeblack if it suits them, I get no support whatever when one of the boots from my company is stolen by another company."

"Indeed, sir?"

"Yes, it happened last autumn. We were issued with four pairs of right-footed boots and after a fearful correspondence it was discovered that four pairs of left-footed boots had been issued to G Company."

"To G Company, sir?" said the Sergeant-major quickly, his eyes brightening. "The Todday company?"

"That's right. Well, Major MacIsaac managed at last to get four right-footed boots over to those infernal islands on the understanding that they would send us four left-footed boots."

"I see, sir."

"And what was the result? Major MacIsaac had an insolent letter from the commander of G Company to say that we had only sent him three right-footed boots and that he was retaining one of the left-footed boots until he received the fourth right-footed boot. What's the result? We have an odd right-footed boot in the company store for which we cannot get a left-footed boot and Captain Waggett, as I understand he's called, complains that he has two—two, mark you—left-footed boots. By the way, you were over in the Islands recently, weren't you?"

"Yes, sir."

"Did you see those two left-footed boots?"

"I don't remember if I actually saw them, sir. But now you've mentioned the subject I do seem to remember Lieutenant Beaton passing a remark about two left-footed boots."

"There you are!" the Chieftain exploded. "Just sitting on a pair of left-footed boots like a hen on addled eggs. Don't you think it's preposterous, Sergeant-major?"

"I expect it's just a little misunderstanding, sir," the Sergeant-major said in a Munich voice.

"Misunderstanding, fiddlesticks!" the Chieftain commented wrathfully. "Why don't you call it kleptomania while you're about it? I call it plain theft. What part of Scotland do you come from?"

"Nottingham, sir."

"I never heard of the place. Whereabouts is it? Somewhere on the East coast, I suppose," he decided scornfully.

"No, sir, it's in England."

"Oh, that place somewhere in the Midlands. Then you're not a Scotsman?"

"No, sir, I'm English."

"But you're in the Clanranalds."

"Only since this war, sir. I was in the Queen's Fusiliers till I went on the reserve."

"The ways of the War Office are beyond me, Sergeant-major. Pikes and boots and putting Englishmen into High-land regiments. More like a lunatic asylum than a Government office. Well, what I was going to say was that if you knew the Islands you'd know that they've been stealing for hundreds of years. And the worst of the lot were the Mac-Ruries of Great Todday. One of my ancestors went over once and hanged the MacRurie of the time in his own chimney. Smoked him like a ham, and sent the result to King James in Holyrood."

"Is that a fact, sir? That certainly was up and doing, that was. No mistake about it."

"I'll tell you what, Sergeant-major," Ben Nevis said suddenly. "I've a jolly good mind to make a raid on Todday myself. I'm determined to recover that left-footed boot. I believe I could get hold of a yacht that would take about eighty of us. What's the strength of G Company?"

"Call it about sixty able to handle arms of one kind or another," said the Sergeant-major. "It certainly would make a pretty invasion exercise."

"You think it would, do you?"

"I'm sure it would, sir."

"I'm very glad you agree with me, Sergeant-major."

"Would your idea be to invade both islands, sir?" the Sergeant-major asked as dispassionately as he could.

"My idea is to recover that boot; but I don't mind invading both islands."

"Because I was thinking, sir," the Sergeant-major went on quickly, "if Colonel Wolseley would give me permission to accompany the invading force I'd very much like to try my hand on Little Todday. They've a very smart little platoon there, and I *would* like to give them something they could really bite at, as you might say."

"I'll ask Colonel Wolseley if he'll let me have your services, Sergeant-major. I should be very glad of them."

"Well, sir, I must say I would like the experience, and I think I could be of some use."

"I'm sure you could, Sergeant-major. Well, I'll say this, if I can't have a Highlandman in a Highland regiment I'd sooner have an Englishman than a Lowlander or an East Coaster. I like the quick way you saw my point about this invasion. None of this miserable Bolshie ca'canny nonsense and disgusting objection-raising. Will you have a dram?"

"Thank you, sir?"

The Chieftain stalked across the Great Hall to ring the bell for his butler.

"Bring glasses and a decanter of Glenbogle's Pride, Toker."

The butler very nearly blinked. It was seldom indeed that Ben Nevis considered a guest worthy of Glenbogle's Pride.

"Soda or plain water?" the Chieftain asked.

"I'd rather have it neat, sir, if you don't mind."

Ben Nevis sighed with relief. He had not misjudged his guest and he poured him out a hefty dram with enthusiasm.

"Well, slahnjervaw, Sergeant-major," he barked, raising his glass.

"Slahnjervaw, sir," said Sergeant-major Odd.

"Ah, I see you've picked up some Gaelic already," the Chieftain beamed. "That's rather a good whisky, eh?"

"It's a marvellous whisky, sir. It has a sort of creamified way of going down."

"Have another?"

"Well, sir, I think if you'll excuse me I was intending to look over the grenades presently and I think perhaps . . ."

"Yes, I daresay you're wise. One doesn't want to be too optimistic about grenades, what?"

The Chieftain guffawed genially.

"The more I think of it, sir," the Sergeant-major declared with enthusiasm, "the better I like the idea of this invasion exercise. To my mind it's just exactly what's wanted. There's too much theory and not enough practice to my mind."

"I quite agree with you. I hate theory. By the way, shall we have to let them know we're coming? I mean to say, wouldn't a complete surprise be the best test of all?"

"It would, sir, undoubtedly. But they're a pretty lively lot, these islanders. And if you surprised them too much they might surprise you."

"How?"

"Well, sir, by using live ammunition."

"Oh, I see. Well, I suppose that might lead to more of this infernal correspondence, though I must say I should like to see how my fellows would behave under fire."

"Yes, sir, but I don't think it would be altogether a fair test to let them be fired at by the defenders and only be able to answer back by clicking their triggers at them. And you could hardly let them use live ammunition, could you, sir?"

"No, I suppose not," said the Chieftain regretfully. "It's a pity we have to be so hidebound. What date do you think would be best for my invasion?"

"I wouldn't put it off too long if I was you, sir," the Sergeant-major urged.

"Well, we're nearly into June now. What about Sunday, June 22nd?" he asked, looking at a calendar. "That's practically the longest day. We'd start before dawn. I'll get Mr Rawstorne to take the *Banshee* round from Obaig to Loch Dooin and we'll go aboard there. I'll ask Captain Cameron of Kilwhillie if he'd like to bring a few of his fellows from D Company. You'll probably be working with D Company then."

"I think June 22nd should be just about perfect, sir," Sergeant-major Odd declared fervidly.

"And you say we must give them notice when we're coming?"

"Oh, I think we must, sir. Mind you, I don't say we need

give them the exact day. If they were to receive a warning to be at their action stations say from the Saturday to the Monday that would keep them on their toes in a manner of speaking."

"All right then. I'll take the matter up with Colonel Wolseley. I suppose I must let him know what I'm proposing to do?"

"Oh yes, sir, I think you must."

"I shan't say anything about that boot I'm going to recover."

"No, sir, I don't think that's necessary. But you'll make a point of asking for me to accompany the expedition?"

"Of course I will, Sergeant-major. Your help will be invaluable. And now, you say you want to go over the grenades?"

"Yes, sir. And one or two other little matters."

"And while you're here I hope you'll practise embarkation and landing and all that sort of thing. I have boats on Loch Hoch and Loch Hoo. Duncan Macdonald, my head stalker, is one of our sergeants. He'll do everything you want."

"You won't forget, sir, that you'll want to take at least two umpires with you? In fact three would be better," the Sergeant-major suggested.

"Umpires? What do we want umpires for? They only cause trouble. I don't want to be stopped by some wretched umpire just as I'm getting that boot and told I'm bunching."

"Why not ask Captain Cameron to be one of your umpires, sir? It might be better to confine the offensive operation to C Company."

" Perhaps you're right, Sergeant-major. And, by the way, you'll be put up in the Castle while you're with us. I was going to billet you in Kenspeckle. But we shall want to plan out this invasion, and you'd much better stay here. My butler will show you where you're to go. He's one of my sergeants. Look here, you'd better have another dram before you go into these grenades and what not."

"Thank you, sir. Perhaps a very small one . . ."

On Mac 'ic Eachainn's idea of a small dram Sergeant-major Odd floated away from the Great Hall to the Company store in one of the Castle barns. Mac 'ic Eachainn himself went off to tell his wife what a treasure he had found.

"Trixie! Trixie!" he went shouting all over the Castle

until he found the Lady of Ben Nevis in a rich confusion of comforts for the three Services. "Ah, there you are, Trixie. Look here, I've got hold of a capital Instructor. A really first-class fellow. He has a thorough grasp of essentials. He's tremendously pleased with my plan to invade the Toddays and recover that left-footed boot they stole from us. I shall get Rawstorne to let me have the *Banshee*. It's such a relief to get hold of a fellow who's not hidebound. He's just what they want·in the company. And he knows good whisky. He comes from Nottingham."

"Oh, he's English, is he?"

The Lady of·Ben Nevis could not resist this little triumph for her own country.

"Yes, extraordinary, isn't it? I've taken a great fancy to him."

And the esteem was mutual. That night Sergeant-major Odd wrote to Peggy Ealasaid Macroon:

> *Glenbogle Castle*
> *Inverness-shire*
> *Monday*

My darling Peggy,

    Thanks for yours and which I duly received. I'm staying here with Major MacDonald who commands C Company. All the people round here call him Ben Nevis and which made Your Loving Fred smile. But he's a real gentleman and no mistake. I never run into a better. He can't be far off of seventy by what they tell me but he's as active as a kitten. Your Dad will know him because they're both on the County Council. He's a man anybody could work with and enjoy himself. The butler too is a decent chap. Name of Toker. I thought him a bit haughtified when he came in with the whisky but he's very free-and-easy in his own room. There's a housekeeper called Mrs Parsall and she is a parcel. Well wrapped up I give you my word. And the cook is called Mrs Ablewhite. Quite a decent woman. But Toker says she can be a terror on her day. In fact I'm in a good place here.

    Well I've got a bit of news for you, Peggy darling. Don't be surprised if you see me sooner than what you expected. I'll say no more about when for the present but I can tell you I'm as excited about it as the King of England. Yes Peggy darling, I'll be seeing you very shortly and I hope you'll have made up your mind to marry me when we meet. I love you more than I can say and I wrote my mother how I'd found the Queen of my Heart at last and she wrote back and said she was very glad I'd setled to setle down and she would welcome you as a daughter. So I hope you're not going to get ideas into your head about me being too old for you. Well I'll now stop and only say I love you more than ever and will continue to do so until I am lying under the daisies. So my darling Peggy, good-bye for the present and we shall soon be meeting again. With love and kisses from

Your ever loving
Fred

Chapter 14

SECURITY

OVER in Snorvig Captain Paul Waggett was as little aware of the aggressive action MacDonald of Ben Nevis was planning for June 22nd as still farther east Stalin was of what Hitler was planning for the same fateful date. He was pre-occupied with the little problems of organization and equipment and correspondence that during the Second World War kept company commanders of the Home Guard in a condition of patriotic deediness, and the red, white, and blue of their morale from browning off.

There was the question of a pigeon-officer, for instance. It began with one of those light-hearted little enquiries on tissue paper sent round to all company commanders of the 8th Inv. Bn. H.G.

Please recommend a suitable pigeon-officer for the company under your command.

G. B. Grant
Capt. and Adj.

Captain Waggett smiled sadly. He was on the point of replying that there was no suitable pigeon-officer on either Great or Little Todday when on Saturday May 31st a priority telegram was received at Snorvig:

Reference my F.A. 562/233 of May 27
Please hasten your reply because sub-stratum command are pressing for an answer

Hog
Fort Augustus

Captain Waggett went to the telephone.

"Put me through to Mr Beaton at Bobanish, please . . . hullo, is that you, Mr Beaton? . . . yes, Captain Waggett speaking . . . I had very nice letters from the Brigadier and the Colonel to say how much they had enjoyed their stay here . . . yes, very pleased, I think . . . but what I rang up for was to ask if you knew anything about pigeons . . . you don't? . . . you wouldn't care to make yourself responsible for a pigeon-cot at Bobanish? . . . no, it's a military matter. I expect it means Hitler is on the move again . . . you feel you have enough to look after without making yourself responsible for pigeons . . . quite . . . yes, I sympathize, Mr Beaton . . . you don't think Mrs Beaton would undertake the responsibility? . . . yes, of course, fowls do take up a lot of time, and she has such splendid eggs . . . no, we've been finding it rather difficult this year to get as many as we should like . . . oh, that's extremely kind of Mrs Beaton. Mrs Waggett will be delighted . . . perhaps you'd give them to Donald Ian when the lorry . . . three dozen? . . . oh, I'll call for them myself with the car . . . thank you very much. . . . No, I quite understand about the pigeons."

He rang off.

"Is Mrs Beaton going to let us have some eggs," Mrs Waggett asked brightly.

"Three dozen, but she won't undertake these pigeons. I think I'll try the banker."

He picked up the receiver again.

"Put me on to Mr Thomson at the Bank, please. . . . Hullo, this is Captain Waggett. I wonder if by any chance you like pigeons, Mr Thomson? . . . no, no, no, not to eat. Western Sub-Stratum Command want a pigeon-officer for the Toddays. If you undertook the job I think I could obtain commissioned rank for you . . . I see, you'd rather remain an N.C.O. . . . no, I'm afraid I don't exactly know what we're going to do with the pigeons when they do arrive. I take it they're intended for messages if our communications are cut . . . no, perhaps they won't be much use . . . I was going to suggest that to Fort Augustus. But I've had an urgent telegram from them and I must try to find somebody."

"Wouldn't Mr Thomson do anything to help, Paul?" Mrs Waggett asked when her husband rang off.

"I think it's Mrs Thomson," he said darkly.

Mrs Waggett sighed.

"Strange how disobliging people can be. I should have thought, knowing how much you have to do, Mr Thomson would have welcomed an opportunity to help. Without any children and without any fowls I should have thought Mrs Thomson would have rushed at the idea of looking after pigeons."

"I suppose it's those cats of hers," he said.

"I think people who keep three great cats at a time like this deserve to be invaded. What would Mrs Thomson do if she had three evacuees battening on her like poor Gladys?"

"Don't work yourself up, old lady. I'll try Norman Macleod." He picked up the receiver again. "Watasett schoolhouse, please. Oh, is that you, Catriona? Is your brother about? . . . he's gone fishing! . . . Fishing where? . . . well, of course strictly speaking he ought to get permission from me whatever he's fishing for in Loch Sleeport . . . I was going to ask him if he knew anything about pigeons . . . oh, he shot two yesterday, did he? . . . no, I daresay, he didn't suppose I would object . . . yes, I know they're destructive . . . but it's the principle of the thing, Catriona. I do want people to understand that I pay rent to the Department of Agriculture for all the shooting and fishing in both islands and if your brother starts shooting pigeons without asking my permission somebody else will be shooting grouse . . . no, I'm sure he wouldn't dream of shooting grouse . . . well, I was going to ask him if he would like to gain a pip . . . pip . . . no, no, p-i-p—pip . . . become a second lieutenant. . . . no, of course I understand you don't know what he'd like . . . but it would be a question of keeping pigeons . . . it's a Home Guard business . . . yes, very well, I'll ring again when he comes in."

Waggett hung up the receiver.

"She's an awfully stupid girl, Catriona Macleod. I *couldn't* make her understand what a pip was. She thought I was talking about a pipe. But I shan't recommend Norman Macleod to be a pigeon-officer. With his communistic ideas he'll just make it an excuse to start poaching again. Catriona said he was out for lythe, but I don't trust him. If he caught a sea-trout he'd eat it in a flash. I did hope that making him a sergeant in the Home Guard would cure him of poaching, but I'm afraid he can't be trusted. It's very discouraging."

"All these communists are alike, Paul," said his wife.

"I'm afraid you're right, old lady," he sighed, with a pessimistic shake of the head. "Well, there's only George Campbell left. He's not really fit for commissioned rank, but I suppose I ought to give him the chance."

Captain Waggett picked up the receiver once more.

"Put me through to Garryboo schoolhouse, please . . . hullo . . . oh, is that you, Mrs Campbell? . . . is George in? . . . it's Captain Waggett speaking . . . he's working in the garden? . . . would it be too much trouble to ask him to come and speak to me? . . . well, it's about his taking on the responsibility for the pigeons we have to keep for the Home Guard . . . no, no, not to feed them . . . I mean not to feed the Home Guard . . . oh, I beg your pardon . . . oh yes, certainly the pigeons would have to be fed . . . on Sunday? Of course, like every other day . . . well, so far as feeding pigeons is concerned, Mrs Campbell, Sunday *is* like every other day. You feed your fowls on Sunday, don't you? . . . Well, I really can't indulge in a theological argument over the telephone, Mrs Campbell . . . if you object to your son's being made a pigeon-officer we'll say no more about it . . . yes, yes . . . but I don't want to listen to grumbles about the Home Guard. You ought to feel very glad that George hasn't been called up."

Captain Waggett cut off abruptly.

"That woman is becoming quite impossible, Dolly. Quite impossible. Well, if the Germans ever do come to Great Todday I hope they'll come on a Sunday, that's all I've got to say. I don't know what to do about this pigeon-officer. Do you think Doctor Maclaren would take it on?"

"Oh, Paul, it would only end in more trouble between you and him. I don't think that's a practical suggestion. I don't really."

"Well, shall I ask Alec Mackinnon?"

Mrs Waggett shook her head.

"He's so resentful of you, Paul. If you gave him this pigeon business to do they'd become his pigeons at once, and you'd never have any say in them."

"If the chicks were here," said their father, "I'd offer to take on the pigeons myself. I suppose you . . ."

"Oh, please, Paul," his wife begged. "You know I'll do anything I can, but I don't think I *can* undertake pigeons."

"Very well," he said in a resigned voice. "I'll have to wire Fort Augustus that I can't recommend anybody here as a pigeon-officer."

And this telegram had no sooner been sent off than a telegram arrived from Fort Augustus to cancel their previous telegram because Western Sub-Stratum Command had decided that owing to the need for conserving shipping space no pigeons could be sent to the Islands.

"All that trouble for nothing," Waggett commented sadly. "However, we *must* remember there's a war on."

After pigeons it was the turn of glasses. A few days later the following letter arrived from Mid Uist, where the Security Intelligence Corps had established themselves in the persons of a captain, a subaltern, two staff-sergeants, two corporals, and four stenographers:

Security Intelligence Corps
Number 12 Protected Area
Nobost Lodge
Nobost, Mid Uist
June 2, 1941

To Captain P. Waggett, O.C. G Company, 8th Inv. Bn. H.G.

Dear Sir,
   No doubt many of the Home Guards under your command are in possession of telescopes, field-glasses, binoculars, or opera-glasses. Under the terms of W.O.I. 23648 S.I. 3624/1509 nobody in No. 12 Protected Area is allowed to make use of telescopes, field-glasses, binoculars, or opera-glasses except in the discharge of his official duties. There is no objection to the Home Guards under your command making use of their telescopes, field-glasses, binoculars, or opera-glasses when in uniform, but if the owners of such telescopes, field-glasses, binoculars, or opera-glasses are desirous of using them in a private capacity permission to make such use of them can only be granted by this office on receipt of an application fully filled in on the duly authorized form T.F.B.O. 525 S.I. 123, thirty-six copies of which are enclosed herewith.

   These forms should be filled in as soon as possible and returned to me at the above address. Applications for permission to make use of telescopes, field-glasses, binoculars, or opera-glasses will be dealt with in rotation as expeditiously as possible, and it is hoped that the necessary authorizations will be issued within the next few weeks. In cases where it has been considered advisable to refuse permission to the owners of telescopes, field-glasses, binoculars, or opera-glasses to make use of them you will be duly notified and I should be obliged if you would report to me any instances that are brought to your notice of any owners of telescopes, field-glasses, binoculars, or opera-glasses who continue to use them illicitly either in a private or a public place.

Yours faithfully,

P. St John Quiblick
Capt. S.I.C.

And with this official communication Captain Quiblick had written a friendly personal note:

Dear Captain Waggett,
  I hope soon to be visiting Great and Little Todday in the course of my duties and I should welcome an opportunity to make your acquaintance and discuss with you any matters in which you think Security Intelligence of No. 12 Protected Area might be interested.

Yours sincerely,

P. St J. Quiblick

Captain Waggett might laugh at the red tape of the Department of Agriculture, but that was a civilian matter. Military red tape gave him extreme pleasure, and it was with a real zest that he set about the task of finding out how many of his Home Guards were in the possession of telescopes, field-glasses, binoculars, or opera-glasses. His only regret was that he had not been asked to investigate the glasses of the civilian population as well. He thought it was ridiculous to entrust such a serious matter to a happy-go-lucky police constable like Macrae, who had been heard to declare openly on several occasions that he thought it was all a lot of nonsense invented to give people with nothing to do something to do at the expense of people like himself with a great deal to do.

To his disappointment the commander of the Todday Home Guard was unable in the whole of his three platoons to discover more than three pairs of inferior binoculars and a small telescope. It was annoying therefore to go over to Kiltod one afternoon and be stared at through Joseph Macroon's rickety spy-glass all the way across the Coolish.

"Have you got a permit from the Security Intelligence Officer to use that telescope of yours, Joseph?" he enquired in a severe voice of disapproval.

"What's an intelligent security officer?" the postmaster asked. "I never heard of him."

"Didn't Macrae the constable notify you that you would have to apply for a permit?"

"Ach, he looked at it, but he didn't think it was worth bothering about. It's only me that can hold it together," the postmaster replied.

Captain Waggett shook his head and walked on. On returning to Snorvig he met Macrae and mentioned having been stared at by Joseph Macroon on his way across the Coolish.

"And he tells me you didn't think it was necessary for him to have a permit, constable," he added reproachfully.

"For that broken-down contraption? It's not worth the price of a twopenny-halfpenny stamp to ask for a permit for the like of that," Macrae declared. "It's only Joseph Macroon himself could hold it together long enough to see an elephant through it across the road."

"But it's the principle of the thing, constable. If the War Office make an order forbidding the use of any kind of glass unless the owner is authorized by the Security Intelligence Officer of the Protected Area, it's surely not for us to decide whether or not any particular glass requires a permit. The order says all glasses."

"Och, Mr Waggett, that telescope of Joseph Macroon's just isn't worth bothering about," the constable insisted.

"Well, Joseph Macroon is not in the Home Guard," Waggett said, "and so I have no authority over him. But if he were in the Home Guard I should certainly insist on his filling up the permit form. I shouldn't like to get you into trouble, constable, but I'm afraid I'll have to report this unauthorized telescope to the Security Intelligence Officer at Nobost."

"Ah well, you'll do what you please, Mr Waggett, but I'll just look after my own business in my own way without intending any offence to your good self."

"Very well, constable," Captain Waggett snapped, his nose discovering a bad smell beneath it, "if that's the spirit in which you take a friendly word of advice I shall say no more."

"I'm not taking it in any spirit, Mr Waggett. But I'll just judge for myself if you don't mind."

And for the second time that day Captain Waggett shook his head and walked on.

"I hate getting Macrae into trouble," he told his wife later, "but I think I must report him to the Security Intelligence Officer."

"Well, dear, you always know best, but he is such a very nice friendly man," Mrs Waggett replied.

"That's the trouble. He's too friendly. There's a war on, Dolly, and we can't afford to be too friendly."

So Captain Waggett, impelled by a strict sense of duty, wrote to inform Captain Quiblick of the existence of an unpermitted telescope on Little Todday. He wished he could stamp his communication SECRET in purple ink, but he did not possess such a stamp. However, he printed SECRET in red ink at the top of his letter and again on the outside of the envelope which he enclosed in a registered envelope and sent off to Mid Uist.

Some days later he received the following reply:

> Security Defence Corps
> No. 14 Protected Area
> Nobost Lodge
> Nobost, Mid Uist
> June 14th, 1941

> Dear Captain Waggett,
>   Many thanks for your letter of June 7th which I only received to-day. Postal communication between the islands is very slow.
>   With reference to the unauthorized telescope in the possession of Mr Joseph Macroon, Postmaster, Kiltod, Little Todday, I would draw your attention to the fact that since the recent reconstitution of Number 12 Protected Area as three Protected Areas, viz. Numbers 13, 14, and 15, Little Todday is now in Number 13 Protected Area and you should address your communication about the unauthorized telescope at Kiltod to Captain H. J. Lomax-Smith, Security Intelligence Officer, Minch Hotel, Obaig. Great Todday as no doubt you know is now in Number 14 Protected Area for which I am responsible.
>   We are so busy up here owing to this reorganization of what used to be Number 12 Protected Area that I have not been able to make my proposed visit to Snorvig yet. But I hope to do it in the very near future.
>   Yours sincerely,
>   P. St John Quiblick
>   Capt. S.I.C.

"But I've heard nothing about this rearrangement of Protected Areas," Captain Waggett exclaimed indignantly.

He picked up the next O.H.M.S. envelope in his mail and saw that it had been opened by the censor. This had delayed it long enough to miss the mail-boat, and thus it had taken five days to reach Snorvig from Fort Augustus.

"What right has the censor to open official correspondence between Fort Augustus and Snorvig?" Captain Waggett again exclaimed indignantly. "What explanation can there be for that?"

The explanation was a simple one. That branch of Military Intelligence which concerns itself with the censorship of correspondence was naturally jealous of the triumph of the Security Intelligence Corps in turning one Protected Area into three Protected Areas and was anxious to demonstrate that it was just as capable as the rival branch of doing its bit to thwart Hitler. Hence the order had gone out that all correspondence to and from 13, 14, and 15 Protected Areas was to be opened and examined in future.

It is impossible to publish the text of the communication in which Captain Waggett was informed of the exact boundaries of the three Protected Areas, because that would be telling the enemy something he is most anxious to know. However, there does not seem any harm in publishing the personal letter from Colonel Lindsay-Wolseley which accompanied the more formal notification:

> *H.Q. 8th Inv. Bn. H.G.*
> *Fort Augustus*
> *June 12th, 1941*

Dear Waggett,

 I'm afraid that this reconstitution of No. 12 Protected Area as Nos. 13, 14, 15 Protected Areas may cause you some inconvenience owing to the line of demarcation between 13 and 14 running between Great Todday and Little Todday. The pundits of Intelligence at the War Office seem to have consulted longitude and latitude instead of the people on the spot. However it has been agreed that members of the Home Guard shall be allowed to pass to and fro between the two islands "without let or hindrance" on condition that the Security Intelligence people receive a list of everybody in G Company with the number of his national registration card and identity card. Grant is communicating with you officially about this. There are one or two other formalities to be carried out, but I managed to persuade them to waive the photographs on condition that you stamp each man's signature with an embossing machine instead of the rubber stamp now in use.

*This machine is being made and will be sent to you as soon as possible.
As a matter of fact for your private information the Security Intelligence
people are not proposing at present to keep any check on the passenger
traffic between Great Todday and Little Todday and as they have
declined my offer to let one of your Home Guards check the passengers
landing at Snorvig, I do not think we are called upon to interfere if the
passenger traffic between the two Toddays continues as it does at
present. I pointed out that the Island Queen did not call at Kiltod
and that therefore travellers to Little Todday must land at Snorvig
first. However, they insist on sticking to the new arrangement, and it
is up to them to make it work.*

*And now for another matter. Ben Nevis is anxious to try out a
rather ambitious scheme of his to invade your domain from the mainland.
I have only agreed on the strict understanding that he is to bear the
whole expense of it. Such an operation is quite beyond anything we
could run to with the funds at our disposal.*

*In order to give you a chance to try out your action stations we shall
make the exercise a 48-hours affair and will notify you by telegram, using
the code-word 'Amphibian' followed by the time. Thus 'Amphibian
15.30 June 21' would mean that from 3.30 P.M. June 21 till 3.30 P.M.
June 23 you would be standing by for the invasion.*

*I understand that when the warning was sent round last September
during the invasion alarm one or two of the islands in the 2nd Bn. Inv.
H.G. did not receive their warning until the All Clear was given next
day owing to the censorship having held up the telegram, but I am
notifying them in Inverness and I don't anticipate any hitch, and you
will be notified in good time to make your defensive arrangements.*

Please remember me very kindly to Mrs Waggett.

Yours sincerely,

A. Lindsay-Wolseley

*P.S. Brigadier Beamish has just rung up to say he would like to
watch the operation, and he suggests that he and I should go to Snorvig
in the Island Queen. If it can be arranged I will bring George
Grant who can act as one of your umpires. You'll have to find the other
two. Of course the Brigadier, Grant, and myself will put up at the
hotel. We are not going to put a strain on your hospitality.*

A. L.-W.

"That's very thoughtful of Colonel Wolseley, dear," said
Mrs Waggett.

"Well," said her husband complacently, "one can't help
feeling rather pleased that one's little command is considered
sufficiently important for an exercise on a scale like this. It
will be interesting to meet Ben Nevis. Very interesting. I

shall have to see that Roderick MacRurie and Joseph Macroon don't try to monopolize him. They're both very fond of trying to monopolize people like that."

"What a pity the chicks can't get leave while Ben Nevis is here," Mrs Waggett sighed.

"I don't know exactly when Ben Nevis is coming, but I'll wire them both to try and get leave for the week-end of June 22nd which I rather think from Colonel Wolseley's letter will be the date."

"That would be lovely, Paul."

So Elsie Waggett and Muriel Waggett each received a telegram:

> *Do utmost obtain leave over weekend June 22*
> *urgent family business*
>
> *Daddy*

But neither the barrage balloon which Elsie was tending somewhere in Lancashire nor the barrage balloon which Muriel was tending somewhere in the Midlands could dispense with either of them, and so paternal fondness was disappointed, although he did have the satisfaction of telling everybody in Snorvig that his twin daughters were more indispensable than ever to the R.A.F.

Anyway, the commander of the Todday Home Guard had no time to indulge in sentimental regrets that his chicks could not have the privilege of meeting Ben Nevis. He had to prepare the islands for the prospect of being invaded from the mainland, and he decided to call a meeting in the Snorvig hall in order to coach the people in their attitude while the invasion was in progress. Feeling sure as he did that the critical day would be a Sabbath, he asked the Minister to take the chair and use all his eloquence to persuade his flock that if ever there was justification for breaking the Sabbath this was the occasion.

Mr Morrison was a broad-minded young man who would have very much liked to be in the Home Guard himself, and he took advantage of Captain Waggett's appeal for his help over the meeting to suggest tentatively that if he required an umpire he should be glad to offer his services.

"That's very good of you, Mr Morrison," said the Company Commander graciously, "I shall be delighted to take advantage of your offer. But you do realize that it is almost certain to be a Sunday? Obviously it will be impossible for Ben Nevis to get all his men together on any other day."

"I'm bearing that in mind, Mr Waggett. But I felt that if I was going to counsel the people against supposing that Almighty God would expect them to hand over Great Todday to these mainlanders just because it was Sunday I ought to set an active example myself."

"Very, very sporting of you, Mr Morrison," said Waggett, with stately condescension.

"I hope it is not so much the spirit of sport which is prompting me to do this, Mr Waggett, as the spirit of duty."

"Oh, I appreciate that, Mr Morrison. Yes, I shall be most happy for you to be an umpire. I'll lend you *The Handbook on Fieldcraft and Battle Drill*. You'll find it very, very interesting."

"I'm sure I shall."

"But you won't mention to anybody that I have lent it you? It's very secret, and nobody who does not hold an official position in His Majesty's Service is supposed to open it."

"Indeed?" the Minister exclaimed in awe.

Captain Waggett went across to his desk, unlocked it, and brought out a small paper-bound volume which he placed in the Minister's hands as cautiously as a powerful explosive.

"I'll put it away in my pocket at once," Mr Morrison whispered. "You need have no fear that anybody except myself will see it."

"And here's another little pamphlet," Captain Waggett went on. "It's called *Military English*. You may find that useful when you're talking to the umpires on the other side. You'll both want to speak the same language."

"Is that secret too?"

"Not so secret as the *Handbook*, but still not the kind of thing that ought to be left lying about for anybody to get hold of. But as you'll read in the pamphlet, "there's no mystery about Military English. Military English is good English." For instance you say 'embuss' or 'embarge' with an 'm' but 'entrain' or 'enlorry' with an 'n'. On the other hand, the converse is always 'de'—'debuss', 'debarge', 'detrain', 'delorry', etc. Then there's bunching and debunching. You'll find that very important from an umpire's point of view."

"I expect I will have a little more idea of what I ought to

do and say after I've studied these two works, Mr Waggett. I sincerely hope that the umpires on the other side will not be too expert for me."

"Oh, no, umpires always give and take. And I've very little fear of the attackers making any real headway at any point. You'll be quite safe in ruling that they were all killed as they came ashore. However, of course we must be prepared for them to effect a surprise landing at some point, and that is why it is important the civilian population should know what to do and what not to do."

Before the meeting was held Captain Waggett received word from Fort Augustus that Brigadier Beamish, Colonel Lindsay-Wolseley, and Captain Grant would be arriving by the *Island Queen* on Saturday June 21st. He knew then that the invasion was practically a certainty for the following day, and he warned the Minister accordingly.

The women of Great Todday had been specially invited to attend and Snorvig hall was full that Wednesday night.

The Minister made a brief preliminary speech in Gaelic to introduce Captain Waggett, who was dressed in uniform with the Squeak and Wilfred ribbons of the last war.

"Mr Chairman, Ladies and Gentlemen,

"I have a very important announcement to make to you this evening. Within the next few days we are likely to be invaded by a strong force of Home Guards from the mainland. I do not know which day they are coming. It may be on Saturday. It may be on Sunday." Here there was a gasp expressive of the shock to public opinion, "It may be on Monday. It may be on all three days. The point is that we must keep our heads and defend ourselves as resolutely against the mock enemy as we should against the real enemy.

"We are to have one great privilege. The attacking force is to be led in person by no less a national figure than Mac-Donald of Ben Nevis, and though we all respect him as a Highland chieftain of renown, I know it will be your pride and my pride to defeat, to utterly, completely, and entirely defeat so redoubtable a foe.

"In days of yore I read that a MacDonald of Ben Nevis once landed at Snorvig and hanged the MacRurie chief of that date in his own chimney. Let us see to it that the present Ben Nevis does not play such a trick with my friends Mr Simon

MacRurie and Mr Roderick MacRurie."

"Ach, by Chinko, no," the latter exclaimed from his seat on the platform, "I wouldn't like that at all."

Roderick was recognized as a humorist. So the audience laughed with relief. They had been inclined to wonder if Captain Waggett might not be speaking seriously.

"You can rely on the Home Guard, but the Home Guard must be able to rely on you," the speaker continued solemnly.

"That's what you want to tell them, Captain," the Biffer shouted from the back of the hall.

"Half the success that the Germans have achieved in Europe has been due to fifth columnists. Well, I don't think we have any deliberate fifth columnists in Great Todday, but without intending it people may do the work of fifth columnists. Therefore do not give any information unless you know the person to whom you are giving it. Don't forget that many of the attacking force will speak Gaelic."

"It's terrible bad Gaelic, the Lochaber Gaelic," Roderick MacRurie interposed.

"Well, of course that's not for me to say," the speaker went on. "But the point I am making is that whether it is good Gaelic or whether it is bad Gaelic, no Great Todday man, woman, or child will give any information of any kind to the enemy. If he asks where the nearest water is, don't tell him. If he asks where the Minister lives, don't tell him. If he asks where his own side is, don't tell him. Don't tell him anything about any place or any person. And if those of you who are on the telephone are rung up and asked something, don't answer. Never mind if you think you can recognize the voice as the voice of a friend. Don't answer. You never can be sure on the telephone. And now I am going to say something which I know will go really very much against your inclinations. If a strange person asks for a cup of tea, don't give it to him. He may be a spy trying to find out where your own Home Guards are. From the moment the call to action stations has sounded across the sea which protects our island against the foe be on the watch, and say nothing to anybody.

"Men, women, and children of Great Todday, we your Home Guards are counting upon you to help us in our determination to beat off Ben Nevis and his invading force. What

I have said to you to-night I intend to say to-morrow night on Little Todday. The two islands have had their differences in the past, but against the Lochaber invaders they are no longer two islands but one island, and who shall sever them?"

"Only the War Office apparently," muttered the Doctor, who had been involved in a long correspondence with the Security Intelligence Officers of Mid Uist and Obaig, the Edinburgh Department of Health, and the County Medical Officer over the question of a permit for himself to go backward and forward between Great and Little Todday in the discharge of his professional duty.

Captain Waggett sat down, and the Minister rose to address the audience in Gaelic on the subject of Sabbath-breaking. The younger members encouraged him with applause, but the older members sat dour and disapproving. However, he stuck to his guns, and, if in the end he failed to convince the majority of his audience that Almighty God was prepared to declare a moratorium on the Fourth Commandment while the invasion from the mainland took place, he did convince them that no amount of head-shaking and lip-pursing would frighten him out of giving his official support to the Great Todday Home Guard in defending their island from a Sabbath dawn to a Sabbath dusk should the enemy dare to violate the Sabbath peace on June 22nd.

After the meeting in Little Todday on the following evening, where the Sabbath problem was less complicated since the defenders might reasonably hope to attend Mass at eight o'clock, Captain Waggett and his second-in-command accompanied Father Macalister back to the Chapel House.

"Will you take a sensation, Mr Waggett?" the priest invited. "It'll have to be rum, not whisky, I'm afraid."

"No, thank you, Father Macalister. Is that some of the barrel of rum they were saying had come ashore on Tràigh Swish?"

"Is that what they're saying?" the priest asked in a tone of the blandest innocence. "Ah well, Mr Waggett, you live in the very jaws of gossip at Snorvig. A barrel of rum on Tràigh Swish! Wouldn't that be convenient now? You know the proverb? It is not the seals that will let Macroon go begging for his supper. A barrel of rum on Tràigh Swish! Fancy that now."

"It's not true then, Father Macalister?"

"I couldn't tell you, Mr Waggett, and that's the literal truth of it," the priest declared solemnly. Then he turned to the platoon commander. "Duncan, I'm not asking you to taste the tiniest snifter. If Ben Nevis is going to invade Todaidh Beag you've got to knock sparks out of him, *a bhalaich*, and you can't do that unless you keep your powder dry."

"Quite so, Father," Duncan agreed in rather a sad dusty voice.

"I was wondering if you could possibly act as umpire for me on Little Todday, Father Macalister?" Captain Waggett asked. "It would give Mr Morrison a certain amount of moral support."

"Ay, ay, the Catholics and the Presbyterians must hold together against this Episcopalian onslaught, they really must," the priest agreed. "Yes, yes, Mr Waggett, provided the enemy doesn't put in an appearance until after the eleven o'clock Mass I'll do my bit towards exterminating him. And on these occasions an umpire can be a pretty destructive weapon."

"You mustn't be prejudiced," Waggett warned him.

"But I will be prejudiced," the priest declared. "I'm going to take care that not a shot fired by the Home Guard of Todaidh Beag is wasted."

"As a matter of fact I rather doubt if Ben Nevis will make any attempt to land on Little Todday. From a military point of view Little Todday would be untenable once Great Todday were occupied."

"Do you hear that, Duncan?" asked the priest. "Are you going to stand for that?"

"No, Father, I won't stand for that."

"Quite right, Duncan. And with my help you won't have to stand for it."

Kirstag, the priest's housekeeper, came in at that moment to say Archie MacRurie was wanting to know what time Mr Waggett would be going back because the tide was dropping.

"Tell him I'm coming immediately," Waggett said.

"But send Archie along here first," the priest added.

The great lobster-claw that was the Biffer's face appeared round the door of the priest's sitting-room.

"You'll take a dram, Archie?"

"*Móran taing, a Mhaighstir Seumas.*"

The dram was poured out and drunk.

"Oh well, that's good rum," the Biffer declared. "You wouldn't get such a glass of rum from Roderick. That's beautiful stuff."

Ten minutes later the *Kittiwake* was chugging back to Snorvig with Captain Waggett on board.

"They seem very confident in Little Today of being able to hold off the invaders, Corporal," said the company commander.

"And they've a good reason to be, Captain," the Biffer replied. "*A Chruithear*, with a barrel of rum like that on the island they would hold off Sahtan himself, horns, hoofs, and tail."

"So it's true, Biffer, about that barrel of rum being washed ashore on Tràigh Swish?"

"I wouldn't know anything about that, Captain," he replied in a non-committal voice. "Is that what they're saying? Look at that now."

And he put the tiller over for the *Kittiwake* to hold her own with the tide.

"Beautiful stuff, right enough," he sighed to himself in luxurious reminiscence. "It's just about time I was taking Father James another good lobster."

When he got home Captain Waggett telegraphed to Fort Augustus that his two umpires would be the Reverend Angus Morrison of Great Today and the Reverend James Macalister of Little Today.

Chapter 15

THE EXPEDITION SAILS

AWAY over in Glenbogle preparation for the invasion of the two Toddays had been going on hard since the beginning of June. Sergeant-major Odd had devoted as much time to rehearsing the various sections of C Company in the action of landing on a hostile shore as if it were a commando. All along Loch Hoch side and Loch Hoo side Home Guards had been embarging and debarging, emboating and deboating, empunting and depunting day after day. When the Sergeant-major's time with C Company was up it made no difference, because Hugh Cameron of Kilwhillie who commanded D Company was quite happy to take part in any operations considered helpful to the great task before C Company.

"Are you looking forward to this expedition?" Kilwhillie asked Toker one day when he was waiting for Ben Nevis to return from a strenuous evening's work in Strathdun with the Instructor.

"I'm looking forward to it with the keenest relish, sir," the butler replied. "Indeed, I may say we all are. Mrs Parsall, who is something of a feminist, sir, passed the remark to me that she wished she was a man for once. And I've never heard such an admission from Mrs Parsall before."

Kilwhillie tugged pensively at his long drooping moustaches.

"Won't the feeding be a bit of a problem, Toker?"

"Well, sir, I'm not going to say it's going to be quite as easy as winking, as the phrase goes; but Mrs Parsall and Mrs Ablewhite and Major MacIsaac and me will master it between us, I think. Is your whisky as you like it, sir?"

"Yes, thanks. I don't want any soda. I'm going to be one of the umpires for C Company," Kilwhillie went on, putting down his empty glass.

"So Ben Nevis informed me, sir. Would you have preferred a more active rôle, sir?"

"An umpire has more running about to do than anybody."

"That is true, sir, of course. But I was employing the word 'active' in the sense it bears in conjunction with service. I meant would you have preferred to be a combatant?"

"I don't mind which I am:" There was a pause. "I've never been out to the islands yet," Kilwhillie observed gloomily at the end of it.

"Have you not, sir?"

"I'm not really a very good sailor."

"Ah, there you've placed your finger on the crux of the whole enterprise, sir. We shall all of us be a little anxious about the weather."

"I've been in that yacht of Mr Rawstorne's once, and I was very badly bruised."

"Indeed, sir? She is what is known in nautical circles as a lively craft, is she?"

"She's more than lively. She's an infernal buckjumper."

"Well, sir, we must all hope for the best. I'm steadily refusing to allow myself to be daunted. I've long had an intense desire to see the Islands. I'm a great admirer of the books of Mr Hector Hamish Mackay. Is he an author you favour, sir?"

"I never read any of his stuff," said Kilwhillie.

"Well, sir, it's not for me to presume to offer you advice, but I think you've missed a real literary treat. He has some particularly inspiring pages about Great and Little Todday in *Faerie Lands Forlorn*. Mrs Parsall, who is not easily impressed, sir, was quite enraptured by his word-painting. But I think I hear Ben Nevis. You'll excuse me, sir?" And the butler withdrew.

"Ah, there you are, Hugh," the Chieftain barked noisily as he entered the Great Hall. "We're gathering off Axedge in Loch Dooin on Saturday the 21st at 10 P.M. Tom Rawstorne isn't sure yet exactly when we shall sail, but that's all to the good. We don't want that fellow on Great Todday to know when we're likely to arrive, and I wouldn't trust Wolseley not to tip him the wink."

"Surely he wouldn't do that, Donald?"

"I wouldn't put it past him. You know he's going over to Snorvig himself?"

"No, I didn't know that."

"He and Beamish are both going. They wanted to come with us in the *Banshee*, but I told Tom Rawstorne to insist there weren't enough berths for them. I'm not going to spoil a jolly trip by arguing all the way with Beamish about those five missing rifles, particularly as two more have gone since. What annoys me is that the only person who has a right to be annoyed is me. After all, it's my stags who will suffer."

"And mine," Kilwhillie added gently.

"And yours perhaps. But if we're not grumbling, Hugh, why should Beamish and Wolseley get annoyed?"

"I suppose the War Office . . ."

"The War Office, rubbish! They're Yankee rifles, all on

lease and lend. You don't tell me Roosevelt's going to worry because a few rifles are missing? I've a much better opinion of Roosevelt than I have of Beamish or Lindsay-Wolseley."

"They may be worried about a shortage of weapons if the Huns were to turn up," Kilwhillie suggested.

"What business have they to worry? They may be poachers in Strathdun and Strathdiddle, but they're patriotic poachers, as you know, and those rifles would soon appear if they were really wanted. Another thing Wolseley annoyed me by doing was asking for my plan of attack. I'm dashed if I'll give him my plan of attack. I will not, Hugh. Suppose these nabobs at the War Office wrote and asked Hitler for his plan of attack? You can imagine what he'd say."

"But won't the G Company umpires want to know what you're trying to do?"

"I don't care whether they want to or not. They jolly well aren't going to be told a word," the Chieftain vowed as he poured himself out a swingeing dram. "By Jove, I've been having a busy evening. Old Duncan Macdonald's too slow altogether."

"Too slow?"

"Yes, he will stalk the enemy too elaborately. It's all right if you've got the whole day before you. But he was two blessed hours this evening getting to windward of Johnnie Macpherson to kill him at 200 yards. And it's no use my arguing with the old boy since Odd gave them this Panther Crawl. Old Duncan was on to that like a bluebottle on to a dead stag. As I said to him, 'You aren't with the Scouts in South Africa now. Things move faster in this war, Duncan.' And what do you think he said to me? 'If I hadn't been with the Scouts in South Africa it's yourself wouldn't be moving at all in this war, Ben Nevis, fast or slow.' Well, I had to give the old boy best. He was reminding me of the time he caught me a crack on the back of my head in a kopje to make me keep it down when a Boer sniper was after me, and, by Jove, a moment later and he would have got me."

"He's a wonderful fellow is Duncan," Kilwhillie murmured.

"Finest stalker in the country," Ben Nevis roared in hearty agreement. "Pour yourself out another, Hugh. Look here, why I wanted you to come over this evening was for a council of war, what?"

"But ought an umpire to take part in a council of war," Kilwhillie demurred.

"Why not? You're on our side,. aren't you?"

"I'm supposed to be neutral."

"You're non-belliregent—belligerent—belliregent, which is it, Hugh?"

"Belligerent, isn't it?"

"I'm dashed if I know. Trixie! Trixie!" he bellowed, catching sight of the Lady of Ben Nevis through the open door of the Great Hall. "Which is it? Belliregent or belligerent?"

"Belligerent, Donald," she replied, passing imperturbably on.

"Yes, I thought it was. It is 'belligerent', Hugh."

"That's what I said."

"Did you? I thought you said it was 'belligerent'."

"So it is."

"Is. it? Well, that's what you are anyway. You're like Mussolini last year."

"I couldn't be like Mussolini."

"I don't know, I used rather to admire the fellah. But I didn't mean you were like him to look at. You'd be more like Hitler if you cut about eight inches off your moustache each side."

"But he's a most fearful-looking tout."

"Oh, I know. Frightful! But you're getting away from the point, Hugh. What I want you to do is to keep the pow-wow going while I get hold of that boot this bounder Waggett stole from C Company. I'm counting on you and Tom Rawstorne and Bertie Bottley to keep the pow-wow going while I get hold of this boot."

Toker came in just then to ask if Ben Nevis wished to speak to the Sergeant-major.

"I take it you're driving him back with you to Kilwhillie, Hugh?" he asked, turning to the Cameron laird.

"I think he ought to have a couple of days with my company. I don't want Wolseley to pester me any more about these proficiency tests."

"I know. He's getting a terrible old woman. As I said to him, 'If the fellows in my company can shoot Huns, that's all I'm worrying about, Wolseley.' Map-reading! Before we know where we are they'll be sending the Home Guard back to school, and that'll mean another sixpence on the rates. Send the Sergeant-major along, Toker."

Sergeant-major Odd followed hard upon this direction and was handed a socking dram by Mac 'ic Eachainn.

"Kilwhillie and I are having a little council of war, Sergeant-major."

"Yes, sir. What does Captain Cameron think of your plan of attack, sir?"

"He hasn't heard it yet. Let's get hold of the map. It's over there, Sergeant-major."

The map was spread out upon a table, and Ben Nevis prepared to expound his strategy.

"By the way, Sergeant-major, what's this nonsense Colonel Lindsay-Wolseley is telling me about my having to send my scheme to him so that he can send it to Captain Wagger's umpires?"

"Beg pardon, it's Captain Waggett, sir."

"Waggett, I mean. I'm not bound to do that, am I? My theory is a blitzkrieg, as you know. You can't run a blitzkrieg like a game of contract."

"No, sir, but I'm afraid you'll have to let the Colonel know what you're preparing to do. Captain Grant will have to send your scheme to Captain Waggett."

"I never heard of anything so preposterous," Ben Nevis burst out.

"Yes, sir, but it will be in a sealed envelope and Captain Waggett himself won't know what's in it. He'll just hand it to his umpires."

"But suppose he opens the envelope?"

The Sergeant-major smiled deprecatingly.

"He'd hardly be likely to do that, sir, I don't think."

"All's fair in love and war, Sergeant-major."

"Yes, sir," the Instructor agreed with genuine warmth. "But this isn't real war."

"So far as that boot is concerned it is."

"But you won't be mentioning that boot in your plan of attack. That's on the side, sir, as you might say."

"Very well, Sergeant-major. I suppose if Colonel Wolseley is determined to be obstructive I'll have to get Major MacIsaac to send him the main outline. Where is Major MacIsaac, by the way?"

"I think he's busy about some Estate matters, sir."

"Well, I suppose this invasion has been taking up a good deal of his time," Ben Nevis admitted. "Now look here, Hugh, this is the idea. You see this sea-loch here—Loch Bob, they call it? The place at the head of it is called Bobanish and the Sergeant-major tells me that the boot will almost certainly be in the company store which is run by the schoolmaster there. Beaton his name is. He's Captain Waggett's second-in-command, isn't he?"

"That's right, sir," the Sergeant-major confirmed.

"And I thought I'd lead a small picked body of men in one of the yacht's boats to recover this boot."

"Yes, but what's the general scheme?" Kilwhillie asked.

"Well, first of all the Sergeant-major has suggested that he shall lead a landing party of about a dozen men to seize Little Todday."

"Excuse me, sir, I don't think you'd better say I'm actually leading them. I'll just go with them, and notice how they carry themselves. I think I ought to be as neutral as possible just in case of an argument afterwards."

"And your idea is that the Little Todday force should be landed first?"

"That's it, sir," the Sergeant-major agreed. "As early as possible. I don't say we'll be able to seize the island, because the Little Todday platoon is about the best of the three, but we ought to be able to keep them from reinforcing the main body."

"Quite," the Chieftain agreed. "I think that's a jolly good scheme, don't you, Hugh?"

"Where is the main attack to be?" Kilwhillie asked.

"Well, after we've landed the Little Todday force at this beach they call Trynamarruf—that's it, isn't it, Sergeant-major?"

"That's as near as I can get to it, sir. I'm not a knock-out on Garlic."

"I used to rattle it off when I was a toddler," said Mac 'ic Eachainn. "I always regret I never kept it up. Well, after they've landed them, the *Banshee* will move across to Loch Sleeport and another party will be landed there. Then she'll continue up what they apparently call the Coolish and cover the main landing at Snorvig. My idea was to have our eight

Lewis guns blazing away at the pier while the attacking party embarks."

"Embarges, sir, if you don't mind me suggesting it. The umpires will understand better what you mean," said the Sergeant-major.

"And after they've disembarked—I mean after they've debarged and everybody's arguing what happened, the *Banshee* will sheer off and get as far up Loch Bob as the tide allows, and I'll recover that boot."

"Well, practically all you need tell Wolseley for the umpires is that you are landing at Little Todday, Snorvig, and Loch Sleeport," said Kilwhillie. "You haven't got to give any time. They'll be under notice of being attacked any time after half-past three on the Saturday afternoon."

"When we shall still be here," the Chieftain guffawed with enjoyment.

"I rather doubt if you'll be considered to have effected a landing at all," said Kilwhillie pessimistically. "The defenders have a great advantage."

"I don't care a button as long as I recover that boot," Ben Nevis declared. "The umpires don't come into that. So I don't see who's going to stop us."

"What happens if the weather is rough?" Kilwhillie asked.

Ben Nevis rushed across the Great Hall and banged on the barometer.

"The glass is perfectly steady, Hugh. We're going to have grand invasion weather."

And Ben Nevis was right. It was superlative invasion weather at eight o'clock of that twenty-first of June when the forces of the Lord of Ben Nevis, Glenbogle, Glenbristle, Strathdiddle, Strathdun, Loch Hoch, and Loch Hoo—seventy-seven strong—enlorried at Kenspeckle to make the twenty-five-mile journey to where at the mouth of Loch Dooin the 200-ton s.y. *Banshee* was waiting for them as once upon a time the French ship *L'Heureux* waited in Loch nan Uamh not much farther up the coast to take off the Prince and some of his followers on that September day in 1746.

"There are two telegrams just come in for you, Ben Nevis," said Willie Macdonald at the Kenspeckle post-office. They were from Third Officer Catriona MacDonald, W.R.N.S., and Sergeant Mary MacDonald, W.A.A.F.

Ben Nevis tore open the first and read:

> *Hope you'll knock billyoh out of the enemy well
> and truly best of luck*
>
> > *Catriona*

"I say that's very decent of Catriona, Hugh," exclaimed the gratified father, passing the telegram for Kilwhillie to read. And who's this from? Oh, it's from Mary:

> *Hit them good and hard for six
> ben nevis you broth*
>
> > *Mary*

"Ben Nevis, you broth?" the Chieftain repeated in astonishment.

"That's the way it came, Ben Nevis," said Willie Macdonald, who was still called young Willie, though he was at least thirty-five and commanded the Kenspeckle platoon.

"It must be Ben Nevis gu brath," said the Chieftain. "Ben Nevis for ever, our motto, Willie."

"Ah yes, that's it," Willie Macdonald agreed. "I knew something was wrong. It's the censorship. They make terrible nonsense of the telegrams, especially if there's a wee bit of Gaelic in any of them."

"I'm glad to see you're coming with us to-night, Willie," said Ben Nevis, eyeing his subaltern's uniform.

"Och, I wouldn't miss the chance of this outing for anything," Willie declared. "Indeed no, we'll all be the better of a little change."

The lorries filled with the steel-helmeted stalwarts of C Company moved off westward. Ben Nevis himself was taking Kilwhillie and his Chamberlain in the new stream-lined car with which, much to his regret, he had been at last persuaded to displace the old roomy pre-last-war Daimler just before the outbreak of the second war.

"Can't stand these new-fangled cars," he proclaimed, as he invariably did when he settled himself down at the beginning of a drive. "Always make me feel I'm in a drainpipe. Now don't go too fast, Johnnie."

"You'll always seem to be going faster than you really are in this car, Ben Nevis," Johnnie Macpherson the chauffeur turned round to assure him.

"And don't argue with me, Johnnie. I must know better than you how fast we're going. You're driving. Nobody driving a car ever knows how fast he's going. That's why we get all these road accidents. Don't you agree with me, Hugh?"

"I don't think I ever drive too fast," said Kilwhillie, tugging his moustache judiciously.

"What are we doing now?" the Chieftain asked.

"About forty, I fancy," said Kilwhillie.

"Thirty-eight," Johnnie Macpherson called back obstinately.

"There you are, you see, Johnnie. You don't know," the Chieftain asserted.

"It would be strange if Kilwhillie was to be knowing the difference between thirty-eight and forty miles," Johnnie Macpherson argued, "and he never going a yard faster than thirty in his own car."

Major MacIsaac, who looked more like the White Knight than ever, dressed in the uniform of a Home Guard subaltern about to invade, thought it prudent to discourage Johnnie Macpherson from turning round any more to argue with Ben Nevis.

"You'd better keep your eyes in front of you, Johnnie," he said. Then he sought to direct the Chieftain's mind away from the car. "I believe we will have it calm, Ben Nevis, for our voyage."

"I hope to goodness we do," said Kilwhillie fervidly. "That yacht of Rawstorne's is a brute when there's the slightest sea running."

"Now for goodness' sake don't start getting pessimistic, Hugh," the Chieftain adjured him. "The Minch will be like glass."

"What about the Atlantic?" Kilwhillie queried. "There may be a heavy ground swell."

"The Atlantic will be a jolly sight calmer than this confounded road, Hugh. We'll never get good roads in the county till they make me Convener of the Roads Committee. I've been saying that for over thirty years now. Who was that went by then in that biscuit-tin, MacIsaac?" he asked abruptly.

"That's the nurse's new car," said the Chamberlain. "She's had it since April. You subscribed £10 to the Nursing Association toward it, Ben Nevis."

"Did I? Why on earth did I do that?"

"Mrs MacDonald thought it was imperative for Nurse Macintosh to have a small car," the Chamberlain said firmly.

"Oh well, I suppose women know best what these nurses want. But I hope she won't use it for gallivanting. She's a real Macintosh, that young woman."

"She won't be able to do much of that with the petrol she gets," said Kilwhillie. "I've tried each month to get some more coupons from that fellow in Dundee who controls the petrol ration, and he will not give me one. Why they should suppose a fellow in Dundee can tell how much petrol we want in Inverness-shire beats me."

"These wise men from the East," the Chieftain scoffed. "No wonder the Germans are such scallywags. They're even further east than Dundee."

However, all the petty annoyances of war-time were swept away in the moment that the car came through the woods round the head of Loch Dooin and its occupants saw the *Banshee* lying off the little pier of Axedge three miles down upon the amber water.

"We're sailing at midnight, Ben Nevis," the owner of the yacht told him. "Are you feeling in good form?"

"I'm feeling absolutely splendid, Tom. I don't think I ever felt better in my life. Glorious weather, what? I knew it would be. Hugh would insist we were going to have a cyphoon—cyclone I mean."

"No fear of that," said Tom Rawstorne, a good-looking clean-shaven man in the mid-forties, wearing a yachting cap. "Do you remember last time you cruised with us, Hugh?"

"I remember a bit here and there," the Cameron laird replied with distaste. "Most of the time I was mercifully only semi-conscious."

"Well, come down below to the saloon, all of you," Rawstorne invited, "and we'll have a dram. Bertie Bottley hasn't arrived yet. Look here, Donald," he said when they were sitting round the table in the comfortable saloon aft, "if I'm going to be one of your umpires I ought to know something about your plans, oughtn't I?"

"Well, you won't have to leave the *Banshee*, Tom. I'm proposing to bombard Snorvig in theory and cover the landing there with eight Lewis guns from behind sandbags."

"Oh, that's what the sandbags are for, is it?" Rawstorne chuckled.

"You didn't mind my sending them along, did you?" Ben Nevis asked.

"Two or three of them burst and made rather a mess of the deck, which riled the skipper a bit; but he's recovered by now. Let's have a look at the chart."

The chart was spread out on the saloon table, and the four of them were bending over it when Sir Hubert Bottley came in, a tall, plump, florid man not unlike Brigadier Beamish. He was in the uniform of a captain in the Home Guard.

"Ah, there you are, Bertie," Ben Nevis barked genially. "It's jolly good of you to be one of my umpires. Tom's going to judge the main assault on Snorvig. Now which would you like to judge? The capture of Little Todday by the party I'm sending over there under old Duncan Macdonald or the assault on Watasett up Loch Sleeport which Willie Macdonald is leading? MacIsaac is leading the main assault at Snorvig."

"Where will you be yourself, Donald?" Bottley asked.

"I'm taking a special party up Loch Bob to get back that boot."

"What boot?" the owner of the yacht asked in astonishment.

"Didn't I tell you about that boot, Tom?" said Ben Nevis.

"Not a word."

"Oh, that's the whole point of the invasion. This fellow on Todday who commands G Company—Waggett his name is, a Cockney fellow—stole a left-footed boot belonging to G Company and I'm determined to get it back."

"A sort of Helen of Troy of a boot, eh, Donald?" Bottley suggested, with the high laugh of the large plump fair man.

"What kind of boot's that?" Ben Nevis asked.

"Come, come, Donald, you're getting on in years," said Bottley, "but you haven't forgotten the Trojan War, have you?"

"Oh, the Trojan War! Helen of Troy, oh, yes, of course. That was the Battle of Marathon, wasn't it? Well, the Greeks have done jolly well in this war. I take off my bonnet to them. But what's Helen of Troy got to do with this left-footed boot of ours this fellow Waggett stole?"

"Never mind, Donald," Bottley said with a grin. "How are you going to retrieve it?"

"I'm going to break into the store and take it. I don't want an umpire for that," Ben Nevis told him.

"I'm not so sure you won't," Kilwhillie put in. "Suppose one of Waggett's umpires comes along and rules you dead or taken prisoner, what will you do?"

"Pay no attention, Hugh. Why should I? This boot business has nothing whatever to do with the rest of the invasion," said the Chieftain.

"Well, I think you'd better take me with you, Donald," Kilwhillie urged. "I may be able to handle another umpire if he rules you a casualty, and don't forget Beamish and Wolseley are both going to be there."

"I know. What they wanted to butt in for I can't imagine," Ben Nevis barked. "I'm jolly glad you told 'em you had no berths, Tom."

"Well, I hadn't," the owner of the yacht said, "unless I put Willie Macdonald and the Sergeant-major forrard. And we're pretty crowded there."

"Jolly good thing," Ben Nevis woofed. "It's much more free-and-easy without them. An invasion isn't a parade, if you know what I mean. I've never forgotten the way Wolseley turned tail when I routed those hikers on Drum-cockie, and as for Beamish he can talk about nothing except a few rifles that are missing in Glenbogle. All right, Hugh, if you think you ought to come with me, you'd better come. The Sergeant-major is going with the Little Todday lot under old Duncan Macdonald, and he can argue it out with the parish priest, who's to be the umpire."

"Is that Father James Macalister?" Rawstorne asked.

"That's his name, yes," said Ben Nevis. "Do you know him?"

"Oh, I know him well. He's a grand fellow."

"Then they ought to have a very jolly time on Little Todday."

"I should think they'll have a glorious time," said the owner of the yacht.

"Well, I don't bear any grudge against the Little Todday-ites. I don't suppose they had any hand in this boot business."

"Any foot you mean, Donald," Bottley giggled.

"Ha-ha!" the Chieftain guffawed amiably. "That's rather a good one, Bertie."

"I think I'll go up and see how the men are getting along, Ben Nevis," Major MacIsaac suggested when Bottley had finished giggling at his own joke.

"Yes, and send along Willie Macdonald and the Sergeant-major for a dram," Ben Nevis told his Chamberlain.

When he had had his dram and heard with satisfaction that there would be no umpire coming to Little Todday, Sergeant-major Odd saluted the company gathered in the saloon and returned to the bows, where he leaned over the side gazing for a long while into the green and golden west.

Eight bells of the evening watch tinkled aft. The windlass creaked; the cable rattled. The *Banshee* began to glide down the Loch. The little pier of Axedge drifted astern.

For an hour the Sergeant-major lingered on deck, gazing into the luminous west while to starboard and to port islands floated past like great silent birds.

"This is quite a trip to fairyland, Sergeant-major," he heard the voice of Sergeant Toker murmur behind him about one o'clock.

"Just about what it is, Mr Toker. You're not coming with me to Little Todday, are you?"

"No, Ben Nevis made a point of me being with him. Loch Bob, I understand is our particular destination. I suppose you'll know that place?"

"Yes, I know it very well," said Sergeant-major Odd. "And a very nice place it is. In fact you can't go wrong on either island. Yes, fairyland's just the word for them. Well, I suppose I'd better turn in. I want to be up on deck when we sight fairyland in the morning."

Chapter 16

ON GUARD

WHEN Brigadier Beamish, Colonel Lindsay-Wolseley, and Captain Grant came down the gangway of the *Island Queen* on that Saturday afternoon, they were met on the pier by Captain Waggett.

"We had your signal this morning, sir," he told the Colonel.

"Good. I left word it was to be sent off as soon as the post-office at Fort Augustus opened," said the Colonel.

"Our action stations were manned an hour ago," Waggett told him. "But I'm not expecting the enemy this afternoon or this evening. The only thing I'm a little nervous of is a night attack. I tried to obtain permission from the Rear-Admiral at Portrose to let me extinguish the harbour lights, but the answer was in the negative. I thought myself the signal he sent back was rather brusque. Here it is."

Captain Waggett handed his Colonel the message. It read:

> *Lights must on no account be tampered with stop question begins who is Captain Waggett question ends*

"Did you tell him who you were?" the Colonel asked.

"Yes, sir."

"And was there any reply?"

"None whatever."

"These sailors are extraordinary fellows, aren't they?" the Colonel said, turning to the Brigadier.

"Extraordinary," the Brigadier agreed. "No conception of cooperation. I think they're worse than those air fellows."

"Do you really?" the Colonel asked doubtfully.

"I do really," the Brigadier insisted.

"Really?" the Colonel echoed. Captain Grant murmured something to him at this point. "Oh, I'm sorry, George. I forgot you hadn't met Captain Waggett yet."

"I expect you've cursed me good and hearty lots of times," said the Adjutant, a tall thin monocled man in a Clanranald kilt with Pip, Squeak, and Wilfred ribbons and the Military Cross—a regular of the last war.

"No, no," Waggett assured him kindly. "We understand your difficulties at Fort Augustus."

George Grant blinked so hard at the lofty patronage implicit in Waggett's tone that his monocle nearly slipped.

"I don't think you need worry, Waggett," the Colonel assured him. "I very much doubt if Ben Nevis will attempt a night attack. I don't fancy Rawstorne will feel inclined to risk the *Banshee* in these waters at night, do you, Beamish?"

The Brigadier shook his head knowledgeably.

Presently up at the hotel the three soldiers were making themselves agreeable to Roderick MacRurie who enjoyed nothing so much as entertaining distinguished visitors in his snuggery.

The host himself had a fondness, unique one might hope in a Highlander, for mixing his whisky with gaseous lemonade, and his notion of the height of hospitality was to offer such a potation to his guests. With the progress of the war this gaseous lemonade had become more and more difficult to obtain, and Roderick had had a bit of a struggle with his baser self before he had been able to persuade his better self to break into his last dozen bottles in honour of the occasion. However, hospitality prevailed, and the whisky in his guests' tumblers was bounteously reinforced with the lemonade. Waggett had often really enjoyed this mixture. The Brigadier and the Colonel supposed it was soda. Only George Grant escaped.

"No thanks. I prefer my dram neat," he said. Roderick exhaled a sigh nicely compounded of regret and relief and did not press him.

"That's one of your Highland habits I can't manage, Grant," said the Brigadier. "I'm afraid I rather offended old Ben Nevis once by drowning some special whisky he brought out for me with soda."

"Glenbogle's Pride, eh?" the Colonel commented. "By Jove, you did commit a crime. But I'm like you, Beamish. I've lived up here ever since I bought Tummie after I chucked the Service, but I still shy at neat whisky."

"Well, slahnjervaw," said the Brigadier, raising his glass. "Isn't that it? I'm getting on rather well with my Gaelic, aren't I, Grant?"

"*Slàinte mhór, slàinte mhath*," Roderick uttered piously.

The Brigadier and the Colonel drank deep, and a moment

later their two countenances registered in rapid succession bewilderment, fear, horror, and disgust. The Brigadier gazed
at his glass incredulously.

"Good god," the Colonel exclaimed. "What is this drink?"

"It's very good, isn't it, Colonel?" the host beamed at his
guests. "It's my own idea."

"I love it," said Waggett blissfully, on whom inappropriate
sweetness exerted an influence such as the cunningly played
flute exerts upon the cobra.

"Well, it's certainly a novelty," said the Brigadier, trying
not to shudder too obviously, and looking across to the Colonel
as a drowning man might look at land.

Colonel Wolseley was on the point of telling Roderick that
it was rather too violent a novelty for the Brigadier and himself when the host said:

"Yess, yess, I thought you'd enjoy that, and I don't mind
telling you that lemonade is very hard to come by just now.
But I was thinking to myself, 'Ah, well, dash it to goodness, it
isn't every day that fine men like Brickateer Beamish and
Colonel Wolseley will be honouring my house.' This is the
first time, Colonel, you've been here, and I've been inviting
you to come to Todaidh Mór often enough when we're at
Inverness together for the County Council meetings." .

"I know you have, Mr MacRurie," said the Colonel, and
summoning to his help the stoicism he had practised for a
lifetime, he courteously drained his glass. He had at least the
consolation of knowing that such an action must force Beamish
to do likewise, and he observed with a slightly malicious contempt the way the Western Sub-Stratum Commander was
hesitating between the unpleasantness of one great gulp and
the unpleasantness of several small ones. In the end he elected
for sudden death and drained his glass.

"You enjoyed that, Brickateer Beamish," Roderick assured
him contentedly. "You'll have another with me?"

"I'm going to try it neat this time," said the Brigadier.
"I'm determined to get hold of this Highland trick of taking
my whisky neat, Grant."

"Good for you, sir," the Adjutant applauded.

"I think I will too," said the Colonel. "I don't want to
rob you of your lemonade."

"Och, it won't be ropping me at all. It's a pleasure to give anybody what they like. I have some beautiful lobsters for your tea."

"I say that sounds pretty scrumptious, Wolseley, eh?" the Brigadier said heartily. "I suppose your family has been on this island for a good long time, what?" he asked the host.

"Thousands and thousands of years," Roderick affirmed.

"Wouldn't you say hundreds, Roderick?" Waggett suggested, with a corrective smile.

The hotel-keeper turned on him indignantly.

"I wouldn't say any such a thing, Mr Waggett. Who was ever on Todaidh Mór before Ruaridh Ruadh?"

"Well, he didn't live before A.D. 1200 at the very earliest," Waggett argued.

"And isn't that thousands and thousands of years?" Roderick asked.

"Well, it's a jolly long time anyway," the Brigadier decided. "Are you joining us over these wonderful lobsters, Waggett?"

"No, I think if you'll excuse me, sir, I'll make my rounds. I want to be sure everything is in order if the invaders do come earlier than they're expected."

Up at Snorvig House Waggett told his wife how much he regretted he had not insisted on putting up the Brigadier and the Colonel.

"They'll get awfully tired of Roderick's eternal bragging," he prophesied. "The best part of Roderick is that lemonade and whisky of his."

"Oh, did he give you some of that, Paul? How nice!"

"Yes, I must say it's far the best way to take whisky. I wish we'd laid in a stock of that fizzy lemonade, Dolly."

"I wish we had, dear," she sighed. "But one can't have enough of everything."

"By the way, I found six kettles this morning in John Maclean's little shop at Knockdown. They were poked away right at the back. He didn't know he had them. So I bought the lot."

"That was clever of you, Paul."

"We don't know when there may not be a shortage of kettles."

"Indeed, no."

"I shouldn't be surprised if there was not a single kettle left on the island presently. They're the most improvident people in the world. Well, I must go round my posts, Dolly."

"What about dinner?"

"We'll have to make it a movable feast this evening, old lady. But don't worry about me. I shall get something somewhere. I'm looking forward to meeting Ben Nevis to-morrow: I wonder if he ever heard of that boot correspondence between Beaton and his second-in-command. I must chaff him about it. Probably I'll get asked to dinner on the yacht. But I think we ought to have them all up here to tea."

"Will it be a very large party?" Mrs Waggett asked anxiously.

"Biggish. There'll be Mr Rawstorne the owner of the *Banshee*, and Cameron of Kilwhillie, and Sir Hubert Bottley of Cloy, Brigadier Beamish, Colonel Lindsay-Wolseley, Captain Grant, Major MacIsaac . . ."

"Who's he?"

"He's Ben Nevis's Chamberlain. And there's a subaltern called Macdonald. He may be a relation of Ben Nevis. So we'd better ask him. Then I suppose we ought to invite the Minister and Mrs Morrison. But I'm not going to ask the Doctor. I don't see why I should. He's done nothing but crab the Home Guard ever since I assumed the command."

"I see no reason at all why you should ask him, Paul. Will you ask Mr Beaton?"

"If I ask him I'll have to ask Thomson. And if I ask Thomson I can't very well leave out Macleod and Campbell. I think it will be wisest to invite nobody except the Minister and his wife. In any case they'll probably be shy at meeting people like Ben Nevis and Bottley."

"That's most considerate of you, Paul. But you always are considerate. I wonder if Sir Hubert Bottley has anything to do with Bottley's Bottled Beans."

"He is Bottley's Bottled Beans. The business was started by his father."

"He must be very rich," Mrs Waggett exclaimed in awe.

"Very very rich," her husband replied; but he did not approve of that note of awe in his wife's voice. "It's strange to think, isn't it, Dolly," he went on in his dreamy voice, "that if I'd gone in for bottling beans instead of cooking accounts we should have been as rich as Bottley?"

"But you didn't cook accounts, Paul," she said reproachfully. "A chartered accountant doesn't cook accounts."

"I was making a little joke, old lady," he explained kindly.

Captain Waggett left his wife and went to get his car out of the garage. He turned to the right from Snorvig to make Garryboo his first call.

At the schoolhouse the commander of G Company was received by Mrs Campbell.

"George is down with the beach patrol, I suppose?" he asked.

The old lady glowered at him balefully.

"George is locked up in his bedroom," she said.

"What? I don't understand, Mrs Campbell. He's not ill, I hope?"

"He's locked in with his Bible and some bread and cheese and he will not be unlocked till the Sabbath is over."

"But this is Saturday."

"I know this is Saturday as well as you do, Mr Waggett; but it will be the Sabbath to-morrow," the old lady said firmly. "And I will not have my son encouraging the men of Garryboo to do the work of Sahtan to-morrow. If the Minister has said good-bye to his senses, I have not said good-bye to mine, Mr Waggett."

"But are you seriously proposing to keep George shut up till Monday morning? I never heard of anything so ridiculous."

"Have you heard of the Fourth Commandment which the Lord gave unto Moses?"

"Of course I have."

"Remember that thou keep holy the Sabbath day," she declaimed. "Six days shalt thou labour and . . ."

"You needn't repeat it, Mrs Campbell. I learnt the Commandments years ago," Waggett interrupted irritably.

"More shame to you then that you should lead George away from righteousness. What would you be feeling, Mr Waggett, if to-morrow night the Lord came for you and you found yourself in Hell with George beside you? Would you be pleased that for the sake of your own vainglory you had dragged my poor boy down with you into the Pit?"

"I can't accept such a supposition, Mrs Campbell. Your son George and I have a duty to our country at a time like this. And if I'm ready to accept any responsibility for what happens to your son I really cannot see . . ."

"Oh, man, man," the old lady broke in, "the shame of you!

Do you dare to set yourself beside the Lord and take another's sins upon you? Be silent, and hide your head."

"And what did George say when you locked him in his room?" asked Waggett, who could have throttled the old lady with gusto.

"George knows better than to argue with his mother. You might make the poor boy break the Fourth Commandment with nonsense about Hitler, but it'll take a bigger man than you, Mr Waggett, to make him break the Fifth Commandment."

"I think it's a mistake to mix up religion with war," he said.

"Not such a mistake as to mix up war with religion," she retorted.

"I insist on your letting George out to perform his military duties. What do you think Brigadier Beamish will say when I tell him that one of my section leaders has been locked up by his mother to prevent him from taking part in this military exercise? And you heard what the Minister said?"

"Not with my own ears, thanks be to the Lord. If the Minister had spoken as he did last Wednesday evening in my presence I would have shamed him before the whole of Great Todday. We'll see what the Presbytery has to say about a Minister who is ready to pi ane the Sabbath to get a pat on the back from the snobs."

"And you refuse to let George perform his military duties?"

"I refuse to let him put his soul in peril of Hell fire," the old lady proclaimed resolutely.

"May I speak to him a minute? I want to know what arrangements he has made for the command of his section."

"No, you will not speak to him, Mr Waggett. And if you went down on your knees to me I would not allow you to speak to him."

"Well, I'm certainly not going to do that," said Captain Waggett scornfully, and turning on his heels he walked out of the room, his nose in the air.

Down at the beach which had seen the landing of the Little Todday men just over a month ago he found Angus MacCormac and Sammy MacCodrum contemplating with rapt interest the almost imperceptible progress of a ship's hatch toward the shore.

"Corporal MacCormac," he said, "you will have to command the Garryboo section until the exercise is over. Sergeant Campbell is ill."

"Ill is he?" asked Corporal MacCormac, blowing suspiciously into the grey forest of his moustache. "He was pretty well this morning."

"He's very ill now. He's had to go to bed," said the commander.

"*Seall sin a nis, Aonghais,*" Somhairle MacCodrum exclaimed. "Och, I was telling you how the *cailleach* would be putting fear on the poor *truaghan*. Ay, she's a proper warrior. I'm married to a bit of a warrior myself, but what's she beside yon terror of a female woman? It's herself is a pitch right enough."

"A pure one," Angus assented fervidly.

"Well, I can't take up any more of my time at Garryboo," Waggett said. "I'm relying on you, Corporal, to see your section is standing by. Keep two men on the look-out through the night, and have everybody ready by five o'clock to-morrow morning. I will telephone through to the post-office where you are to go. I'm arranging for a lorry."

"Will we be likely to meet any of those rascals from Todaidh Beag?" Sammy asked.

"They have their own island to look after," said the commander firmly.

"It's just as well for them, Captain," Sammy declared. "We'd have been putting pullets into the dirty blaggarsts, and that's the truth. And they with a cask of rum. Och, well, well, well, the Lord took a queer notion into His head right enough when He sent that cask of rum ashore on Todaidh Beag."

"Let bygones be bygones," Captain Waggett advised.

"I'll let any bygone be a bygone," Angus offered. "But how can this be a bygone when it isn't a bygone?"

"Well, what you have to concentrate on now is beating off this invasion from the mainland, Corporal. This illness of Sergeant Campbell's has put a heavy responsibility on you all at Garryboo."

"Don't you worry, Captain. You won't find the Garryboo men will fail you," Angus promised. "But if we come back home and find every woman and child in the place screeching like mad craytures, the bygones are going to be pretty fierce."

From Garryboo the commander drove round the north of the island past Sròn Ruairidh to the tiny township of Knockdown where there were two Home Guards of nearly seventy and one of seventeen, an outpost of Sergeant Campbell's section. A landing here was unimaginable and they were told to join the muster at Garryboo next morning.

To this the two ancients objected. They were near enough to the allotted span to feel that it was unwise to take any risks with their eternal future by breaking the Sabbath.

"I'm surprised at you, Hector," said the commander to Hector MacRurie, a tall bearded old crofter. "You didn't refuse to fight on a Sunday when you were out in South Africa with Lovat's Scouts."

"I wouldn't refuse to fight now, Captain, if Hitler himself was to be jumping on our back to-morrow. But Ben Nevis is no Hitler. Och, I remember him well. He was a lieutenant in my own troop—a fine upstanding young chap Always talked very loud. Ay, he was a big talker. But he wasn't just only a talker. No, no. He was very handy with a rifle. Nothing would please him better than if he would get a good shot at a Boer."

"Well, surely you'd like to see him again after forty years?"

"I'd like to see him right enough, and I've a good mind to walk along to Snorvig on the chance of shaking his hand. But I don't like the notion of soldiering on the Sabbath."

"But the Minister made a special point of its being perfectly all right to break the Sabbath for patriotic reasons."

The old man tugged his beard in perplexity.

"Ay, Mr Morrison gave us permission right enough," he admitted. "But he's pretty young at his job to be putting himself up to be giving permission to go against the Word. Not that there's any harm in the wee man. Ach, well, I'll think it over when we're taking the *leabraichean* to-night at family worship. I might come along after all, Captain. I'd like fine to shake hands with Ben Nevis."

From Knockdown Waggett drove on round the east side of the island to Bobanish, stopping for a moment to see if anybody was taking advantage of his preoccupation with military affairs to fish in his favourite Loch Skinny. There were no poachers except the water-lilies, which he eyed distastefully. They must be eradicated after the war, he decided. This resolution he confided to Paddy, his outsize setter, who thumped his plumose tail in approval.

"Good old boy, good old dog! You understand every word I say to you, don't you, old man?" he maundered.

But this soft side of him was hidden behind a mask of ruthless efficiency when he reached the schoolhouse at Bobanish and saw his burly second-in-command waiting for him.

"All in good trim, Mr Beaton?" he asked briskly.

"I think we're ready for them, Captain."

"You'll want to use your judgment when the attack begins, Mr Beaton. Personally I expect the main assault to be delivered at Snorvig because the yacht will probably be chary of coming too far up Loch Bob or Loch Sleeport, but there may be a feint attack on either. However, I shall be in touch with you over the 'phone to give you my orders. I shall say 'Hullo', and then I shall say 'Gibraltar, Gibraltar, Gibraltar' three times, and you will answer, 'Trafalgar, Trafalgar' twice."

The honest brow of John Beaton was wrinkled with perplexity. He doffed his bonnet and patted his sandy hair.

"I don't quite understand, Captain, I'm afraid."

His commanding officer smiled patiently.

"The point is that you won't give anybody speaking over the 'phone any information who doesn't say Gibraltar three times first, and I won't say anything until you've said Trafalgar twice so that I know you're not a fifth columnist. It's quite simple, I think."

"Yes, yes, I have the idea now. Very good, very good," the schoolmaster jerked out.

"Then if you hear me order your platoon to reinforce us in Snorvig as quickly as possible you'll know that it really is me and not one of the enemy pretending to be me."

"Ah, well, you're very far-sighted, Captain Waggett. You don't mean to be caught napping I see."

The commander accepted his subaltern's tribute with a modest smile.

"Well, of course, I've studied military theory a great deal," he admitted. "I often wish I was twenty years younger. I should like to have had a chance to see what I could do with a tank. I don't think that even the Germans have really mastered tank warfare. However, it's no use regretting what none of us can avoid. If we beat off this invasion to-morrow I shall feel quite content. By the way, I'll tell you who you'll probably see to-morrow—MacIsaac."

"Is that so? My goodness, he wrote me one or two pretty stiff letters. We still have that boot, Captain."

"Yes, I shall pull Ben Nevis's leg about that boot to-morrow."

"Perhaps it would show a nice friendly spirit if we were to hand over that boot to-morrow after the battle is over," the schoolmaster suggested. "It's no use to us."

"I'll hand over that left-footed boot when we receive the right-footed boot C Company said they sent us, and which we never received."

"Oh, it's for you to decide, Captain," said his second-in-command hastily. "I just made the suggestion."

"I'll see about it to-morrow. Meanwhile, you'd better take the boot out of the store and give it to me. I'll take it back with me to Snorvig House. And now I must tell you about a rather awkward incident that occurred at Garryboo."

"Dear me, I'm sorry to hear of awkwardness there. That's bad."

"It's very bad indeed. Mrs Campbell has locked up George Campbell in his room to prevent him from taking part in the battle to-morrow."

"The woman's mad," exclaimed John Beaton.

"Mad or sane, that's what she's done. Of course, if George Campbell had any guts he'd get out of the window. But you know what he's like where his mother is concerned."

"You've really staggered me, Captain. I never heard of such a thing in my life."

"I rather fancy they suspect at Garryboo what's happened, but we'd better keep this to ourselves, Mr Beaton."

"I wouldn't say a word to anybody. Oh, well, well, poor Seoras. He'll feel it very keenly. *A bhobh bhobh!* Poor soul, I'm really sorry for him. It's mortifying right enough for a man of his age, and a schoolmaster at that, to be locked up in his bedroom like a boy."

John Beaton tutted away to himself at the reflection.

"Well, there he is. I put Angus MacCormac in command of his section. I don't anticipate any attempt by the enemy on the west. So I shall have the Garryboo lot with us in

Snorvig. But it's very very annoying. Are you having any trouble here about this Sunday business?"

"Some of them don't altogether like it. But och, there'll be no trouble. They're very sensible if it's properly explained to them."

"Well, I must be getting along, Mr Beaton. You won't forget 'Gibraltar, Gibraltar, Gibraltar'?"

"Trafalgar, Trafalgar," John Beaton gulped, blushing hotly with self-consciousness over the countersign.

"That's right. You'll have look-outs posted during the night, and by five o'clock to-morrow morning everybody should be at their stations. Keep in touch with me by 'phone."

"I will, Captain. Excuse me, Captain. If I ring you first, do I say Gibraltar or Trafalgar?"

"In that case *you* say Gibraltar three times and I answer with Trafalgar twice. Norman Macleod at Watasett will have the same instructions. George Campbell would have had them too, but I was afraid they might muddle Angus MacCormac."

"I think you were wise, Captain. Some of them are not too happy with the telephone even in Gaelic."

"Oh, by the way, I'm going to commandeer the post-office for Company H.Q. to-morrow."

"Will Donald MacRurie agree to that on a Sunday?"

"There's no question of his agreeing or disagreeing," Captain Waggett replied coldly. "It's a military order. If I use Snorvig House as H.Q., time will be wasted running up and down the hill between there and the pier. And now if you wouldn't mind getting me that left-footed boot I'll be getting along, Mr Beaton."

From Bobanish the Commanding Officer proceeded to the schoolhouse at Watasett.

"I have a presentiment, Sergeant Macleod, that the enemy will launch a strong attack up Loch Sleeport," he told the section leader.

"We'll be ready for them. They'll get a pretty warm reception here. What are you looking at, Captain?"

The Commanding Officer's eyes were looking out of the window to where below the schoolhouse the little Slee was tumbling into the narrow head of the loch.

"Are those corks I can see?" he asked.

"Corks?" Norman Macleod echoed innocently. "Och, I

wish to god I could see even so much as one cork. It's terrible the way the right stuff has gone all wrong these days. I really feel ashamed I can't offer you a dram. You'll just have to excuse me, Captain. When the revolution comes we'll manage things more shipshape."

"I wasn't referring to corks in bottles," said Waggett severely. "I was asking if those were corks I could see across the head of the loch."

Norman Macleod looked in the direction indicated by the accusing finger of the fishing tenant.

"Ay, I believe you're right, Captain," he said presently. "Ah, I forgot I told the boys to put down the net."

"You told them to put down the net?" Waggett gasped, staggered by the impudence of the admission. "But you know perfectly well that I have prohibited nets absolutely in my fishing waters."

"Ay, but that was for fish. That net there was never put down for fish. No, no, no. Who would ever put down a net for fish in Loch Sleeport?"

"Then what is that net put down for if it's not put down for fish?" Waggett demanded sternly.

"Oh well, that's a good one right enough," the section leader of Watasett chuckled. "Fancy you thinking we would be putting down a net for fish! Och, that'll give all the boys a good laugh when I tell it to them. No, no, no, no, that's for the enemy. We'll be hiding some of the section behind the rocks on either side in a state of highly suspicious alertness, and when the enemy's boat gets tangled up in the net we will open up on them and massacre the lot."

"It won't improve the net," Waggett commented.

"Och, that's nothing, Captain. The poor old net was just lying about idle, and I thought, 'Oh well, by Jove, I'll make you do a bit of war work, old fellow.' Ah, dash it to goodness, the boys will have a really good laugh when I tell them you thought it was for fishing we were putting it down."

The sporting tenant was not in the least convinced by Norman Macleod's innocent explanation, but there was nothing for him to do save accept it with good grace. However, he did not intend to allow the net to intercept any salmon or sea-trout on its way up the Slee to spawn.

"I don't consider that net has the slightest military value

where it is, Sergeant Macleod," he ruled. "So you'd better have it taken up at once."

"Very good, Captain. Have you been having much sport yourself lately?"

"I've very little time for sport in these days," the sporting tenant replied, an adamantine rebuke in his tone.

"Ay, I know you're kept very busy with the Home Guard. But talking of sport, you wouldn't have any objection to me going out sometimes after school to have a try for a *sgarbh* or two on Poppay?"

"Cormorants, you mean?"

"Ay, the very same."

"No, I don't object to your shooting cormorants if you have the cartridges."

"I believe I might be able to scrape together a few here and there. Did you ever eat a *sgarbh*, Captain?"

"Never."

"It's pretty tasty, if you bury it for a wee while. Catriona's a good hand with a *sgarbh*."

"Is she a good hand with a grouse?" Waggett asked, with a piercing look at his section leader.

"Ah, I don't believe she'll ever have tried her hand at a *cearc fhraoich*, Captain. She was just a wee girl when you became the shooting tenant, and what chance at all has she ever had to cook a grouse?"

"Well, we mustn't spend any more time discussing grouse. Keep your look-outs through the night, and have your section standing to arms by five o'clock sharp. Company Headquarters will be the post-office in Snorvig. If I have to communicate with you over the 'phone I shall preface my remarks by saying 'Hullo! Gibraltar, Gibraltar, Gibraltar' and you'll reply, 'Trafalgar, Trafalgar'."

"Look at that now, Captain, isn't that good? General Franco talking to Lord Nelson," the section leader grinned.

"It's not a joke, Sergeant. The speaker over the 'phone will always say 'Gibraltar' three times and he will not say who he is until he gets 'Trafalgar' twice from the other end."

"I see. Sometimes you'll be General Franco and sometimes you'll be Lord Nelson. Is that the latest bit of paper they've been sending round from Fort Augustus?"

"No, no," said Waggett petulantly, "it's my own arrangement. Suppose the enemy managed to obtain possession of the post-office he might telephone all sorts of misleading orders, and the defenders would be in confusion."

"Just in a proper muddle."

"So we must know that it's ourselves telephoning to one another and not the enemy. My arrangement allows for you wanting to telephone to Mr Beaton at Bobanish."

"Will John have to say 'Trafalgar' twice to me?" Norman Macleod asked, beaming at the prospect.

"Of course."

"Oh, god almighty, I'd like to see the face on him when he's doing it," Norman Macleod chuckled.

When Captain Waggett was on his way back to Snorvig Norman Macleod picked up the receiver.

"Bobanish schoolhouse, please. . . . Hullo! Gibraltar, Gibraltar, Gibraltar."

He heard from John Beaton a self-conscious cough. Then came the answering 'Trafalgar' twice, in nervous succession.

"Is that you, John? . . . I just wanted to tell you Waggett expects that every man will do his duty." Then he hung up the receiver abruptly, and presently rang George Campbell.

"Hullo! Gibraltar, Gibraltar, Gibraltar."

But there was no answering 'Trafalgar'. There was only the voice of Mrs Campbell demanding coldly who was speaking.

"Is that you, Mrs Campbell? . . . it is? . . . ah, well it isn't me."

And Norman Macleod cut off.

The Bank House was Captain Waggett's next call.

"Good evening, Sergeant Thomson. Well, the enemy look like having splendid weather for their attempt."

"Imphm."

"Have you posted your look-outs?"

"Imphm."

"I don't expect any excitement to-night."

The banker was silent.

" Do you?" Waggett asked.

The banker shook his head.

"I fancy the main assault will be delivered against the pier."

"Imphm?"

"We'll have everybody standing to arms by five o'clock sharp."

"Five o'clock," the banker repeated tonelessly.

"You don't think that's too late?"

The banker shook his head.

"I thought we'd have a nest of Lewis guns on the roof of Iain Dubh's house."

The banker's eyes opened wide to allow a look of contempt room to escape.

"You don't agree with that idea?"

The banker shook his head.

"What's the objection, Sergeant Thomson?"

"They'd slide off it," he replied with a sour look at the company commander for extracting from him a sentence four words long.

When he left the Bank House the commander of the Home Guard ran into Alec Mackinnon, the head of the Civil Defence.

"Can I be of any help to you to-morrow, Captain Waggett?" the tall thin headmaster of Snorvig school asked eagerly. It was the first time he had ever accorded Waggett his rank, and the heart of the latter, slightly depressed by Andrew Thomson's apparent lack of enthusiasm about the invasion, warmed towards him.

"That's very kind of you, Mr Mackinnon. I wanted to ask you to be one of my umpires, but owing to this Sunday business I thought it wise to ask Mr Morrison and Father Macalister."

"You were quite right, Captain Waggett."

"And then Captain Grant the Adjutant came over with Brigadier Beamish and Colonel Lindsay-Wolseley and I couldn't very well refuse his services."

"I quite understand. I would have been only too pleased to be of use, though," the headmaster said, a shade of disappointment in his tone.

"I'm sure you would, Mr Mackinnon. . . ." Waggett hesitated. "I wonder if you would care to undertake a confidential mission for me? Look here, come up to the house. I'm feeling rather hungry. Have you eaten yet?"

"Yes, thank you, I had my tea quite a while ago, but I'll be very pleased to discuss anything while you're eating,

Captain Waggett," said the headmaster.

Mrs Waggett was as much astonished to see her husband alighting amicably from the car with Alec Mackinnon as she would have been to see him alighting on such terms with Dr Maclaren.

"Mr Mackinnon has very kindly offered his services to me for to-morrow, Dolly," she was told, and the smile of gratification into which she was surprised had the effect of a sudden crack in the china of her face.

"Did you get anything to eat on your way round the island, Paul?" she enquired anxiously.

"Nothing. There was far too much to discuss and arrange."

"You must be famishing, dear."

"I am pretty hungry," he admitted heroically.

Mrs Waggett bustled round getting cold viands laid before the starved warrior, and Alec Mackinnon was given a dram to occupy him while the warrior ate.

"Did you notice that boot I brought in with me, Mr Mackinnon?" he asked presently.

"I did notice you brought in a boot."

The commander of G Company gave him the boot's history up to date.

"I would have done exactly what you did, Captain Waggett," the headmaster affirmed emphatically. "That's the kind of thing that makes me see absolutely red."

"Still, having made my point, I can afford to give way a little now," said Waggett. "I don't propose to afford Ben Nevis the gratification of solemnly presenting him with this boot in front of everybody. I think that would be undignified. So what I wondered was if you could somehow arrange to slip on board the yacht with it and put it in Ben Nevis's cabin. I thought I'd tie a label to it *With Captain P. Waggett's compliments to O.C. G Company.* If I sent it back by one of my own men in uniform that would make it a sort of official action, and it might be construed as an admission that G Company was in the wrong about that boot, which I am *not* prepared to admit."

"Exactly. I quite appreciate your idea."

"I had thought of asking the Minister to return it, but I know the little man will have to stand a good deal of criticism from his parishioners to-morrow for acting as umpire, and if he were to be seen walking about Snorvig with a boot, even if it was wrapped up in paper, it might be misunderstood by these strict Sabbatarians, especially if he were noticed going on board the yacht."

"I think it undoubtedly would be misunderstood," Mackinnon agreed.

"Whereas if you take the boot on board the yacht nothing can be said, even if you *are* seen with it."

"I'll be very pleased to do this for you, Captain Waggett. I suppose they'll let me on board the yacht?"

"Oh, I'm sure they will, once the battle is over. I'm going to invite them all up to the house then. And that'll be your opportunity."

"There's one thing that occurred to me, Captain Waggett, about to-morrow. . . . I don't want to seem to be butting into your arrangements, but . . ." the headmaster hesitated.

"Please don't be afraid to make any criticisms that occur to you, Mr Mackinnon," said the Home Guard commander graciously. "I have a very open mind, you know. Very open."

"You say that Father Macalister is to be your umpire on Little Todday. What will happen if a landing by the enemy should take place while he's at Mass? Simon MacRurie will be taking morning service here for Mr Morrison, but Father Macalister has Mass at nine o'clock and again at eleven, and Roman Catholics manage these things differently from the way we do. Father Macalister won't be able to get anybody else to take his service for him."

"Yes, I see your point," Waggett admitted. "Of course, when I asked Father Macalister to be an umpire I didn't know when they would arrive. I don't know now for certain, but it's almost bound to be some time to-morrow morning. They probably won't want to get back too late to-morrow night on account of the men."

"How would it be if *I* stood by to-morrow morning, Captain Waggett?" the headmaster asked eagerly. "Then if they did come while Father Macalister was at Mass I could deputize for him."

"I think it's a very, very good suggestion, Mr Mackinnon. But can you be over at Todday to-morrow morning by five?"

"Wouldn't it be better if I went over this evening right away?"

"Can you manage that?"

"Easily," the headmaster enthused. "I'll get a bed at Joseph Macroon's."

"Well, it's very kind of you, Mr Mackinnon. I had intended to go over to Little Todday myself this evening, but if you're willing to go I can send a note by you to Duncan Macroon. I want him to have his look-outs posted through the night and everybody to stand by at five o'clock sharp. Of course, there may not be any attempt to land at Little Todday."

"By Jove, I hope there will be, Captain Waggett," the headmaster exclaimed, as much excited as one of his own pupils.

And thus it was that Alec Mackinnon, after criticizing the Home Guard for a year, went over to Little Todday in the *Kittiwake* on that June evening, determined to leave nothing undone that an umpire could do on its behalf, even if he should be up all night.

"And you won't forget about your little confidential mission?" Captain Waggett reminded him as he went down the steps of the pier to board the *Kittiwake*.

Alec Mackinnon patted his bag. The boot was packed up inside.

Before turning in, the commander of the island defences went up to the hotel.

"Ah, there you are," said Brigadier Beamish cheerily. "You've been having a busy evening, Waggett. All in good order?"

"I think so, sir. I've been right round the island, and now we must wait for the balloon to go up."

"Good. We've had a grand blow-out here, haven't we, Wolseley?" said the Brigadier. "Your Roderick MacRurie is a great fellow."

"The lobsters were certainly a treat," the Colonel agreed.

"A great treat," the Adjutant echoed.

"You live like fighting cocks out in these Islands," the Brigadier declared. "I never knew anything like it. Look here, what are you going to drink, Waggett?"

The commander of the island defences decided upon a whisky. Then he caught sight of one of Roderick's bottles of gaseous lemonade.

"Oh good, that's just what I want," he sighed luxuriously.

The other three looked at him in amazement as he added

the frothy sweetness to the whisky already in his tumbler. Their bewitched silence gave him his chance.

"This evening reminds me of the night before the German attack on Grand Marnier. I'd been right through our front-line trenches with the Brigadier, and he said to me, 'Waggett, I don't believe they're going to attack to-morrow after all,' and I said, 'Well, sir, I feel absolutely sure that they are,' and he said, 'Well, Waggett, you're usually right,' and of course I didn't say anything, but as a matter of fact I was usually right. Well, we went back to his dug-out, and he said, 'What are you going to drink, Waggett?' "

"And you drank lemonade and whisky?" Brigadier Beamish asked in awestricken tones, wondering what manner of man that other Brigadier was.

"No, no. There wasn't any lemonade in the Brigadier's dug-out," Waggett related gently. "But I had some sherbet in an envelope, and that makes a wonderful mixture with whisky."

The Adjutant's monocle fell with a sharp tinkle upon the table. Colonel Lindsay-Wolseley passed a hand across his forehead in a dazed gesture. Brigadier Beamish loosened the collar of his shirt. And Waggett himself, sipping the lemonade and whisky, went on telling them about that German attack on Grand Marnier.

Chapter 17

THE BATTLE OF LITTLE TODDAY

IT was shortly before six o'clock when the summer-time sun was flashing into the tender sky of dawn that the *Banshee* stood off the little island of Poppay to lower two boats in which Sergeant Duncan Macdonald and a dozen of the steel-helmeted warriors of Ben Nevis embarked with Sergeant-major Odd to effect a landing on Tràigh nam Marbh.

Duncan Macdonald was a superb figure of a septuagenarian with a beard on him like a major prophet who stood six feet two inches and carried himself as upright as the Sergeant-major himself. Tràigh nam Marbh was held by Alan

Macdonald and Hugh Macroon, a stocky, clean-shaven crofter with a bald domed head, slow of speech but with a quick shrewd pair of eyes.

"*Seall, Uisdean,*" exclaimed Alan, picking up his rifle, "there they come."

Hugh contemplated without emotion the two boats pulling for the strand.

"Ay," he said slowly, "I believe it will be them right enough. What do we do now?"

"We just shoot away at them," Alan replied.

"But how will they be knowing we are shooting away at them?" Hugh asked. "I can't make no more noise with this rifle of mine than a crickett."

"Ay, it's a poor kind of a noise right enough," Alan agreed.

"It's no kind of a noise at all," Hugh declared contemptuously. "It's just a nothing. I could make a finer noise with my own tongue."

"I believe you could, Hugh. A pity we cannot be shooting at them with our cartridges," Alan said regretfully.

"The way you was shooting the *sgadan*," his companion reminded him.

The allusion was to Alan's encounter with the barrel of phosphorescent herrings on this same strand the night the Germans were expected.

At this moment Alec Mackinnon, who with the umpire's sealed information was expecting the enemy to land on Tràigh nam Marbh, came up on a bicycle in a state of great excitement followed by young Kenny Macroon.

"I'll have to give you both casualties if you stay here," he warned the defenders.

"Casualities?" Alan Macdonald echoed indignantly. "Who are you to be saying if we are casualities or not?"

"I'm the umpire," the headmaster of Snorvig announced, with a touch of grandeur that stung the defenders to protest.

"You *say* you're the umpire," said Hugh Macroon slowly and solemnly. "But how do we know you're the umpire? I think you're a spy."

"Can't you see my armlet?" Mackinnon asked.

"Ay, I can see your armlet right enough," Hugh replied. "Can you hear my rifle?"

There was a click as the trigger was pulled.

"Who's the casuality now?" the marksman demanded.

"You can't shoot at an umpire," the headmaster expostulated.

"Ah, but I know I can," Hugh retorted. "And that's why it's a dead man you are just now, Mr Mackinnon."

"Look here, Hugh, I'm only trying to be helpful," Alec Mackinnon insisted.

"You can't do nothing. You're dead," Hugh Macroon asserted in a tone of absolute finality.

"Ay, you're dead, Mr Mackinnon," Alan Macdonald affirmed in support of his companion. "Just as dead as you can be."

"Well, whether I'm dead or not doesn't matter," said the umpire. "But if you two stay here when those Ben Nevis fellows come ashore you'll be a jolly sight more dead than I am."

"Who can be more dead than a crayture who is dead? And that's as true for a Protestant dead as a Catholic dead," Hugh argued.

"The point is that if you two fall back at once," Alec Mackinnon said, "you can warn your commanding officer in good time and give him a chance to put the invading force out of action. But if you stay here I can't warn him, because I'm the umpire, and they may capture Kiltod."

Alan Macdonald fondled his trim square beard.

"There's a lot in what Mr Mackinnon is saying," he decided.

"It's a pretty long walk all the way back to Kiltod," Hugh pointed out. "And if we have to crawl like panters all the way we will be just as dead as if we wass shot. And not such an easy end at that."

"Will I go on my bicycle?" Kenny Macroon seized the opportunity of Hugh Macroon's indolence to ask eagerly.

"That's just what you will do, Kenny boy," said Hugh. "Alan and me will stay here and fight it out, and you'll tell Duncan Bàn how Alan and me just died fighting like Victoria's crosses. Ay, ay, just gave up our two lives for the sake of the rest of them."

The boats of the invaders were near enough inshore by now to make out their numbers.

"Tell him there's fourteen or fifteen of them unless Alan and me will have killed them all first," Hugh Macroon added.

The umpire shook his head.

"I'm sorry, Hugh, but the way you're sitting there without any cover you're dead already," he insisted.

Hugh Macroon gazed at him with an expression of melancholy disgust as Kenny plunged off upon his bicycle in the direction of Kiltod. Then he aimed his rifle at the boats and started to click at them, Alan Macdonald doing the same.

"Hullo!" he exclaimed suddenly. "Do you see who's with them, Alan?"

"It's the Sergeant," Alan declared. "Isn't that splendid now?"

"Ay, it's himself right enough," Hugh affirmed.

The two defenders of Tràigh nam Marbh stood up, and walked down to the beach, where the invaders were by now landing, to welcome the Sergeant-major back to Little Todday.

"You're both casualties, you know," the umpire called after them.

"Ay, ay, two casualties doing the Spirit Walk," Hugh called back over his shoulder. "Ah, well, Sergeant," he said a minute later in his deliberate way, his shrewd eyes twinkling, "*Fàilte do'n dùthaich*. Welcome to the country." He offered his hand in a hearty grip, and Alan did the same.

"How are you both?" enquired the Sergeant-major.

"Ach, we're both dead, but we're pretty well for two corpses. And how's yourself?"

"I'm in the pink, thanks. Hullo, is that the umpire?"

"He says he is. He's the schoolmaster in Snorvig—Mackinnon. He's not a bad fellow at all. Just a bit interfering, but there's no harm in the man."

"Oh yes, I know him well," said the Sergeant-major. "Good morning, Mr Mackinnon. What a lovely morning, eh?"

"Good morning, Sergeant-major. I'm acting as umpire for the defenders. Isn't there an umpire with the invaders?"

"No, Mr Mackinnon. I had orders to arrange with whoever was umpire on the spot. Well, what's the verdict?"

"Landing effected," the headmaster ruled. "Both these men are casualties." He indicated Hugh Macroon and Alan Macdonald. "I don't know what your next move is."

"I believe Sergeant Macdonald intends to attack Kiltod,"

said the Sergeant-major. "This is Sergeant Macdonald."

Ben Nevis's head stalker put out his huge fist, and the conversation was carried on for a while in excited Gaelic.

"The orders were that the boats were to return to the yacht," the Sergeant-major reminded old Duncan Macdonald.

"Yes, yes, that's right," said the old man. "We'll just sit down for a wee while and have a look round. Ah, well, it's a pretty country. Beautiful, beautiful," he sighed with pleasure. "Just as beautiful as a picture hanging up on the wall."

The boats pulled off again in the direction of Poppay, and for the next half-hour the invasion became an extremely cordial *céilidh*.

Back in Kiltod, Kenny had brought news of the landing and Duncan Bàn had made his dispositions to give the invaders a hot reception. South of the harbour there was an outcrop of stone against which the sand had piled itself in a miniature range of tiny green hills the hollows of which afforded perfect cover to a defending force, against whom any attack from that direction must be carried out across the wide level stretch of machair that ran for nearly a mile southward, creamy with sweet white clover at this time of year but completely devoid of any shelter against the marksmen of the defence. In this miniature range of hills the whole force of Little Todday was concentrated that June morning, and it says much for the strict neutrality of Sergeant-major Odd that when Sergeant Duncan Macdonald proposed to lead the men under his command right into this death-trap he did not indicate by so much as the flicker of an eyelid any misgivings about the tactical expediency of such a move.

"I rule that every man in the attacking force is either dead or taken prisoner," the umpire decided, after the rifles of the defenders had clicked a murderous fire into the invaders at fifty yards. "What's your opinion, Sergeant-major?"

"I agree with you, Mr Mackinnon. Perhaps you'll notify the umpires over in Great Todday in due course that the attempt by the landing force to capture Little Todday completely failed after a partial success in effecting a landing. Meanwhile, the troops landed must consider themselves prisoners until the *Banshee*'s boats come to fetch them off."

"Prisoners?" old Duncan Macdonald echoed. "Does that mean we mustn't move from where we are?"

"Oh, I don't think it need mean that," said the Sergeant-major. "I'm sure Lieutenant Macroon will accept your parole. You've no objection to your visitors just amusing themselves as they want, Mr Macroon, till the time comes for them to rejoin the main body?"

"It's not they will have to be amusing themselves," Duncan replied. "It's we will be amusing them if they'll just sit and smoke a pipe until church is over. Father Macalister will be wanting to see them all."

"Ay, I'd like very much to meet Father Macalister again," said old Duncan Macdonald. "He's a great man for the Gaelic. We had a crack together once at the Fort William Mòd."

"And when do you think I ought to go over to Snorvig and report what has happened here?" Alec Mackinnon asked the Sergeant-major.

"You could go across in the *Morning Star* when church is finished."

"Will you come with me, Sergeant-major?"

"No, I think I'd better wait here, Mr Mackinnon, and keep an eye on things. There's one or two little jobs I have to do," said the Sergeant-major.

One of the little jobs that Sergeant-major Odd had to do took him into Joseph Macroon's sitting-room where Peggy Ealasaid, who had been to early Mass, was looking after the establishment while the rest of the family were at the second Mass.

"Is the fighting all over?" she asked.

"Yes, there's no more fighting. It was what anyone might call a foregone conclusion. With luck you and me might get a nice long walk together before I have to start back to the mainland, Peggy. Still, just in case we don't . . ." he sat drumming his fingers on the table.

"I'll be kept pretty busy by my father with all these soldiers you've brought here, Sarchant Odd," she pouted.

"What's Fred done?" he asked reproachfully. "If you can write it, Peggy, you can say it. My notion was we could get married this autumn. There's no use putting it off any longer if I'm so old as what you like to make out."

"I didn't think you'd be coming here to talk foolishness."

"Why is it foolishness?"

"Just because it is," she murmured.

"Don't you *want* to be married? I mean to say, have you got anything in particular against marriage *as* marriage? Or do you want to marry somebody else?"

"I don't want to be married at all. It's just a nuisance to be married."

"That's what I used to think till I bumped into you, Peggy. Yes," he went on in the tone of one surprised by the follies of his youth, "when I used to hear the Wedding March lah-lah-ing away on the organ it sounded to me once upon a time more like the Dead March in Saul."

"What are you saying?" she exclaimed in fretful bewilderment. "I don't know at all what you are talking about, Sarchant Odd."

"Fred."

"If I say 'Fred' will you leave me to do what I have to do?"

"Terms of surrender offered by the garrison not accepted. Besieging forces refuse to withdraw."

"I never knew anybody who talked so strange as you," she pouted. "And if I laugh you look so crabbed."

The Sergeant-major jumped up from where he was sitting at the table and caught hold of Peggy's hand.

"You're squeessing me terribly hard," she protested.

"That's because I don't want to let you go. Listen, Peggy, I'm serious. Will you marry me this autumn? Or don't you love me at all?"

"I told you I liked you very much. And if you weren't so old . . . oh, but you are terribly old. I wouldn't like anybody to laugh and say Peigi Iosaiph had married a *bodach*."

"Here wait a minute, who's Peggy Yosif? That's a new one on me. And what's a bottuck?"

"Peigi Iosaiph is me. Iosaph is my father. And a *bodach* is an old man."

"But look here, Peggy, it's not hardly right to call me an old man. I've got a good thirty years to go before you can call me that. All the same, if there's a boy of your own age you like better than me, say the word and I'll clear off and accept my discharge."

She was silent.

"Is there, Peggy?"

"And you're a Protestant," she murmured.

"I've been into all that," he said cheerfully. "By what I can make out, so long as I promise all the children shall be brought up Catholics . . ."

"Sarchant Odd!" she protested from a blush.

"Fred," he corrected firmly. "You won't want to look so shocked if you call me Fred. Well, to go on with what I was saying . . . so long as the children are brought up Catholics your padre won't raise any objections. I told my old mother about you being a Catholic girl and she wrote and said she was only too glad to hear I knew there was any difference between Catholics and Protestants and took it as a sign I really had begun to think for myself at last. But you didn't answer my question, Peggy. Is there anybody else of your own age you like better than me?"

She was still silent, and when he put his arm round her and drew her close she did not struggle away from him.

"Suppose you tried kissing me of your own accord, Peggy darling? Try. It might give you a bit of confidence."

And she kissed him.

"Well, well, Sergeant," Father Macalister said to him an hour later when he went up to pay his respects at the Chapel House, "Ben Nevis suffered a fearful defeat on Little Todday."

"Yes, Father Macalister, so he did. But I never expected anything else. However, he was set on capturing the island, and I didn't like to try and put him off. Mr Mackinnon's just gone over to let them know in Snorvig what's happened. I understood you were going to be the umpire."

"So I would have been if you'd landed at a reasonable time, but I had two Masses to say."

"Excuse me, Father, but I'd like to tell you something."

"Go ahead, my boy."

"Well, I've just asked Peggy Yallasich to marry me, and she's said 'yes'. And what I wanted to say to you was I wouldn't like you to think I was just asking her anyhow in a manner of speaking. I mean to say I really love the girl and I wouldn't try to change her from what she is for anything and I thought if you knew it was like that with me you'd feel it was all right with you. I'd like you to marry us this autumn here, if that's all right. I spoke to her father, but he was so flummoxed with all these Ben Nevis chaps I'm not sure if he's taken it in yet."

The Sergeant-major stopped and waited for the priest's verdict. It was given immediately.

"You've chosen a beautiful lovely girl," Father Macalister declared. "And a good girl, which is more important. But well, well, by Jingo, my boy, I don't think she's done so badly herself. Ah, well . . ." The priest went to the cupboard and brought out a bottle of rum from which he poured out two drams.

Chapter 18

THE BATTLE OF THE BOOT

WHEN Alec Mackinnon reached Snorvig with the tidings that the whole of the force which had invaded Little Todday was out of action he found that the battle for Great Todday was over also. The *Banshee* was lying alongside the pier. The assault troops, for all the furious clicking of the Lewis guns which had covered them from behind sandbags, had been declared obliterated by an equally furious clicking of the Lewis guns controlled by Sergeant Thomson and the Biffer and the rapid clicking of the defenders' rifles. News of what had happened to the diversion up Loch Sleeport had not yet come in; but lorries had been sent to Watasett to bring the combatants in to Snorvig, where Brigadier Beamish was to address the combatants gathered in the square at one o'clock, and nobody supposed that the invaders would be anything except dead men or prisoners.

Alec Mackinnon after receiving this gratifying intelligence thought he would take the opportunity to go on board the yacht and execute the confidential mission with which Captain Waggett had entrusted him. This he did not have the slightest difficulty in doing. The left-footed boot was deposited in Ben Nevis's cabin, and the headmaster went ashore down the gangway. Half-way across the pier he was stopped by a lantern-jawed man in the uniform of a captain, with the expression of a professional palmist, who asked to see his permit.

"My permit?" the headmaster of Snorvig school exclaimed in amazement. "What permit?"

Behind the lantern-jawed captain stood another captain, a round chubby man with the gimlet eyes of the store detective always on the look-out for shop-lifters.

"Your permit to travel between Great Todday and Little Todday," said Lantern-jaws portentously.

"What's this about permits? I'm a resident of Snorvig," Alec Mackinnon protested. "I don't require a permit."

"There you are, Smith," said Lantern-jaws, turning to address Gimlet-eyes, "I knew it was high time the position here was cleared up."

"Will you come along with us to the police station, please," Gimlet-eyes demanded sternly.

"I'll do nothing of the kind," Alec Mackinnon declared with some heat. "Who are you to order me to the police station?"

"I am Captain Quiblick, Security Intelligence Officer of Number 14 Protected Area," said Lantern-jaws in the hollow voice of mystery. "And this is Captain Lomax-Smith, Security Intelligence Officer of Number 13 Protected Area," he added, indicating Gimlet-eyes.

"And I am one of the umpires in this invasion exercise," Alec Mackinnon explained.

"Let me see your authority," said Captain Quiblick grimly.

Alec Mackinnon pointed to his white armlet.

Captain Quiblick smiled the weary smile of one who has plumbed too often the uttermost depths of human deception to be caught by the flashy glitter of such surface bait.

"I think you had better come along with us to the police station," he advised, with a menace at the back of the invitation.

"I refer you to Captain Waggett," Alec Mackinnon said. "He commands the Home Guard on both islands."

"The local commander of the Home Guard has no status in a matter concerned with Security Intelligence," Captain Quiblick replied.

"None whatsoever," Captain Lomax-Smith added with fierce emphasis.

Twenty-four hours earlier the headmaster of Snorvig school would have been immensely gratified to hear such an un-equivocal statement about Captain Waggett's limitations. Now since the *rapprochement* between them the slight filled him with indignation.

"Do you mean to suggest that the Home Guard has no importance in the defence of these islands?" Alec Mackinnon asked.

"None," Captain Quiblick snapped.

"None whatsoever," Captain Lomax-Smith amplified.

The headmaster looked round him; but at that moment there was nobody in sight from the pier to whom he could appeal against the arrogance of the military. He decided to accompany the two officers to the police station. In the middle of the invasion nobody would suspect him of being as it were provisionally under arrest. Snorvig was too full of uniforms on this Sunday.

The reader more familiar with the long arm of coincidence than the long arm of intelligence may be wondering how Captain Quiblick and Captain Lomax-Smith found themselves together on the Snorvig pier on this Sunday in June. It befell thus. Captain Lomax-Smith had made the long journey from Obaig to Mid Uist in order to confer with Captain Quiblick about measures to make the bureaucratic armour in which their protected areas were encased still more impregnable to the bullets of individual liberty. At Nobost Lodge, which had been commandeered by the War Office on behalf of the Security Intelligence Corps, Captain Quiblick had pointed out to Captain Lomax-Smith what a threat the Coolish was to the whole theory of Protected Areas.

"I mean to say if Milperm"—this was at once a telegraphic address and a term of endearment for the Military Permit Office—"issues to somebody a permit to visit Great Todday," said Captain Quiblick, "what's to prevent the holder of such a permit from crossing over to Little Todday, which is in your protected area?"

Captain Lomax-Smith scowled at the idea of such audacity.

"Do you think anybody would do that?" he asked incredulously.

"I don't know. We had a lot of trouble with this fellow Lindsay-Wolseley who commands some Home Guard battalion up here. He actually put his Home Guards at our disposal to check up on the passenger traffic."

"Good god, I never heard of that. These elderly dug-outs in the Home Guard have the most fantastic notions about their own importance."

"I know. It's beyond belief, isn't it?" said Captain Quiblick. "I pointed out in a secret memorandum that Colonel Lindsay-Wolseley ought to think himself lucky the S.I.C. didn't insist on his Home Guards having to apply for permits every time they crossed from one island to the other."

"Yes, I saw a copy of that," said Captain Lomax-Smith. "I thought it put the case unanswerably."

"All the same he tried to answer it," said Captain Quiblick.

"Did he?" Captain Lomax-Smith exclaimed in astonishment. "What did he say?"

"He wrote a very offensive letter to this Brigadier fellow commanding Western Sub-Stratum to ask what was the idea of putting either of the two Toddays into a protected area because there was nothing on either island to protect."

"Good god," ejaculated Captain Lomax-Smith, "how foully last war! Doesn't he understand that Intelligence has been speeded up like everything else to keep pace with mechanized warfare?"

"I suppose not," said Captain Quiblick contemptuously. "These re-inflated blimps are pretty soggy in the head. It wouldn't occur to a fellow like Lindsay-Wolseley that the whole point of constituting a protected area is to make the Hun think it is protected, and so save shipping space."

"Well, of course the whole business is too utterly last war even to be funny," Captain Lomax-Smith said in disgust. "These Home Guard fellows complain about being issued with pikes. Good god, they ought to be thankful they weren't issued with flint arrowheads. Ha-ha! Well, I must say that was a good one. Can't understand why the two Toddays are in a protected area, because there's nothing on either to protect! Ha-ha-ha!"

"It's a great pity there ever was a last war," Captain Quiblick muttered sombrely. "It's handicapped us terribly in this one. Well, what about you and me paying a visit to Snorvig on Sunday and snooping around a bit?"

"I think that's a very sound notion. How will we get there?"

"We'll charter MacWilliam's boat at Loch Stew," said Captain Quiblick.

And it was from MacWilliam's motor-boat that at a cost of £30 to the taxpayer he and Captain Lomax-Smith had just landed at Snorvig when Alec Mackinnon coming over from

Kiltod after that suspicious visit to the *Banshee* had run into the pair of them on the pier.

"But this is Mr Mackinnon, the headmaster of Snorvig school," said Macrae the constable. "You've made a mistake, gentlemen."

"The point is not who he is, constable," Captain Quiblick observed. "The point is, what is he doing on Little Todday without a permit?"

"Ah, I know now who you are," Macrae exclaimed. "You're the gentleman who wrote to me about permits for glasses. What a waste of your time, eh?" he added sympathetically. "Ah, well, it's· wonderful what they'll think of in war-time to waste people's time. This permit business between Great and Little Todday is another piece of nonsense just to waste time."

"I can assure you," said Captain Lomax-Smith severely, "the War Office attaches very great importance to permits between Great and Little Todday, and pending the establishment of Security Intelligence controls at Snorvig and Kiltod you are responsible for seeing that no travellers with permits for Great Todday visit Little Todday."

"And of course *vice versa*," said the Security Intelligence Officer whose realm included Great Todday.

"And what about myself?" Macrae asked. "Do I give myself a permit to visit Little Todday? And *vice versa* of course."

"I sent you full instructions about the procedure to be adopted," said Captain Quiblick reproachfully.

"So did I," said Captain Lomax-Smith.

"So did the Chief Constable," Macrae added, beaming. "And I've had a lot of instructions about the procedure to adopt with German submarines who come to either of the two islands without a permit."

"Well, I don't know anything about German submarines . . ." Captain Quiblick began.

"Nor do I," said Macrae.

"They don't come under Security Intelligence."

"What a pity," said Macrae sympathetically. "I believe you'd make a good job with them, sir."

Captain Quiblick darted the penetrating glance of a Security Intelligence Officer at the constable, but Macrae's eyes were innocent of sarcasm.

"Well, neither Captain Quiblick nor I want to get you into trouble, constable," said Captain Lomax-Smith.

"Thank you very much, sir," Macrae interposed with an apparent warmth of grateful relief.

"But in future," Captain Quiblick went on quickly, "Captain Lomax-Smith and I shall expect you to keep a strict check on all passenger traffic between the two islands. Anybody who wishes to travel from Great Todday to Little Todday . . ."

"Or *vice versa*," Captain Lomax-Smith put in.

"Must write to the Military Permit Office, Aberdeen, setting out in full their reasons for wishing to proceed from Great Todday to Little Todday. Or *vice versa* of course. A form will then be sent to the applicant which must be accurately filled in and returned to the Military Permit Office, when if the application is favourably considered the permit will be issued in the course of two or three weeks."

"And what's the idea of all this?" the constable asked.

"The idea of all this," said Captain Lomax-Smith sternly, "is to get on with the war."

"Och, well," said Macrae, "I think it's a good thing Hitler has had a crack at the Russians."

"What do you mean?" asked Captain Quiblick in astonishment.

"Didn't you hear the wireless then?"

"No."

"Och, they're into Russia right enough," said Macrae. "And Mr Churchill will be telling us all about it to-night at nine o'clock."

"I never heard anything about that on Little Todday," said the schoolmaster, all agog. "By Jove, Norman Macleod will be pleased. He's a great believer in the Russians."

"Is this Norman Macleod a communist?" one of the Security Intelligence Officers asked with ready suspicion.

"No, no, no," said Macrae soothingly. "Just what we used to call a Liberal when I was a boy. Ah well, now, if you two gentlemen have finished with Mr Mackinnon, will you excuse me while I go down to the square? I'll want to keep the children quiet while Brigadier Beamish is talking about the invasion."

"Mr Mackinnon has not yet explained what he was doing on

board that yacht lying alongside the pier," Captain Quiblick said.

"I was engaged in performing a confidential mission for Captain Waggett. I refer you to him," said the headmaster stiffly.

"I'm afraid that's rather too vague," said Captain Quiblick. "What exactly were you doing on board the yacht?"

"Well, if you must know," said the schoolmaster, "I was leaving a boot there for Ben Nevis on behalf of Captain Waggett."

The two Security Intelligence Officers exchanged meaning glances.

"We shall not detain you longer," Captain Quiblick said to the schoolmaster. "You realize of course that if you proceed to Little Todday again without a permit you are liable to be expelled from the protected area. If I may give you a word of advice, Mr Mackinnon, you should be very very careful what you do in future."

"More than careful," Captain Lomax-Smith corroborated.

"Your story about the boot will be investigated," Captain Quiblick went on. "And if it should turn out to be a false statement, any inconvenience you may be caused in consequence will be entirely your own fault."

The two S.I.C. officers walked out of the police station.

"Och, I wouldn't let them worry you, Mr Mackinnon," said the constable. "These fellows aren't used to authority, and it just goes to their heads. They'll have been ordered about by other people all their lives and a war like this gives them their chance."

While the constable and the schoolmaster were making their way down to the square where Brigadier Beamish was to address the combatants of both sides, Captain Quiblick and Captain Lomax-Smith strolled as nonchalantly as they could manage in the direction of the yacht. It was simple work for men of such experience to effect an entry to Ben Nevis's cabin where the boot with Captain Waggett's card attached was still on the bunk where the schoolmaster had left it.

"I'll take this back with me to Nobost Lodge and have it tested for secret communications," said Captain Quiblick.

"That's a very sound notion," Captain Lomax-Smith agreed.

And at that moment the entrance into the cabin was darkened by the kilted bulk of Ben Nevis, in his hand another left-footed boot.

"What the devil are you both doing in my cabin?" the Chieftain roared. "Who are you? What are you?"

But before we hear Security Intelligence's answer to this question it will be necessary to follow the course of Mac 'ic Eachainn since he and Kilwhillie, with Toker in attendance, were rowed up Loch Bob and put ashore by one of the yacht's boats at Bobanish.

"Mind you, I don't like this expedition, Donald," said the Cameron laird. "I'm not at all convinced it's a legitimate operation for an invasion exercise."

"Legitimate fiddlesticks," the Chieftain scoffed. "Do you suppose Hitler stops to ask if some operation is illegitimate?"

"Isn't that why we're at war with him?" Kilwhillie suggested.

"And aren't I at war with this fellow Waggett? By the way, did you notice Beamish standing on the pier when we ran alongside with the *Banshee* the first time and raked it with the Lewis guns? I thought he looked completely idiotic."

"I don't think he looked so particularly idiotic."

"You're in a very contradictory mood this morning, Hugh."

Kilwhillie stroked his moustaches without replying.

"Well, they've gone back now for the final assault," Ben Nevis said.

"I wonder if they'll be successful," said Kilwhillie.

"I don't care a button whether they are or not so long as I get this boot. This must be the schoolhouse, I think. Is this Bobanish schoolhouse?" the Chieftain called out to Mrs Beaton, who was in the garden looking at the way her peas were coming along.

The wife of the second-in-command of the Home Guard had been well trained. She stared at the strangers in uniform as mute as one of her own fuchsia bushes.

"She may not speak English," Kilwhillie suggested.

"Where's the bottuck?" Ben Nevis bellowed.

There was no reply.

"She certainly doesn't speak Gaelic," Ben Nevis affirmed. Both he and Kilwhillie tried various questions on the schoolmaster's wife, but to all of them she answered only with silence.

"I think she's a deaf-mute," said the Chieftain. "Most embarrassing, what? I'll try once more. Are you deaf, my good woman?" he roared at her through cupped hands. "By Jove, she heard something, Hugh. I noticed a distinct blink."

But the blink was all they could extract from Mrs Beaton, and the two invaders walked on past the schoolhouse toward the road. Along this they perceived coming from the north an ancient Home Guard with a full white beard.

"Come on, Hugh," Ben Nevis shouted, "we must take this chap prisoner."

"I can't. I'm an umpire, Donald."

"Well, I'll take him myself. Hullo, you're my prisoner," he shouted to the old man.

"Ah, I'm not fighting at all to-day," said the old man. "I left my rifle at home. I'm just walking to Snorvig to shake hands with Ben Nevis."

"But that's me," the Chieftain exclaimed. "Who are you?"

"Ah, well, well, well! I see now it is yourself, Ben Nevis," the old man declared, peering into his face. "But my goodness, you've changed in forty years. Man, I wouldn't have known you if you hadn't said it was yourself. You don't remember me?"

It was now the Chieftain's turn to peer.

"I'm afraid I don't. Who are you?"

"Hector MacRurie of Lovat's Scouts. I was in Q troop with yourself, Ben Nevis. And I mind well when Duncan Macdonald caught you a crack on the head and put you flat when a Boer sniper was near getting you."

"Good lord," Ben Nevis barked, offering his hand, "I remember you perfectly. Kemmararshif? And old Duncan's over in Little Todday at this moment."

"*Cia mar tha sibh fhein?* Ah well, well, well, it's proud I am to be shaking your hand, Ben Nevis. Och, I said to the *cailleach* I'll not be breaking the Sabbath fighting, but I'm going to put on my uniform and walk along to Snorvig to shake the hand of an old friend. Ah, well, man, you're looking splendid."

"So are you, by Jove, Hector. This is Hugh Cameron of Kilwhillie."

"Kilwhillie, is it?" exclaimed the old man, shaking the Cameron laird's hand. "Look at that now! My great-great-grandmother was a Cameron from Glenbore, and I believe she was pretty nearly related to the laird of that time. Ay, yes, I believe she was his eighth cousin."

"Then you and I must be related," said Kilwhillie.

"Och, yes, we're related right enough," Hector agreed. "And I've always been proud of my Cameron blood. They were always bonny fighters. Ay, I believe the Prince thought a lot of them."

"My great-great-great-grandfather was out in the '45," said Kilwhillie.

"Ay, he would have been. Great days right enough. Fighting the Germans then just the same as we are now. Isn't that strange?" said the old man, shaking his head.

"Well, you can tell me something I want to know, Hector," said Ben Nevis. "I lost a boot some time ago, and Sergeant-major Odd told me it was in the company store at Bobanish."

"Sergeant-major Odd, eh? A fine man. We liked him very well in Knockdown."

"Knockdown? That's where you live, is it?"

"Ay, just about three miles up along the road. I settled on the croft when I came home from South Africa, and I've never been off the island since. Ah, well, if Sergeant-major Odd said your boot was in the store it will be there right enough. We'll go along and have a look for it."

But when they reached the store it was locked.

"Never you mind, Ben Nevis," said Hector. "I'll be getting the key from Mrs Beaton. She's a cousin of my wife's."

"She's deaf, isn't she?" the Chieftain asked.

"Not she. She has quicker ears than most."

"She wouldn't say a word to me when I spoke to her just now."

"Ah, she would be shy. They're pretty shy, the Great Todday women."

"Well, it may have been that," said the Chieftain doubt-fully.

It took an argument before old Hector MacRurie persuaded Mrs Beaton to give him the key of the store. She declared that her husband had already given the boot Ben Nevis wanted to Mr Waggett.

"Och well, if he did I believe Mr Waggett will have taken it for himself," said Hector. "He came to John Maclean's shop yesterday and took away six kettles for himself. And I had a beautiful curliflower in my garden last year, and he praised it so high it put shame on me not to be giving it to him. And so he had that too. But Ben Nevis is a fine gentleman and if he's wanting a boot it's he who should be having it, not Mr Waggett."

So Mrs Beaton parted with the key to old Hector MacRurie and a few minutes later Ben Nevis seized triumphantly a left-footed boot.

"That's what I came to Great Todday for," he announced gleefully. "Well, we'll go back to Snorvig now, Hugh. There's no point in going on with this invasion. And, look here, Hector, if you get down as far, come and have a crack with me on board the yacht. I'll give you the biggest dram you ever saw in your life. And we'll drink to old days in South Africa, what? Toker!" he turned round to roar.

The butler-sergeant came forward discreetly.

"If Hector MacRurie comes on board when I'm ashore give him a dram and look after him till I get back."

"Certainly, sir. I shall be most eager to hear some of Mr MacRurie's stories of insular life."

"All right, Toker. Come on, Hugh. We'll get along to Snorvig now."

Thus it was that Ben Nevis reached the *Banshee* to discover Captain Quiblick and Captain Lomax-Smith in his cabin and asked them who and what they were.

"I'm the Security Intelligence Officer for Number 14 Protected Area," said Captain Quiblick. "And this is the Security Intelligence Officer for Number 13 Protected Area."

"What right does that give you to come into my cabin on a private yacht and . . ." the Chieftain's eyes glared at the second left-footed boot, and he snatched it away from Captain Quiblick. "Where did you get this?" he roared. "Why, *this* is the boot I've been trying to recover for months, and look here, you ruffian, it was restored to me by this . . ." he gulped, "by-er-Captain Waggett."

"I must protest, sir," Captain Lomax-Smith interposed. "You must realize that Captain Quiblick was only doing his duty."

Ben Nevis rushed to the companion and shouted:

"Tom! Tom! Send some of your men below to my cabin. I want to put two fellows in irons and take them back with us to the mainland."

"I warn you, sir," said Captain Lomax-Smith, "that Scottish Command will take a very serious view of your behaviour."

"My behaviour? What right has a bounder like you to talk about behaviour? You don't know what behaviour is. Tom! Tom! Where *are* those men of yours?"

But it was Colonel Lindsay-Wolseley who came down the companion in response to the roar of Ben Nevis, and he was immovable on the subject of carrying off the two S.I.C. officers in irons to the mainland.

"It cannot be done, Ben Nevis," he said firmly. "And it will not be done," he added even more firmly. At the same time he allowed the two S.I.C. officers to perceive plainly that he regarded their activity on Great Todday without approbation, and in some mysterious way, in spite of being so foully last war, he managed to reduce both to something like a condition of obsequiousness before they left the yacht.

"Beamish is going to talk to everybody about the exercise," the Colonel told Ben Nevis when the S.I.C. men had departed.

"I don't have to be there, do I? He bores me to death."

"Yes, certainly you must be there, Ben Nevis."

"Well, I've got my boot. Waggett returned it to me of his own accord."

"That was very decent of him, I think," said the Colonel.

"Yes, I suppose it was," the Chieftain admitted grudgingly.

Later on, after the pow-wow in the square in the course of which Brigadier Beamish made one of his usual speeches to gathered Home Guards, Ben Nevis gave Hector MacRurie that immense dram.

"And look here, Hector, you might put this boot back in the store, will you? Captain Waggett gave me the other one."

The old man seemed to be levitated from the yacht to the pier, an unearthly glow in his eyes and on his face a smile Enoch or Elijah might have worn at the moment of their bodily transportation aloft.

"Well, it has been a very successful day, old lady," the commander of G Company said to his wife with a complacent sigh that evening when the *Banshee* had left Snorvig with the invaders and also Brigadier Beamish, Colonel Lindsay-Wolseley, and Captain Grant whose presence, now that he had recovered his left-footed boot, Ben Nevis no longer resented on board. "Very successful," he repeated in that tone of dreamy satisfaction he usually reserved for days in which he had excelled with the shot-gun. "I think Ben Nevis was very pleased with the boot. I wonder if he'll ask me to do any stalking at Glenbogle Castle in September? I suppose I could leave John Beaton in charge here if I went away for a week or two. I think Winston was quite right to take that line about the Russians. I should have done exactly the same. Sergeant-major Odd spent a very quiet day on Little Todday. Of course, the attacking force walked right into it. He says he hopes Colonel Wolseley will send him over to give some more instruction soon. I hear two Security Intelligence Officers were here, but they left before I saw them. Alec Mackinnon was in trouble over not having a pass to Little Todday. Well, the only way to check passenger traffic between the two islands is to make it a Home Guard responsibility. The Brigadier was very complimentary about my dispositions. So was Colonel Wolseley. Yes, it's been a very successful day. The Minister quite enjoyed himself. Father Macalister didn't act as umpire after all. Apparently he couldn't give up his service. Very strange. I always thought Roman Catholics paid very little attention to Sunday. Well, I think the people here are beginning to appreciate at last all the work I've done to make the Home Guard really efficient."

And with this reflection the further activities of the Home Guard on Great and Little Todday must be left unchronicled. It is tempting to relate how Captain Waggett, on receiving secret instructions to apply the scorched-earth policy in case of invasion . . . but no, the temptation shall be resisted.

G Company are still turning. They have just learnt to substitute tempo for suspicious alertness and to speak of being checked instead of being held up. They are trying hard not to bunch. Their ceiling has been whitewashed and distempered and deplastered and emplastered. Their weapons have been dealt and re-dealt as often as a pack of cards at progressive whist. Their boots are getting worn out, but they are still proud of them, and it is as well they are, for they are not likely to get any more for a long while. And since the two islands are still in two different protected areas, the people of Great Britain can feel secure. Hitler is not likely to land on either island without a permit, and if he does, the pikes are waiting for him.

GLOSSARY
OF THE GAELIC EXPRESSIONS

*The pronunciation indicated in brackets is only
roughly approximate*

CHAPTER 1

page

60 *charaid* friend

61 *An t'Eilean Muileach* (an chaylen moolach) The Isle of Mull

61 *céilidh* (cayley) literally: visit, but used for any entertainment

62 *papanaich* papists

CHAPTER 8

73 *a Choinnich* O Kenneth

73 *Nach ist thu?* (nach isht oo) Will you not be quiet?

73 *matà* then

74 *a Mhaighstir Seumas* (a Vysh-chir Shamus) O Mr James

78 *A bhalaich* (a vahlich) O boy

78 *A chlann an diabhoil* children of the devil

80 *A Mhuire mhàthair* (a Voorye vahair) O mother Mary

80 *bòcan* bogy

CHAPTER 9

88 *A Chruithear* (a Crooyer) O Creator

93 *athair* (ahair) father

CHAPTER 10

99 *nach sibh tha carach?* (nach shiv hah carach) are you not cunning?

CHAPTER 12

121 *Tha gu dearbh* (hah gu jerrav) Yes, right enough

121 *poit-mhùin* (poytch vooin) chamber-pot

124 *Istibh* (ishtiv) Be quiet

124 *amadan* (amatan) fool

CHAPTER 14

157 *Mòran taing, a Mhaigstir Seumas* (moran tang, a Vysh-chir Shamus) Many thanks, Mr James

CHAPTER 16

178 *Seall sin a nis, Aonghais* (shoul shin a nish, Aonas) Look at that now, Angus

178 *cailleach* (calyach) old woman

178 *truaghan* (trooagan) poor creature

page
179 *leabraichean* (lyaurichan) literally: books, but used for the Bible
184 *sgarbh* (scarrav) cormorant or shag
184 *cearc fhraoich* (kyark raoch) literally: hen of the heather, *i.e.* grouse

CHAPTER 17

191 *Seall, Uisdean* (shoul, Oosdjan) Look, Hugh
191 *sgadan* (scatan) herring
193 *Fàilte do'n dùthaich* (fahlche don du-hich᾽
196 *Peigi Iosaiph* Peggy of Joseph (*Iosaph*᾽

CHAPTER 18

206 *Cia mar tha sibh fhein?* (kemmar hah shiv hain) How are you yourself?

Fantasy, comedy, magic and high adventure in three great novels by the world-famous fantasy writer·

James Branch Cabell

"Witty, subtle and magnificently entertaining fantasy fiction" *Lin Carter*

Figures of Earth

How Manuel the swineherd set out to make a figure in the world, and ended his quest as overlord of Poictesme. ·

"So inventive, so funny and so beautiful that it is a joy to read" *James Blish*

The Silver Stallion

How the nine barons of the Fellowship of the Silver Stallion, who had ruled Poictesme under Count Manuel, came to most colourful and unusual ends.

"One of the wittiest, most delightfully entertaining of all fantasy novels" *Lin Carter* ·

Jurgen

The ribald adventures of Jurgen, who regains his lost youth and wanders joyfully through the mythical lands of Poictesme and Cocaigne, meeting the world's fairest women and dealing fairly with them all—after his own fashion.

One of the few truly comic and erotic classics: "it will amuse, bemuse and delight you" *James Blish*

Published in Tandem editions at 35p each

Best-selling fiction in Tandem editions

Elizabeth Lemarchand

Death of an Old Girl 25p
The Affacombe Affair 25p
Alibi for a Corpse 25p

Three first-class detective stories featuring Chief Detective-Inspector Tom Pollard of Scotland Yard, and sure to appeal to anyone who enjoys Agatha Christie.

"A superbly told tale of blackmail and terror"
Manchester Evening News

"A real genuine police detection story . . . a hundred per cent winner"
Sunday Times

Kate Thompson

Great House 30p
Mandevilla 30p
Sugarbird 25p
Richard's Way 25p
The Painted Caves 25p

"Family chronicles are among the most popular of novels and high on the list are Kate Thompson's stories centred on the South African family of the Derains"
Bournemouth Evening Echo

Catherine Cookson

Hannah Massey 25p
The Garment 25p
Slinky Jane 25p

Compelling and moving novels, set in the North Country which Catherine Cookson has made famous.

"In an age when so much rubbish is published and writers are two a penny, Mrs Cookson comes as a boon and a blessing. She tells a good story. Her characters live"
Yorkshire Post

Historical fiction in Tandem editions

Edith Pargeter's memorable trilogy
of medieval England and Wales

The Heaven Tree 35p
The Green Branch 30p
The Scarlet Seed 30p

Romance and history combine in a swift-moving story of
border warfare, power politics and private feuds on the Welsh
border in the reign of King John.

"A highly dramatic and intense story, beautifully written"
Glasgow Evening Times

Talbot Mundy

Tros 30p   Liafail 30p
Helma 30p   Helene 25p

The saga of Tros of Samothrace, warrior hero, pledged to
frustrate the schemes of great Caesar, ruler of Rome and master
of half the world, who would lay Britain under the yoke of the
conqueror.

John James
Votan 30p
Not for all the Gold in Ireland 35p

On the edges of the civilised world eighteen hundred years ago
and more, when men and gods rubbed shoulders, a wily rogue
like Photinus the Greek could set whole nations to warring and
emerge with some profit. Whether making kings or killing them,
fathering most of the royal houses of the north, or leading an
army into battle, Photinus is irrepressible.

'. . . excitement, mythology, the splendour and barbarity of the
Dark Ages, and vividly imagined adventures'   *Northern Echo*

Men Went to Cattraeth 30p

It is a century or more since the Legions left Britain, and Myny-
dog, King of Eiddin, has raised a war-band three hundred strong
who will ride south through the devastated lands beyond the
Wall to combat the menace of the Saxon marauders from across
the seas . . .

'Rich and fascinating and intense. . . . There is splendour in
this saga'   *Western Mail*

Name ....

Address ....

Titles required ....

....

....

....

....

....

....

....
